The roses lay in dewy perfection on the draining board. At the last possible moment I folded the rug in half and dropped it, en masse, over the flowers.

There was a loud, stunning crack and my back hit the edge of the open door. I ran to the phone where Patrick was still shouting my name.

"I'm OK," I said, and had to sit quickly on the floor. The rug now had a smoking black hole in it, the kitchen reeked of burnt wool.

"I'm OK," I said again. There was nothing else to say. We both knew if he hadn't rung I'd probably be blinded or minus my hands.

A MURDER
OF CROWS

MARGARET DUFFY

FAWCETT CREST · NEW YORK

EPITAPH

The street lights were flickering on in groups of three or four as Peter Clyde turned into Royal Parade. He had paused for a moment by the Civic Centre, his mind registering reflections of buildings and tall trees in fountain ruffled water but dismissing the images as an irrelevance. Against a background of street sounds a pattern had been repeated, footsteps ceasing as he himself became motionless and resuming as he started to walk again. For an hour he had strolled on the Hoe, for no other reason than to confirm his suspicions; imagination played no part in this game.

Hands in pockets, he turned right again and walked behind Saint Andrew's church, down Finewell Street, past the Prysten House, hearing, almost with satisfaction, the two sets of footsteps echoing his own. The ancient street became narrower, the sounds of covert pursuit louder. Involuntarily, he quickened his pace.

It had been raining and a damp fishy breeze wafted in from the harbour to ruffle his hair. As he crossed the road by the brewery the dense, familiar smell of hops enveloped him. He consciously slowed his pace as he walked into the Barbican, passing restaurants, gift shops and public houses. There was usually something here to catch his eye—3D post-cards from Japan, antique jewellery—but not today. Dimity, the country people of Devon called this time of day; deep dusk.

North Ope was a passage some fifty yards in length that ran between two warehouses recently converted into flats. As he came to the narrow opening Clyde paused but all he could hear was the petulant slapping of halyards on metal masts from the yachts moored on the Cattewater. He waited, finding himself holding his breath.

He was expecting confirmation but when it came the hairs on the back of his neck stirred as though tiny feet were brushing through them. First, the merging into shadow of a figure directly ahead of him at the far end of the passage. Then, as he glanced behind him, a man stopped more abruptly than seemed normal to look in a shop window. There were other people walking their dogs, couples, children on cycles, but only these two mattered.

Clyde dived into a nearby doorway, the first in the passage, and jammed his thumb on to a bell push, the middle one of three. The doorway itself was in deep shadow, the lightbulb having been removed from an overhead lamp, Clyde knew that without glancing up. He had been this way the day before.

There was an aching pause, during which Clyde steadfastly fought down panic. Then, voice distorted over the intercom, his wife's former husband invited him to identify himself. Clyde did so and moments later heard the click as the door was released.

It was like stepping into a more civilised world; the staircase before him had immaculate ivory-coloured paintwork, jade green carpeting, and there were Japanese prints on the walls. He went up to the first floor, wondering how Gillard could afford a flat in Plymouth as well as one in London.

The front door of the flat stood ajar. Clyde pushed it all the way back, hesitating to enter. "Come into my parlour," said the spider to the fly. He went in slowly, aware that he was being watched in a series of mirrors, large gilt-framed ones, carefully sited. Of course, Gillard was not as mobile as he used to be. Nevertheless, Clyde's skin crawled.

By the light of a solitary table lamp, Patrick Gillard sat in the living room in an easy chair, legs crossed. This was a surprise, and the sudden premonition that he was in line for a few more left Clyde feeling spent and light-headed. Perhaps he was losing his grip.

"Sit down."

He sat.

"D'you want a drink?" The offer sounded as though it stemmed from curiosity and not hospitality.

He declined, politely, and Gillard's grey eyes narrowed slightly. Clyde made a conscious effort to relax, not even looking at the gun which now swung gently, pointing towards the floor, in the lax fingers of the other's right hand.

"Don't they give you whistles to blow these days?"

So he looked as scared as he felt. "I'm being followed."

Gillard smiled, then said, "Who and why?" He did not sound bored.

"I don't know."

Gillard raised his eyebrows in an exaggerated pantomime of patience. "You work for an organisation well equipped with the means of finding out," he observed dryly.

"I'm not sure . . ." Clyde's words died in his throat. It sounded so bloody pathetic. He leant back in his seat and closed his eyes.

". . . whose side they're on?" Gillard prompted.

Clyde was beginning to wish he had accepted the drink. "In a way."

"Would you like me to kill them for you?"

The detective sergeant looked sharply at Gillard, knowing he was being mocked. "Mental cruelty," he said slowly.

Gillard smiled again, not understanding.

"The grounds for the divorce," Clyde persevered. "Ingrid wouldn't talk about it for ages but I got a good idea after a while. The cold sneer's your stock in trade."

Frowning, Gillard shifted slightly in his chair. Then, astoundingly, he grinned and Clyde realised that he was witnessing Gillard's first genuine emotion of the encounter.

"I seem to remember her throwing me out of her house one cold winter's night. We came to quite a polite arrangement as to what to call it—she hit on mental cruelty. Always had a real way with the English language did Ingrid." He put down the gun on a small table. "Have a drink, for God's sake."

Clyde fixed them both drinks. So, Gillard was not going to be stung into talking about it.

Uncannily, his thoughts were discerned. "If there's an overwhelming need first to flay me in public . . ."

"No," said Clyde. "Not now."

"You never harbour grudges?" Gillard asked sharply.

"I wouldn't be here if I did."

"That's not much of an answer."

Clyde considered, perhaps not appreciating he was being

given a chance to relax. "No," he said after a short silence, "I don't harbour grudges."

Again, that small fretful movement. "So, someone's getting at you."

Gratefully, Clyde took a mouthful of his drink, whisky and water. "I came to you for advice because I've been followed for a week, on and off, and so far there's been no real official backing."

There was no immediate response, giving him time to study the man before him. In the days before service and serious injury in the Falklands War, Gillard had been a lithe, arrogant, scathing snob, and long ago, more years than he cared to remember, a good friend of Peter Clyde's. They had entered the police together though Gillard had left to join the army. He was thinner, almost painfully so, and the black curling hair had more than a light frosting of grey. He still looked like a man who could kill with his bare hands.

"You don't get taken seriously?"

"You're not taking me seriously."

The complaint was ignored. "Are they outside now?"

"They were when I came in."

"How many?"

"Two."

"Are you armed?"

"Of course not. This is Plymouth, not the Wild West."

"You've reported this?"

"I've already said so."

Gillard's face tightened in amazement. "And no one's checked?"

Clyde slammed down his drink on the arm of the chair, spilling some. "On the days they checked nobody came out to play."

"What are you working on? Anything sensitive?"

"Nothing important."

"Tell me," Gillard said.

Clyde counted on his fingers. "Three small cases of breaking and entering—probably kids. Cattle stealing from farms on the moor. A hit and run that was almost certainly someone from outside the county, and—"

"How do you know?"

"From the car, a black Rolls. All the ones round here belong to people born with silver spoons in their mouths."

"I get your point," Gillard said. "None of whom would have the spine to knock off the copper investigating the hit and run. Any real godfathers?"

"We've checked them all out anyway. No, this place is like a church vestry."

"Because it's well sewn up or because everyone's law abiding?"

"A bit of both but mostly the former. Not boasting," he added.

"No international terrorists?" This with the merest hint of tongue in cheek.

"No," said Clyde, stolidly.

"Have you upset any VIPs lately?"

"Not so far as I know."

"Think," came the inexorable reply.

No, Gillard had not changed. Think, he had said as head boy, having caught a second former running down the staff corridor before applying the all too familiar terrier shake; think, he had said as a police cadet in role play stopping a motorist for speeding. That was where they had parted. In the police people refused to think the Gillard way so he had joined the army, risen through the ranks like bread dough on a hot day and was now, no doubt, destined to become an instructor on the more sadistic survival courses.

"No," said Clyde again.

"Drugs?"

"Not the big time. Plenty of pushers . . . gutter rats. That's when I wish I was armed."

Gillard tut-tutted. "Most unprofessional of you, officer."

Clyde kept quiet.

"I can't help you, Peter," Gillard said after a pause.

"What do you suggest is my next move?" Clyde asked evenly, succeeding in keeping bitterness from his voice.

"Dial 999."

Clyde swallowed. "There was a time . . ."

"You said it yourself. This isn't the Wild West." Gillard cocked his head, listening. "All the windows have burglar proof locks."

"These aren't burglars," Clyde said.

"But regrettably," Gillard continued as if he had not spoken, "the doors . . ."

Downstairs there was the sound of splintering timber.

"Dial 999," Gillard said, pointing to an alcove.

Clyde crossed the room, picked up the receiver and then replaced it. "Dead," he said. He looked back at Gillard, senses heightened. "Are you just going to sit there?"

In the distance a crash of woodwork.

"No time," said Gillard. "Climb out of the kitchen window. There's a pretty strong drainpipe just below to the left. This door will keep them busy for a while."

Clyde ran across to the kitchen door and then halted, staring back. Gillard sat still, looking at him, an unholy Buddha in a small temple of light.

"Go," he said.

Clyde flipped down all the switches on a nearby panel and brilliant light flooded every corner of the room. There was no doubt, Gillard flinched.

When he spoke it was with the slightest tremor in his voice. "All actors prefer to choose their own lighting."

"A stage," Clyde said in a fierce whisper. "For what? Why do you have to act to me?" The door to the flat was being systematically kicked in.

"Go," Gillard said again.

"No, I'm going to get you out of here."

"There's no time."

Shuddering, Clyde approached him, "For God's sake . . ." he began, and then the gun came up, pointing.

"Get out," Gillard said.

Clyde stood still, transfixed.

"Go on!" Gillard yelled. "Move!"

Many had jumped to that command but Peter Clyde did not belong to the small esoteric world that Gillard inhabited. So he stayed and, when the door finally yielded, moved in a very deliberate and purposeful manner thereby being instrumental in his own death as well as that of the two men. Before he died he discovered that Gillard could just about walk without the aid of the crutches propped discreetly in one corner and that he had strong comforting hands. Strong hands . . .

CHAPTER 1

I wrote that reconstruction of the last hour of Peter's life the same night that Patrick came to see me. He gave me his version of the events twice. The conversation between the two men and what happened is verbatim as Patrick recounted it to me the second time. I'm sure of this because I took it all down in shorthand. It's his version and I don't believe him. Not yet.

It didn't put him off when I whipped out a notebook and pencil. Soldiers with photographic memories get used to people writing down what they say. It's part of the job. He just sat there and went on talking in his dry, crisp voice, even making sure that I was keeping up with him. I was, my shorthand's still pretty good.

Being a writer helps in moments of crisis. You can bash it down on paper, getting rid of all the poison, or you can hang on to it. Beware all you neighbours who cut me dead or butchers who cheat on the price, you all get put into little bottles of formaldehyde inside my brain to be stored for future use. I haven't been able to use Patrick, ever; there isn't a bottle large enough to hold him.

The day began as had its fourteen predecessors: I came out of a heavy sleep with a jerk as the alarm clock went off at seven-thirty. Not sleeping pills but hard work, trying to get within a decent distance of a publisher's deadline. You can't just curl up and die because your husband's been murdered. I shifted Pirate, my cat, off my chest rather more impatiently than she would have liked and then had to spend the next couple of minutes soothing her ruffled feelings. She's good company now.

Thank everything holy for Agas. Mine held court like a captive smiling red sun in the kitchen and I leant against its warmth, waiting for the kettle to boil, ignoring Pirate's entreaties for breakfast.

Two weeks. Two weeks to this day Peter had gone out of the door and I hadn't seem him alive again. Three weeks to our first wedding anniversary. Oh, hell! I made the tea, splashing my hand with boiling water, ran it under the cold tap for a while, drank tea and fed the cat.

After more tea and toast and honey I felt that I could face the final draft of *Moonlake*, the story of a young woman's struggle to run a country hotel in a small Devon town after the death of her mother, and her sister stealing her fiancé. I started work, feeling even more guilty than usual that I wasn't feeling guilty about not doing the housework. It's surprising how clean a small cottage can keep with just one tidy woman living in it.

I have been writing almost as long as I can remember: plays with me acting all the parts; terrible, facetious essays at school that were somehow tamed into something acceptable to examination boards by a long suffering English teacher, and later at least a dozen romantic novels steeped in purple prose that were incredibly boring to read. I tried Science Fiction but even when I exercised unrelenting discipline these tended to undergo metamorphosis into romantic novels about people wearing space suits.

Life began to improve when I finally struggled out of my teens. I wrote a semi-autobiographical novel about a girl and her relationship with her father, who had just died. The story was a very private, personal one and publication came as a strange shock. I know I felt horribly guilty and my mother didn't speak to me for about six weeks for my own father was dying, of a ghastly creeping illness that turned him into an old man when he was in his early forties. When the book came out, and his brain was still all right when it did, I showed him a copy and he took it and read it and I could see by his face how happy it made him. It was all I could give him, my love.

He lived for another two years and one of the last rational things he said to me was that he was sorry he would not be able to go to my wedding. So it was the bride who cried instead of her mother as she walked up the aisle on the arm of an uncle, my father's brother, Leo. The funeral had taken place a month earlier.

This was not a good morning for concentration. Through the window, stare at the wall as I might, Dartmoor glistened in the summer sunshine after a night of heavy rain. It seemed as if I could stretch out a hand and touch the granite and heather a mile and a half away. Peter and I used to walk for miles. Used to. I was getting around to using the past tense. Was that a good or bad sign?

I left my writing room, the cool spare bedroom tucked under thatched eaves, and went downstairs, made a mug of coffee and took it out into the yard. It was a tiny gravelled area, not large enough to swing a car around in, but it looked pretty with its tubs of begonias and trailing lobelia. Across the yard was the barn, a haven for swallows and large hairy spiders. We used to keep the car in there but Peter became so disenchanted with performing fifteen point turns on cold winter's nights that he built a garage halfway up the private lane to the main road.

I wandered up the lane towards the village, mug in both hands. An ancient Saxon way, it had led from the high moor to Lydford, two miles away, a road used by people bringing their dead for burial in the old stannary town's churchyard. Next to this were the ruins of the castle where the Stannary Courts had been held to deal with the tin miners. The justice of those times was of ill repute, neatly summed up by a local poet, Browne:

> *"I oft have heard of Lydford law*
> *How in the morn they hang and draw*
> *And sit in judgement after."*

Why did I keep thinking about death today?

I went back indoors, slamming the door to shut out ghosts. I was well into my stride by two, dismal thoughts banished. It's stupid to live off scraps so I made my working lunch a proper meal of Brie, crackers, a chunk of home made fruit cake and an apple from the tree in the garden; this a windfall, tiny and immature but surprisingly sweet. Nothing alcoholic, not in the middle of the day, that was fatal. I'd seen more than one friend drink herself into the ground after personal disaster.

Afterwards I took another mug of coffee into the yard—and that's where it all started.

Halfway up the lane was a man on a motor bike, sitting quite still, all in black, the bike, leathers, helmet, everything. The helmet was one of those with a tinted visor so you couldn't see through it. My heart began a panicky thudding inside my ribs and he sat there, like some bloody fifth horseman of the apocalypse.

In the end I called out, "What do you want?" and watched as he took off the brakes and rolled silently towards me. The way the bike came to a halt, less than poetry becoming motionless, gave me my first clue, quite unnecessarily as my visitor pushed up his visor.

"You frightened me," I said, keeping my voice as disinterested as possible.

"I'm sorry," said my ex-husband, his tone equally flat. The one he utilised with those he didn't like.

He got off the bike, pushed it across the yard and leaned it against the barn wall.

"Why don't you use the stand?" I called out.

"Because I can't stand on one leg yet to kick it down with the other," he replied without turning round.

I didn't offer to help. You don't with people like Patrick. I said, "Where's the car?" He had kept the elderly Austin Maxi with my blessing when we were divorced.

"Gave it away," he said, removing the helmet. "Same kind of problem."

The problem, if it could be described as such, could not be hidden and was quite appalling. The limp distorted what had been almost a dancer's body, his right leg seeming now to be shorter than the left. Positively the worst aspect of his halting progress towards me was the knowledge common to us both that without the limp he would have been listening to me screaming at him to leave.

He came close, took me lightly by both shoulders and kissed me, cool and distant, but on the mouth, his breath smelling slightly of peppermint. I did not draw back. There was nothing to fear. He had never been a man to shove his tongue down your throat, not even when we were married. Patrick had exquisite sexual manners; surprising, really, as I knew what he was capable of when really wound up. But then again, he was perfect in everything he did, and knew it, one of the reasons I had decided to live my life without him.

"Not strong enough for emergency stops," he said, and smiled warily.

"Why have you come?" I asked. A natural question, I suppose, but to me it sounded utterly inane.

"I want to talk to you."

I gave him a good hard stare and warm triumph washed over me like a bath with expensive bath oil as he dropped his gaze. "You mean you want to talk about Peter's death?"

"In a way."

"There's more than one way to speak of murder?"

He still needled easily. "I haven't come to winge about the past or upset you more than necessary."

I said, "It's necessary to upset me at all? To come at all?"

He took a ragged breath. "I didn't mean it like that. There are things you ought to know."

I carried on staring at him. "I read all about it in the paper."

"Ingrid . . ."

I can't walk past a lost kitten and always trail round the village on the animal charities' collecting days. In my bad moments I had probably day-dreamed of him one day arriving on the doorstep looking like a whipped cur, and me shutting the door in his face. Now, I discovered that day-dreams do not necessarily follow traits of character. Seeing Patrick in this condition was simply unbearable. The coward in me meant that I walked indoors, hoping he would follow. He did.

I challenged him immediately. "Perhaps I had sussed out all by myself that he wasn't hard on the heels of two desperadoes bent on snatching your jade collection, during which episode there was a struggle and he was shot. What really happened? Were you in the middle of some SAS reunion, taking pot shots at seagulls when he asked you to desist?" To my chagrin my eyes filled with tears.

Infuriatingly, he decided to play along. "And the other two?"

"Innocent passers-by, what else? Undercover units don't have to worry about the law." He could have done with sitting down but my charity didn't extend to that.

"I'm not in the SAS, Ingrid," he said patiently.

I knew full well he wasn't but his undercover unit wasn't that different. A rose by any other name . . .

He said, "Do you want to read a letter or hear the truth from me first?"

I went to the kitchen and banged the kettle on to the hot hob of the Aga. "Are they trusting the widow with the truth?" I shot back at him. He limped after me, unzipping his ridiculous jacket, and I had to take the letter from him. He went to stand by the Aga while I read it.

"Who's this Colonel squiggle dash blot?" I demanded.

"Daws," said Patrick. "I agree—lousy handwriting. My new boss. What does he say?"

I gave him the full benefit of my green eyes then. "You mean you don't know?"

"Hardly," he said.

My carefully controlled temper snapped. "I'll tell you what he says," I raged, ripping up the letter and throwing the pieces at him. "After the usual condolences he says that in no way are you responsible for the death of my husband which appears to have been a motiveless killing. They were a lot more imaginative than that in the local paper when they said it was an attempted robbery! He also says that you've been assigned to look after me for a while in case there are repercussions."

I came up for air. "I don't need a bloody minder, Major Patrick Gillard, least of all you." I went right up to where he stood holding on to the towel rail of the Aga. "You didn't know about that?" I hissed, right in his face.

He was quite white under his tan. "Ingrid, if you kick my shins the way you used to . . ." He swallowed. "I knew about the last bit, of course, but . . ."

"But?" I saw a drop of my spittle hit his cheek.

"He can only tell you the bits that aren't covered by the Official Secrets Act . . . officially the murder's motiveless." Again he had to stop speaking.

"But you can fill me in on some of the rest." I turned away from him. "Get out of here. Leave me alone."

"When they burst in they went for me first," Patrick said, breathing in a most peculiar fashion. "Peter saw how it was and used his body as a shield. I shot them. He saved my life, Ingrid."

I turned to face him. "What a bloody awful waste," I enunciated slowly.

"Yes, wasn't it?" he agreed, and fainted dead away.

I'm never one to mollycoddle and wasn't about to start now but neither am I the sort to stand crowing over another's downfall. I rolled him on to his stomach in case he vomited, and the movement brought him around. After half a minute or so he was able to take a tot of rum and drank it down in one, eyes watering. It seemed inhuman not to suggest he lie on the settee under a travel rug.

Other than a temporary resemblance to an unshrouded corpse, four years had not been too unkind to him. His hair was still thick and wavy, his face unlined but for a few crinkles around the eyes. He'd had a crooked front tooth capped which made a big difference to the rare occasions when he smiled, revealing white slightly uneven teeth with only a few fillings in the back ones. I knew. His whole body was as familiar to me as Sheet 202 of the Ordnance Survey.

"You've been staring at me like that ever since I arrived," he complained when a cup of hot sweet tea was inside him.

"Exactly how long have you been out of the hospital?" I countered, sitting opposite.

"Not long." His gaze was roving the room as he spoke, taking in the Waterford crystal vase my mother had given to us as a wedding present, a blue Jasper Wedgwood plaque, framed and mounted on golden velvet, which he had produced one Christmas morning before spilling a cup of tea all over me as I sat up in bed. Not one hundred percent perfect perhaps.

"*How* long?" I persisted.

He was too weak to bang up the shutters. "About three weeks. I have to keep going in because bits of rock are embedded and they move around. My right leg's a real mess . . . the pins aren't really holding."

"Is that what you meant by, 'Peter saw how it was'?"

He nodded.

"So you'd been out a week and couldn't walk."

"Only on crutches."

I heard my own voice slither up a full octave. "And you've been sent to protect *me*?"

"I'm a very good shot," he said, unable to keep the resentment from his tone. "Horizontal and vertical." Then he told me what had happened in his flat and when he had finished there was a long silence.

"Do you think that dangerous criminals were after him?"

"It's possible."

"You'll have to do better than that."

After another silence Patrick said, "There are two theories. One is that, unwittingly or not, and the police aren't being at all helpful on this, he had stirred up a hornet's nest with some enquiries he was conducting. The other theory involves me, but my money's on the first."

I knew that he didn't feel up to further explanation and there was another silence during which we avoided each other's gaze.

At last I had to say something. "It's just as well there's a barn, isn't it?"

"Save your overwhelming hospitality for the more deserving," he said, throwing aside the blanket. "I'm under orders. I've brought a tent, fish hooks, snares and a very sharp knife."

I stared at him.

"Not even allowed to field low flying cups of tea," he added.

That night there was a thunderstorm that lasted five hours.

In spite of the fact that he was outside and the door securely locked on his instructions, life for me inside had changed, undergone a subtle shift of emphasis. I resented it. There was also, nagging away, the realisation that today was the first time he had been inside the cottage since I had thrown him out all that time ago. It had not been entirely selfish of me. It was my house, paid for with my earnings. I thought about that night; how I had smashed his classical guitar, screamed obscenities at him—and all because he had tried to explain to me how to cook a soufflé that didn't collapse. It wasn't the only reason, of course. It was just the last straw that broke the long-suffering wife's back. No other women, no heavy drinking—well, not very often—I was just up to the eyebrows with him being so insufferably superior. My writing had hit a bad patch, too, Alan, my agent, had tut-tutted in a way that had made me want to wring his neck. He was right, though. That novel, *Seafarer*, had gone to the wall forever.

The divorce had come through while he was in the South Atlantic, living in sheep pens, and right now he was somewhere down by the river, in a tent in the pouring rain. Despite how I'd hated him, a juvenile emotion I'd grown out of by now, this wasn't quite the kind of revenge I'd had in mind. Another daydream had crumbled.

Before he'd gone outside he'd obediently related the whole story over again. You could see his brain ticking away behind the tiredness, and understand why the army thought so highly of him. He was a sort of walking computer cum lie detector with a big sting in the tail.

I had an idea why he'd been sent. Someone, perhaps the faceless Daws of the lousy handwriting, had come to the opinion that it was about time a certain soldier was out of hospital and back into active service. A few nights under the stars and with an empty belly might remind him what he was getting paid for.

I went up to my writing room and sat at my desk. Patrick's earnest white face kept swimming in front of my eyes. That is what the armed services are all about, I reasoned, getting shot or blown up if you're unlucky. You could be killed or maimed for life on exercise let alone active service. And Patrick was the kind of damn fool diehard who would leave hospital too soon and kid himself he was fit and strong enough to stay on a big motor bike. I'd had a look at it when he collected his stuff from the panniers and locked it in the barn, a BMW R80 with full fairing which must be more difficult to cope with than the Maxi. Men!

We had made a very handsome couple, Patrick and Ingrid. He was tall with black curly hair, I was dark, too, and fairly attractive though not the mirror cracking type. He'd only been a captain in those days but a couple of years later had survived a special course and come home as good as promoted. He'd told me about some of it afterwards, enough to make my hair stand on end. He became one of the youngest majors there was but it hadn't done him much good. He was still major at thirty-eight and, from his reference to Daws as his new boss, it was apparent that they had invalided him out of the heavy brigade.

I wrote down my reconstruction and then read it through and cried.

CHAPTER 2

The feeling that everything was going to be different from now on overwhelmed me as soon as I opened my eyes the following morning. The alarm clock had not gone off and when I looked at it I made the discovery that it was only six thirty-five. There was no sign of Pirate. She had climbed out of the top window during the night and shinned down the wistaria, an ancient one that could easily support the weight of a human body never mind a cat.

For as long as I can remember I've been able to handle whatever life throws at me: buying and selling houses, mending fuses, understanding insurance policies and publishers' contracts, putting a new hose on the washing machine, riding horses and mending punctures in bike tyres. None of this was a whit of use when faced with an ex-husband camping in the garden, a crippled ex-husband who looked as if he needed several weeks of square meals in order to get back to normal weight. I'm not motherly either, but how do you explain to a coroner that the body on your property had been under strict orders not to accept victualling?

I made tea and called Pirate. No cat. Everywhere outside was sodden and dripping, shrubs bowed down to the ground with the weight of water on the foliage. Directing my thoughts toward *Moonlake*, I took my tea upstairs to the typewriter. Three hours later I had changed a vital aspect of the original draft on a whim and thus channelled myself into a savage case of writer's block. Should I tear up several thousand words or sweat it out?

Confound the man. Had he died of exposure out there?

I walked right past where he had dug himself in three times

before I noticed the green canvas under broken off branches. By this time I was in a mood that could have confronted a stiffening corpse with serenity. I had been tripped over twice on the journey to the river bank by wires concealed under grass camouflaging.

He was crouched on a flat rock by the river's edge, and despite the sound of the water heard me coming. I was close enough to see him take a fresh grip on the knife he was using to joint a small animal, a rabbit judging by the furry remains on the bank. He stood up and I knew he was swearing under his breath to exorcise the pain. His lips were moving in a grimace I hadn't seen since he'd been rushed to hospital years ago with appendicitis.

"You're soaking wet," I said inanely. He was dripping from the waist down. After I'd spoke I hated him a little bit, like of old, as he gave me that wide aperture stare with those unholy grey eyes of his. Then, visibly, he changed his mind about being supercilious.

"I fell in the river," he said, and pointed to a tree trunk that had spanned the water. Obviously rotten, it had given way under his weight.

"If you're living off the land," I said, "you can break into the barn and throw that lot in the tumble dryer. Would it save several new locks if I gave you the key?"

Patrick shook his head but his grin outweighed the negative by a good fifty percent. He beckoned with a long forefinger. Ye gods, I had forgotten those hands. When I reached him he took one of mine and plonked the dripping bits of rabbit meat into it. I had to call up the other one as a reinforcement.

"Take those up to the tent for me?" he wheedled.

I glanced round. There was a wood fire on the bank, a good hot one with hardly any smoke, and Pirate, finishing off what looked like three small brown trout. As for the man himself, despite being wet he was warm, shaved and looked as if he'd had a good night's sleep.

"Point made," I said. "I'll come back in a week's time."

"Mind the wires," he called after me, and then chuckled. It was not a particularly pleasant sound.

It was day one of a war of attrition that lasted almost a week. I became irritated beyond belief, a mood that soon took on all the symptoms of stress; restlessness, lost appetite and inability to sleep properly.

Strangely, my irritation was not directed against Patrick but at a situation over which I seemed to have no control. On that first morning I found other wires stretched across the lane at knee height and left them there, telling myself that he had never shown signs of being a dangerous maniac in the past so no doubt they would not be left to ensnare visitors who arrived at conventional calling hours. This proved to be perfectly correct; he removed them long before the postman was due just after seven. I watched him take them down and that was the last time I consciously checked on his activities.

I was working so I stayed at home, only walking up to the village post office cum general store for small items and when I felt I needed to talk to someone.

On each and every one of these visits to the village I was aware of Patrick's presence. He was there and yet he was not, no rustling in the hedge or footsteps behind me, only a presence. Perhaps he was using binoculars? Whatever, I could feel his eyes boring into my back. At first it was a novelty, a game even, and if there were dangerous men about, it was rather comforting to have protection.

After four days it was no longer such a game.

Ruthlessly, I tried to put Patrick out of my mind, and my powers of concentration are formidable. I continued with *Moonlake*, changing a large part of the plot, and each night, surveying the pile of neatly typed sheets, was vastly dissatisfied. The rain sluicing down the window of my writing room was partly to blame. The barn had not been broken into and I had not given him the key so I knew he had stayed wet with very little chance of drying out. So to bed, to a repeated snippet of nightmare about a man climbing the wistaria.

In between the heavy showers I wandered aimlessly in the small garden behind the barn. The apple tree appeared to be losing its meagre crop of fruit and once, for a full ten seconds, I contemplated tying further goodies wrapped in cooking foil to the branches. No.

I grew no vegetables but there was a herb garden—mint, parsley, sage, thyme and rosemary—and as the days went by these began to look as though a colony of rabbits had made a meal of them. I doubted it. Not with such an efficient poacher living in the vicinity.

On the fifth morning, the day after a neighbour had phoned the police to report that a strange man was lurking by the river and, cheeks flaming, I had explained, I saw Patrick in the yard.

It was early, first light, I had my bedroom window open and was leaning on the sill, watching the tors play hide and seek in the swirling grey cloud. I found myself biting the tip of my tongue hard as he limped through the garden gate, shambled almost, hunched into his sodden parka against the rain. He was unrecognisable, unshaven, his hair a mess. I froze, not daring to move in case he saw me, but he had halted already, scenting the air like an animal. Slowly his head turned and he saw me, or rather, I felt, had smelled me, my perfume perhaps or the soap with which I'd just washed my hands. He drew himself up and gave me a quaint salute, clicking his heels painfully. Then he went away, back towards the river.

A kind of madness took hold of me. I dressed, pulling on the first clothes that came to hand, bolted toast and coffee that I didn't want and headed for the garage with shopping baskets.

The car wouldn't start.

After half a dozen tries I knew why and transferred my attentions to the horn. He came quite quickly, but not before the entire village was awake and probably reaching for their phones. Not a word was spoken while I yanked on the bonnet release and he raised it and replaced the rotor arm. Then he opened the passenger door and sat alongside me.

"You can't come to Plymouth looking like that," I said.

"I most certainly can," he replied.

"I'm going round the stores," I told him. "If you think I intend to tolerate a smelly shadow—"

"At five-thirty in the morning?" he interrupted.

"When they open at nine," I said coldly.

He looked me straight in the eye for the first time. "It takes you three and a half hours to drive fifteen miles?"

I knew I'd already lost, I'd lost as soon as I locked the front door. "No," I said. "Alright, not now. Later on I must go shopping."

He got out of the car, lifted the bonnet again and removed the rotor arm. Through my wound down window he said, "Sound the horn when you're ready. Meanwhile I'll endeavour to have a wash.''

I sat still after he'd gone, ready tears of anger and self pity pricking the inside of my eyelids. At least I now knew what had happened to the herbs—he was chewing them to allay hunger pangs. His breath, unlike the rest of him, was as fragrant as a bouquet garni.

I didn't go to Plymouth. How could I? How can you take a starving man around the shops and buy tea and coffee?

By the sixth morning I had decided what I was going to do. It was just after nine-thirty when I carefully picked my way over the wires towards the tent. The rain smacked on the taut canvas and wilting branches and was running down the back of my waterproof on to my legs.

A perfect orphans in the storm tableau. As I opened up one flap of the tent Pirate poked her head out of the layers of plastic fertiliser bags he had wrapped himself in to keep warm.

''I thought she'd ended up in that toffee tin you're using for a cooking pot,'' I said, seeing a knife poised for throwing.

He didn't smile.

''I'm going to London for a few days. I thought I ought to tell you so you can call off this . . .'' For the first time in ages, words failed me, something to do with the expression that flitted across his face. Anger? Surely not fear.

''Charade?'' he offered.

''I wasn't going to say that.''

''It makes no difference. Plymouth, London, Hong Kong . . .''

I said, ''I'm going on my own, Patrick.'' He was acting, damn him. When had I ever known what was really going on inside his head?

''I won't be the complete bastard and ask if there's a boy-friend.''

''You already have,'' I pointed out coldly. ''There isn't.''

''Then I won't be a gooseberry,'' he said with perfect logic.

''I thought of staying with my friend Maggie. Going shopping, to the theatre . . . You'll find it an awful bore.''

He laughed, tickled pink at the prospect of being bored rather than hungry and cold.

''I'll take my sleeping bag,'' he said.

"Why is this necessary?" I shouted. "Did you talk Daws into doing this to me?"

"I told you the truth," he said quietly.

I took a deep breath. "There's more though, isn't there? A hell of a lot more that you're only prepared to tell me when I get off my high horse and apologise for what I did to you."

He just sat there like an owl with a hangover under his blue plastic bags.

"Come to dinner," I said, curiosity as usual my doom. "I'll give you the money for a new guitar. Smashing that was unforgivable."

"For starters we can have those two salmon steaks you bought from the fish van yesterday and didn't eat."

"The forcible billeting of troops is called dragonnade," I said, holding a glass of wine up to the lamp light to admire the colour. "Louis XIV used it to persecute the French Protestants."

"I bet he didn't send them along with the main course," observed my guest, helping himself to more calabrese.

Two rabbits which I had found skinned and jointed on the kitchen window ledge, wrapped in dock leaves, had been marinated in red wine, oil and garlic and then casseroled very slowly. Plain mashed potatoes soaked up the wonderful sauce.

I wore an apricot silk dress. It was very modest and I had bought it for the rare occasions when Alan took me out to dinner and I wanted to do battle with him without giving him ideas. Arguing with females makes some men randy.

"Not even allowed to field low flying cups of tea?" I said, spooning the remains of the sauce on to Patrick's plate.

"This is different," he said. "What I meant was—"

"A one-off invitation is all right," I interrupted. If I was going to beat him it would be with his own weapon. Interrupting people because he knew what they were going to say was one of Patrick's worst traits.

"Right," he agreed. "As of old you read me like a book."

I sighed. This was going to be a long job. "How can we bear this? How can we sit here as though Peter wasn't dead and we hadn't gone through a divorce, as though everything was the same?"

"Because we're pretending," he said. "It saves all the old

rows and unpleasantness. After all, we're both highly civilised people."

"Are we?" I retorted. "Isn't it just a veneer that is easily scraped off?"

"You pretend after the veneer's gone," he told me, picking up a rabbit bone to nibble off the meat. He had eaten everything I had put before him, but not as though half starved.

I thought about it, watching him.

"I lost mine when the grenade exploded," he said. "The sergeant who was with me, a real tough cove, only got his arm broken when he was thrown into the wall. He held me with the other one and I couldn't understand how he was screaming with his mouth closed. Then I realised it was me."

You pay dearly when you write because it means you have a vivid imagination. The picture his words brought to mind would wake me tonight.

Patrick was observing me closely.

I said, "I think we ought to drop the civilised posturing."

His face was inscrutable. "Perhaps."

"After we split up," I began, "I didn't feel any different for ages. You were away so much when we were actually man and wife and then when you went to the South Atlantic, Peter had come on the scene again . . . I felt like a service wife with a boyfriend, a complete trollop." I had said this to Peter and, predictably, he had told me not to be a fool; if I couldn't see an old school friend while a divorce was in the pipeline then something was wrong with my head.

Patrick said, "A female friend would probably say you'd married him for mental respectability."

That touched a raw nerve. "But didn't cave in until last year. That makes me sound very weak, but then again you've always put me in an inferior position, always in the wrong, always the one who needed guidance. Your guidance. Shepherded gently through life on the arm of an expert."

He grinned, a real one. "Dad always did want me to follow in his footsteps."

That did it. I banged down the plates I had begun to stack, words flying like arrows at Agincourt. "The bloody insufferable Gillards, vicars of Little Puking since the Civil War! How they must love this son of their loins. It's always been the army or the Church, hasn't it? No one's ever run a betting shop or worked in Woolworth's.''

His grin went all the way into the smirk I remembered. ''It was rumoured that Uncle George served in a fish shop for a while.''

Written down all this looks rather funny but with his face wearing contempt with a capital C and that dry familiar drawl we were back four years ago.

''Your suggestion,'' he said, ''that we drop the civilised posturing.''

He had baited the hook and thrown it and I had swallowed it down. Smooth as melted honey, I said, ''Why has it taken you three years to get over your injuries?''

''Almost no legs,'' he said after a short silence. ''Smashed bones in a soup of the day with flesh and muscles attached. No skin left. Nowadays it's on long-term loan from other places. Other injuries, too.''

He spoke like that, painting pictures in my imagination, knowing what it would do to me. Knowing also how to make me stop asking questions.

I attacked farmhouse cheddar with the cheese knife, guillotine style.

''What made you ask?'' he said, frowning.

''I thought you might have been up to something else,'' I lied.

''I joined Daws' department last week,'' he said. ''In person . . . he's been in touch for quite a while.''

''If you'd been born disabled, would you have entered the Church?''

He blinked quickly a few times. Never, not once, not even with my grasshopper mind, have I been able to make him lose his way in conversation. ''There's no duress,'' he murmured. ''My cousin David was the last one to—''

I viciously chopped him off in mid-sentence. ''Would you?''

''I don't know. I might have done.'' This time it was through my agency that he had stopped acting.

''What about now?''

He didn't answer for a moment, then shrugged and said, ''Why not?''

I really walloped the spurs into my war horse. ''That pig-brained assurance that it's the Gillards of this nation who have always bred everyone who matters! You're all the same—you, your father, and your mother for that matter. Self-satisfied. It makes me want to throw up.''

He rose from the table. I'd got him on the run.

"You stand there," I went on, hearing the choking anger in my voice, "fitting the mould all too well—dangerous, profane and foul-mouthed, the perfect soldier in her Majesty's modern army—and tell me you'd consider becoming a priest?''

"Am I?" he said.

I lopped off more cheese, defeat blurring my vision.

"Am I?" he repeated. Why wasn't he angry? Why was I saying these things? We had never quarrelled along these rather profound lines.

"No," I said quietly. "The first and the last but not the middle." I put some chips of cheese on a plate and helped myself to crackers. "Please sit down again and finish your meal.''

After a moment or two he came back and sat down, resting his hands on the table, watching me. I looked at them—musician's hands, murderer's hands, lover's hands—and shivered.

I said, needing to return to less perilous ground, "Those men followed Peter all over Plymouth and only decided to attack when he entered a building where, presumably, they knew he didn't live. It doesn't make sense.''

Patrick took some cheese. "Unless they had a good idea of his destination and that a cripple lived there who wouldn't represent a threat. That's part of the first theory.''

"But you said that the second involved you, too.''

"The second excludes Peter completely. As far as I'm concerned it's a non-starter.''

"You and Peter drank together years and years ago, not long after you left school. Why should he go to you for help?''

He smiled at me, a trifle crookedly. "Up until the time I left with the task force we met quite often, just for a pint or two. We made a point of not mentioning you.''

I preferred to let that slide over my head. "You hadn't seen him since you came back?''

"I haven't been to Plymouth very often.''

"So he'd no idea how badly hurt you were?''

He moved restlessly. This happened every few minutes and I was sure now that it was as pain shafted through his legs. "Of course not. Would you go to a cripple if you were in fear of your life?''

"You shot them after Peter was killed shielding you?''

"If you can't run you have to be well prepared. Yes, I shot them." He shifted again, holding his breath, and I waited, knowing there was more to come.

"I'm under orders now but I volunteered. Laugh if you want to.''

I nearly cried.

We washed up, just like old times, me washing, him drying. I would have preferred him to curl up in his tent or even stretch out on the settee but he was restless and edgy. It was not that he was objectionable to be near, somehow he had achieved a bath and a shave in the river and was wearing a sweater and an acceptable pair of jeans. No, it was the domesticity, the two in a kitchen, the memories of living with another person.

I made coffee and took it into the living room. "Would you like some music?'' I asked him. "I've still got your record of the Brandenberg Concertos.''

To my surprise he came and sat by my side on the settee, with an arm draped along the back of it near my shoulders.

"What's on your mind?'' I said, whispering and not really being sure why.

"You're too perceptive," he said.

I gave him a cup of coffee, stirring in one spoonful of deme-rara. Old habits were refusing to die. "What about?''

"Me." He carefully placed the cup on the low marquetry topped table, hesitated, then put both arms round me and kissed me. It wasn't a real kiss, more the kind done for the benefit of cameras. He was uninvolved. I didn't struggle, go rigid or bite him, just let him know that it wasn't required. He drew back and looked at me.

"Why did you do that?'' I enquired, really wanting to know.

"I've been told to look for a working partner.''

A simple statement. Like regarding a pink plastic laundry basket and someone telling you it was full of cobras.

"Not full-time," he elaborated. "Could you travel around the country with me acting as man and wife?''

007 didn't have assistants like me. "And abroad?'' I asked.

"Perhaps. Loads of material for books," he added craftily.

He was never a man to take you for a ride. "Why me?" I said, needing time and knocked sideways by the implication that there was a lack of glamorous young volunteers only too willing to do the married couple bit with him all the way.

He said, "I know you. You're level-headed, educated, and we get on famously in public."

This was perfectly true. "But there must be others . . . girls who've signed the Official Secrets Act." Why was I even talking about it?

"Known girls," he replied. "If I suddenly started swanning around with one of our girls, someone would smell a rat. You and I were once married, for ten years if my memory serves me right. It's not too far-fetched if we take up together again sometimes." He paused. "You'd have to put your name on that small piece of paper."

I shook my head, picturing each mission disintegrating into petty quarrels. We had quarrelled incessantly. In private.

"You'll get paid."

I chose to ignore that. "Hotel staff will soon get to know that we're sleeping in separate rooms."

"Could you bring yourself to share a room with single beds?"

I could not and, gazing at me, he received his answer.

"It's part of the deal," he said softly.

"No," I said. "No deal."

"No sex," he said. "Promise."

"No," I said again.

He smiled, shrugged sadly. Then he glanced across to Pirate stretched out on the hearthrug. She had her head up, listening with her ears pointed. Someone or something was outside.

Patrick leaned over and switched off the lamp. At that precise moment a large stone smashed the window and landed at my feet. I yelled, more from surprise than fear, and after that everything happened very quickly. He gathered me to him like a combine harvester and we both ended up on the hearthrug, roughly on the spot just vacated by Pirate. I could hear her paws as she hammered up the stairs.

From outside came a raucous bellow of laughter.

"The river's bloody cold tonight," the same voice shouted. "Coming for a dip?"

"A count of ten and then we're inside," came another high-pitched voice with a north country accent.

"Who are they?" I whispered in Patrick's ear. "What do they want?"

"Blood," was all he said as he slid away from me into the dark.

CHAPTER 3

My father always used to say that I was more cat than woman and he wasn't throwing insults, we were very close, Dad and I. Even when very young I used to love standing in the garden at night, just listening and watching—stars, the moon, rustles in the grass, hedgehogs for whom I put out saucers of bread and milk—anything that nature had to offer. So, when Patrick left me and a blanket of silence dropped over our little encompassment, I went after him.

This was what he had been waiting for, the end of the survival course when the volunteers are carted away and interrogated. Starved, dizzy from lack of sleep and exhaustion, they are loaded into lorries and driven off to be taken apart by anonymous strangers, giving them a taste of what to expect if they are captured behind enemy lines. He had gone through it before, lived off weasels and rats, shivered in makeshift shelters, and tolerated the ceaseless searches for forbidden, usually stolen, provisions.

Patrick had not gone outside but into the walk-in larder. I blended into the shadow of the open doorway and stopped breathing. Peeping round it moments later I saw a darker shape outside the window. It was open and an arm slid inside, deftly opened it wider and proceeded silently to remove various jars and bottles that were on the window ledge. The next seconds were confusing, the kind of episode you need to see again on an action replay in slow motion. The shape began to come in the window, which was quite low and large enough to admit a man, came in a hell of a lot faster than both he and I were expecting, and was felled with a sound that added another item to my nightmare repertory. Then Patrick had gone. Pausing only to return for the poker I followed, using the unconscious man as a step.

My weapon was superfluous judging by the moonlit pas de deux being performed just outside the window. A man was bent in an interesting L-shape, suggesting that Patrick had dived to the ground in a forward roll and hit him in the stomach as he stood up. The bent one had his throat encircled by an unsympathetic elbow.

"How many of you?" I heard Patrick breathe. When there was no response he applied science and small shake.

"Five," came the choking reply. "Please . ."

No chance, he should have known better. I looked away.

"You'd have the Russians in tears," said Patrick to the man who could no longer hear him. He dragged him into deeper shadow, ignoring me.

Number three was in the barn. Even I heard his nervous sniff from behind a winter's supply of logs. After that there was silence and I could see nothing from my hiding place just inside the open double doors. They had been shut and locked earlier, before it got dark.

I heard the moment that Patrick found him. A shout stifled by fingers, those wiry, wringing fingers.

"Where are they?" A penetrating whisper that would have gone from one end to the other of the Albert Hall.

Silence, and then a soft snapping sound that made me feel sick. The man shrieked and someone put the lights on.

The one outside the larder window had either been lying or couldn't count. There were four Royal Marines left unscathed, in camouflage gear, their faces blacked, the one by the light switch an officer.

"Horse soldiers," Patrick said.

The man at his side held his broken wrist, moaning under his breath. Patrick put the flat of his hand on his face and shoved him violently into the log pile. It was a comment of a sort. This type of confrontation was not conducted by any rules I would recognise.

"Maxwell," said the officer with his hand on the light switch. "Good try. My orders are to—"

''Gillard,'' Patrick interrupted. ''Major. Captain Maxwell, I suggest you remove your little troupe before I lose my temper.''

Maxwell eyed him up and down. ''My orders expressly forbid that we touch your legs. If you resist I'm afraid I'm likely to suffer from temporary amnesia.''

Patrick, on his own on one side of the barn, three of them closing in on him.

I threw the poker at Maxwell and the head of it hit him in the chest, expelling the air from his lungs with a whooshing sound. He grabbed his ribs to find out if they were still there and I leapt for the light switch.

If the thought had crossed my mind for a moment that Patrick would slip away, it was soon dismissed. I couldn't put my hands over my ears to block out the sounds, found it just possible to stand with one finger on the switch, leaning against the wall so that my knees didn't give way.

A thin crescent moon came out from behind a cloud, glimmering weakly through the dirt and spider's webs that festooned a small window set high up in one wall of the barn. It shone into my eyes, doing nothing to obliterate the relentless images projected into my brain. Was it my imagination or had two of them got hold of Patrick while another slammed short powerful punches into his body? A wild hope surged inside me when someone swore shrilly, not Patrick. There was more activity but of a deadly, quieter nature.

After a while the sick making sounds ceased and I put on the light. Maxwell was standing right by me, where he had remained all the time.

They had had Patrick on the floor several times by the look of his clothes. Sawdust, coaldust, blood; his own, someone else's, in his hair, on his hands, everywhere.

''It was a try out,'' said Maxwell.

''For them or me?'' The undoubted winner spat a mouthful of blood on to the floor of the barn and then his voice rose in crisp parody. ''Got something big for you chaps. One of ours has gone soft and is lying low with a bit of crumpet on the moor. Take it as a great favour if you'd lift him and teach him how it's done in the Marines these days.''

It was clear who had received a lesson.

* * *

"Probably. Tomorrow . . . perhaps the day after. We won't be here."

I scrubbed my eyes on the sleeve of my ruined dress. A soapy hand caught mine and held it, then he put his other one on top, mine in the middle.

"They're making sure I'm on my toes."

"And punishing you for Peter's death?"

He merely squeezed my hand a little tighter.

"It's a filthy way to treat a man," I burst out.

"I'm sorry you were involved in it," he said. "Please get me a drink."

I gave him a double brandy with a little ginger ale added to make it slide down easier.

He said, "I don't mind if you talk."

So I talked, washing him as I would a child, even the bits under the suds, telling him about *Moonlake* and how it had gone wrong. When I couldn't postpone it any longer I said, "I didn't put the light out so I couldn't see you being hurt."

He registered real surprise. "It never occurred to me that you had. I was praying you would as a matter of fact." He rested his head on the back of the bath, surveying me through half closed lashes.

"I might play charades with you if I'm stuck on a chapter," I said lightly, committing myself. "Now and then. If it suits me."

"Because you've seen me naked?" he asked shrewdly.

He had guessed my suspicion that he had exaggerated his limp in order to gain my sympathy. He had not been pretending. Both his legs were travesties of what they had been before, scarred, twisted deformities. It seemed a miracle that he could walk at all.

I said, "I haven't changed my mind for that reason, no. And I think you've just proved that you can look after yourself."

He drained his brandy glass.

"Please sleep in the house tonight," I said.

He shook his head.

The scene in the barn presented itself in all its merciless detail. The man with the broken wrist sprawled in the logs, another sitting dazed on the floor with blood streaming down his face, a third tidily out cold on his back and Maxwell backing away behind me as Patrick walked towards him. Strange, I couldn't remember what any of them looked like.

"They won't touch you," Patrick said, reading my face correctly but not the reason for my fear.

"If they're mad enough they might turn up with friends tonight," I said but he wasn't listening. I gave him a clean towel and Peter's dressing gown and as he appeared to be mobile let him cope. When he came into the living room I was sitting with my feet up on the settee, drinking cocoa and stroking Pirate to soothe both our nerves.

"Lowers the heart rate," Patrick said, seating himself carefully on the other end of the settee. "Proved." He took the cat from me and she sat on his chest, purring.

"Cocoa?" I asked but changed the query when he gazed at the whisky bottle on the sideboard.

With the same kind of detached scientific precision that he had utilised outside the larder window he drank neat whisky until life became worth living, hardly speaking, staring into space, stroking Pirate. Then he rose painlessly, deft with artificial grace, and put on the clothes I had brought from Peter's wardrobe. Pants, socks, sweater and jeans. The latter were both too big and not long enough. Finally he topped them with his parka, removed his gun from under the cushion upon which I was leaning and went into the morning.

One thing was quite certain. If anyone woke him during what remained of the night they'd get a bullet.

I slept where I was, huddled under the dressing gown. It smelled of Peter's after shave and the awful bubble bath. Drifting off to sleep I wondered what Patrick's own dressing gown smelled of. Carbolic probably, he'd wash with anything and splash on anything, odd behaviour in a man so conscious of excellence in everything else. A mass of contradictions.

It occurred to me, waking up for a moment, what I'd done and that now I'd be sharing a room with him from time to time. He'd told the truth about something else as well: his legs weren't all that had suffered serious damage.

CHAPTER 4

Due to what she referred to as "a minor accident" in her spare bedroom, Maggie couldn't put us up. We discovered when we saw her that it had been almost completely gutted by fire after an electrical fault. On the phone, in the morning, she said she had room for one on the sofa, was terribly sorry but couldn't manage two. When I told her who I was bringing she seemed to think there might be room for two on the sofa but I declined politely. Unfortunately, Patrick came in through the front door without my hearing him as I was explaining that he was not exactly his old self, and got hold of the wrong end of the stick. He was also quite normal insofar as he was clearly spoiling for a second Hundred Years War.

"Does it make you feel secure or just superior?" he threw at me by the way of a first salvo as I put down the phone, not shouting and in a manner that would have frozen ethylene glycol solid.

I handed him a mug of strong coffee. "Good morning."

He sat down with his back to me. "Well, now you know."

"I wasn't referring to that," I said, stung by the unfairness of his not giving me the benefit of the doubt. "I wouldn't . . . not even with Maggie."

"I suppose it'll be like having a eunuch for a bodyguard."

I tried to tell myself that his eyes weren't dead, blank. I said "I'll read *The Arabian Nights* and let you know," and made my escape upstairs, taking my time with showering and washing my hair, and attempting without much success to camouflage the dark circles under my eyes. We were both too old, he and I, for this kind of excitement.

35

I phoned my sister from the bedroom. When I'd finished giving her the latest bulletin on my life there was such a long silence that I thought we'd been cut off. Then her voice came down the line with far fewer decibels than usual.

"You're mad, Ingrid . . . absolutely raving mad."

"I don't need that kind of comment," I told her crossly. "What would you have done?"

Sally had always liked Patrick and had flirted with him briskly, not all that tongue in cheek, every time they met. She had a husband of her own, of course. Derek was a historian and looked like one, shy, absent-minded and untidy. He was also incredibly handsome. Against all expectations the men had got on famously, Derek taking Patrick beach fishing and teaching him how to cast. I had never been sure if Patrick's reciprocal generosity had met with Sally's approval—he had set Derek on the road to a black belt in judo.

"You could never walk past a stray kitten," Sally said.

"Or a worm drowning in a puddle," I added. And once, not even a cockroach with all six feet gummed firmly to a piece of sticky parcel tape. Perhaps, after all, I was only obeying my genes.

"It sounds rather fun," said Sally. Ye gods, did I detect a hint of envy in her voice?

"According to you," she continued, "he used to have cloven hooves and a long forked tail."

"Now it's a well-Brasso'd halo." Was the necessity to fabricate this brave perky humour the penalty you paid for being a modern emancipated woman?

"You'll not say a word," I continued.

"Like a tomb," she promised, and after telling me that her youngest, Julian, had mumps, rang off.

During one fateful conversation before Peter and I were married he had made me promise never to wear black if anything happened to him. So I hadn't, not even at the funeral, guiltily easing my conscience with a suit in slate grey. I put it on now, with a cornflower blue blouse beneath, white earrings and a white silk scarf tied cowboy style. I studied my reflection in the mirror. A serious person stared back, black bobbed hair quite shiny like the nose, the legs not too skinny if I stood like a model. Not bad for thirty-five. I removed the jacket and scarf and went downstairs, postponing make-up until later.

He was mooning around the kitchen. There seemed to be some inner struggle as to whether he should help himself to breakfast or wait for me to get it for him. His face set masklike when I walked in.

I ladled out some muesli into a bowl, poured milk on it, plonked it on the breakfast bar together with a spoon then busied myself cutting bread for toast. He didn't move, another crunch time.

"Traps empty this morning?" I enquired, not intending to sound so spiteful.

"I came in to ask if I could use the phone," he said.

"Have you eaten?"

"I'm not hungry, thank you."

"Carry on," I told him. "You know where it is."

The ice capped volcano went out, closing the door. I ate the muesli, made tea, reduced three slices of bread to charcoal and was just getting rid of the evidence, the extractor fan going full blast, when he put his head round the door. Someone had cured his hangover. I could tell because a grin made a surprise raid on the corners of his mouth and almost won. He squinted at the blue air and then the rest of him came round the door.

If you now give me a demonstration of how to make toast, I thought, I'll stick the bread knife into your ribs.

A limp rabbit hung from one hand. He found an old newspaper, in the place where they'd always been kept, and skinned it, thankfully having already removed its insides. I'm not squeamish about skinning, I'd watched him do it plenty of times before, like pulling off a glove. He jointed it, washed the pieces, put them in a polythene bag and thence into the freezer.

We were both going to London. Final.

One pathetic specimen of emancipated womanhood then collected the wages of freedom. A huge sob erupted from me, gathered allies and reduced me to a blind, shaking fool. I make a lot of noise when I cry and fully expected him to react the way he always used to, like a horse shying at a scarecrow. When I felt his hands on my shoulders turning me round to face him, I nearly fainted. I had it all—singing in the ears and greyed out vision.

I don't know how long we stood there. It was straight out of Mills and Boon, me with my stupid head on his chest listening to his heart beating. The decision of how to end it was taken out of my hands. He simply gave me a couple of sheets of kitchen roll and went outside to stow his tent.

With numbed resignation I phoned a local builder to ask him to mend the window, visited my neighbour of the nervous disposition to give her a ten pound note to buy food for Pirate, returned to the cottage and packed a suitcase. Patrick had already ordered a taxi and presented himself, remarkably spruce, only one or two visible bruises, when it arrived in the yard. In total silence we caught the eleven o'clock train for Paddington.

We travelled first class under the auspices of my credit card and he wrote out a cheque for me for his share. I wondered if his expense account would stretch to a hotel bill.

"Apparently Maxwell's mob are considered a force to be reckoned with," said Patrick smugly, watching Devon roll past the window.

I said, "They didn't fall foul of any of your booby traps." After all, there had been no debriefing on my tears which were merely, I now realised, the result of delayed shock.

"Pretty basic stuff," he murmured. "They came across the fields. Maxwell got a carpeting for not having a go himself."

"From Daws?" I enquired innocently.

"Hardly. He's the source of the information . . . it's nothing to do with him really."

"If the position had been reversed, what would you have done?"

He replied without hesitation: "Led from the front."

"Through the front door?"

"Naturally."

"That would have made it seven to one."

"No, evens."

I couldn't believe my ears. One moment in tears or stretched out decoratively on the kitchen floor; the next, Jack the Giant Killer.

"Evens," he insisted. "Think."

"They expected you to be underpar," I said.

"A presumption instantly reviewed when they found that I was inside the house . . . or should have been. No," he continued, "underpar, half-dead, starving, call it what you will, their target was a big question mark. It was evens because we went to different schools, evens because I was taught to fight filthy. They were up against an alien education."

I shrugged. They had done their best and hurt him badly, but there had been two axes within his reach in the barn, one small one for chopping firewood and another full sized for splitting logs. Also on the wall had been a sickle, a garden fork and spade, and two pairs of shears. He had used his hands, and unless I was very much mistaken, both feet, reaping self-inflicted agony. What price chivalry?

He took the minder bit very seriously. We went for coffee to the restaurant car where I persuaded him to have a proper breakfast and afterwards he stood guard outside the lavatory door while I availed myself of its facilities. Attempting grimly to remain in contact while the train rounded a sharp curve, I remembered that my escort was armed. If this Daws approved of his choice of partner then I, too, might be expected to pack hardware. Then an idea of such nastiness raised its head that I couldn't wait to unlock the door and tackle him with it.

"Is it me being tried out as well?" I said sharply, ignoring the fact that several other travellers were nearby.

Patrick gave me a look that his father might have used on women who tried to pick him up when he was in mufti. When we were back in our seat he said, "Why don't you put it over the main broadcast? Female spy for sale, two previous owners and low mileage."

I didn't speak to him again until the train drew in at Paddington and only then to ask him to lift down my case. This was one of his favourite weapons, making the one instigating the sending to Coventry break the silence first. He reformed after that, holding open doors, bowing me on to the escalators, finally bringing the house down at South Kensington by laying his parka over a puddle. By this time I had a headache of such monumental proportions that I was only too happy to oblige him and step on it.

We booked into the hotel just off the Fulham Road that I always use when I'm in town to see Alan, my agent. That gentleman once invited me to stay at his flat, but only the once. Ingrid Langley ten percents are too precious to risk losing. I don't actually dislike Alan. He is too good-natured and well-mannered, the sort of person you can hate whole-heartedly for five minutes before inevitably succumbing to his charm. He had, after all, quadrupled my earnings from foreign sales.

I was thinking about him as I was shown into my room, the usual one overlooking the garden at the rear, and was toying with the idea of taking Patrick with me when I called to see him. Nay, the shadow would insist upon being included. The meeting might be rather amusing, if Patrick didn't have him stuffed and mounted for his collection.

Immediately the door closed there was a knock on it and I had to admit the reason for my presence in London. He wandered in, eating an apple, already tired, and checked window, wardrobe, behind the pictures. Then he stretched out on the bed, feet on the covers.

I ignored him and rang Maggie. She said that she would love to see us at any time after six and could we all go out for a meal as she'd had workmen in all day and the place was a shambles? After a short chat with her I rang Alan who decided, when I told him that I was being escorted, that he was only available for an hour, at ten the following morning.

Patrick was asleep, Granny Smith cradled in one hand. Perfection stretched to looking shipshape when slumbering, he never snored or lolled with his mouth open but I could not remember ever seeing him asleep during the day before. He looked dead.

I took his apple and finished it, standing by the window, glancing at him now and again. His face was almost totally unmarked, and sucking several ice cubes had reduced the swelling of his tongue. Under the denim jacket I knew he wore a shoulder holster with a gun. Major Patrick Justin Gillard, late of something not far removed from the SAS and now recruited into a unit equally secret. My ex-husband, I had to keep reminding myself, a different man from the one I had cast from my life, a difference that had nothing to do with serious injury, with nothing I could put into words.

Two hours later I was mulling over how to wake him without provoking a violent High Noon reflex action. I had showered, changed into a sage green dress that wasn't too formal, done my hair and made myself up with just a little evening glitter around the eyes.

I steeled myself. "Patrick?" I whispered, and then again, kneeling, speaking close to his left ear. He breathed deeply and evenly, the long black lashes far thicker and more glossy than mine.

It had to be done. I kissed him on the forehead.

No movement.

He was having me on, a joke of old, in order that I'd forgive his earlier behaviour. Neat, also demonstrating that he hadn't lost his sense of humour. One upwomanship demanded stringent action, a munching wet kiss full on the lips.

He wasn't having me on. A tremor went right through him, the broadside to his nervous system crashing into the ops room and catapulting him right off the bed. I saw it all. He not only didn't know what day of the week it was but couldn't remember coming into my room. I had been watching someone functioning on automatic pilot.

"Where did you get the apple?" I asked in an effort to divert him.

He woke up fully and the look of intense hatred on his face was fleeting but enough to send me backing away. He came towards me and for the first time in my life I faced violence of the mauling, mindless variety. My shoulders hit the bedroom wall.

"I'm sorry," I said, through fear. There was nothing for which to apologise.

"Behave anyway you like but that way," he whispered, turned on his heel and left the room.

I sank on to the bed, cursing a slow bumbling brain that had failed to penetrate crystal. He wanted me for a partner because, out of every woman on this globe, I was the only one who wouldn't want to go to bed with him. He was safe from distractions and that kind of challenge, a tidy arrangement for a man who had suffered injury of the worst possible kind. By the time we went out, half an hour later, he had cooled to waspish and I knew better than to try to jolly him out of it. The panniers on the BMW had proved to contain a comprehensive wardrobe and he had risen to my little green dress with a dark suit, white shirt, and claret silk tie. I studied him when he wasn't watching, flagging down a taxi, and thought about drugs and hormones and what I had seen in my bathroom in Devon, then dismissed it from my mind forever.

Or at least, tried to. There were complications.

Maggie's flat was contained in a large house that had started life rather genteel, plummeted into semi-ghetto and now, as the district once more became fashionable, had been bought by someone with imagination, gutted and turned into several opulent apartments. There were black-painted railings with gold points, a newly varnished front door with a massive brass knocker, and window boxes crammed with bright pink Regal pelargoniums.

Patrick's gaze raked the front of the building, trying to guess which was Maggie's flat. "That's the one . . . cacti trying to die on the window ledge, and the cat. It's probably stuffed. Inside there'll be one of those natty tiled fifties fireplaces that she got from a demolition yard because it reminds her of Mummy, and a row of those glass domes which you fill with water then consign flowers to a watery grave. We'll be given seed cake on plates with doilies under them.

"Or possibly the floor above," he continued in ringing tones. You can recognise an ex-choirboy even when they're ninety. "The one with the airport art antelopes and macramé plant holders. She swathes herself in ethnic cottons with silver tassels, those things that make even thin women look perpetually pregnant. She'll greet you with loud cries of—" and here his voice swooped down the street like a dying cor anglais—" 'Daaaarling!' "

He eyed the eleven steps and limped up them determinedly. "On the other hand," he went, no less loudly, "your Maggie's probably Jessie Adams in *Moonlake*. An Earth Mother, lives in the basement surrounded by seething pots of homemade yoghurt and sprouting fenugreek. There's a wartime Anderson shelter in the middle of the living-room in the event of the whole lot being blown to Kingdom come."

We made our way to the lift. My mouth wasn't actually hanging open but the little précis of one of my characters was perfect and delivered in quite different phrases from those in which I had described her to him. Patrick had obviously been thinking about my work. When we were married, he had never bothered.

On the top floor our feet sank into pale fawn carpeting which silenced all footfalls and made one want to speak in an undertone. It had this effect on my companion to the extent that he stopped altogether and followed me meekly to Flat Three.

The door was opened by an Irish Wolfhound which placed paws the size of feather dusters on Patrick's shoulders and knocked him flat. Lissom as willow he shut his eyes and waited until the face washing had ceased in response to loud cries of female consternation. Maggie looked down at him with a remarkably brave smile.

"I always thought the Irish were little people," Patrick said, allowing both of us to assist him to his feet while he assimilated Maggie's five feet eleven inches.

"It's the bitch that's Irish," said Maggie, removing long dog hairs from his jacket. "I'm just stretched with the speed that she takes me round the park."

Shepherded by both inmates of the flat, we entered. The four-legged one was almost immediately banished to her basket in the hall, a wicker creation that looked as though it might feel more at home beneath a hot air balloon, for hurling a rubber bone into my lap as soon as I sat down. We sank into vast armchairs, squashy red velvet ones with gold tassels, but not before Patrick had kissed Maggie's cheek to show that there were no hard feelings.

I had not met Maggie when Patrick and I were married. She was an ex-paramour of Alan's. Not that he is married, it was her own description of herself and sounded dramatic.

"Maggie's an interior designer," I explained to Patrick. Everyone gawps when they first enter one of her creations and Patrick was no exception. His gaze roved from the woodburning stove in the centre of the room, at the moment in its summer guise as the respository for an arrangement of flowers, over the deep red walls that matched the chairs and velvet drapes, you simply could not refer to the miles and miles of fabric as curtains. There were floor cushions in more red velvet with the same gold tassels to move them around by, ikons and an antique Delft dinner service in an illuminated alcove. Below all this lay acres of deep pile white carpet and, here and there, crimson and gold Rya rugs.

"Where on earth do you get logs in London?" I asked.

"I know a little man," said Maggie with a wink for me alone.

She had a whole bevy of these little men—stocking her favourite brand of French coffee, perfect potatoes she could bake in their jackets to mouth watering tenderness, exactly the right shades of fabric, doing her hair precisely how she wanted it—an army of adorers. She forgot not one of them at Christmas.

Patrick was examining the contents of the log basket. "Dead elm from the Royal Parks," he announced. "Blue sap."

"Ten out of ten," Maggie cried. "Brought up in the country or CID?"

"Both," he replied, and she smiled triumphantly and went into the kitchen for more ice.

"I'd have laughed like hell if you'd shot yourself in the armpit just now," I said to Patrick under cover of a passing vehicle with a defective silencer.

"I heard that," said Maggie through a serving hatch which I'd forgotten. She appeared, framed in pine. "And you can take that Cheshire cat grin off your face, too."

"Me?" Patrick said. "I've breath to grin?"

"You," she confirmed, disappearing to come back through the door with an ice bucket. "The ex to end all ex's according to Ingrid here." She fixed him with a penetrating blue stare. Quite formidable is Maggie, pretty, too. She'd kill me if I told Patrick she was forty-five. "How many Argies did you kill to make it worth while being blown up?"

"I shook hands with one," he said, smiling.

"Take no notice," I told her. "He fits no earthly pattern."

"It was by way of being a serious enquiry," Maggie said, presenting me with a vodka and fresh orange juice without asking my preference. "I wouldn't joke about things like that. What will you have to drink?"

"You got a serious answer," Patrick replied. "I'll have a pint of Marston's Pedigree for first choice, or a whisky and soda second."

"That comes by the barrel," she retorted and fixed him a whisky.

I said, "What I like about you, Maggie, is that you don't turn a hair when I roll up with a man only three weeks after being widowed."

A small frown appeared above her immaculately plucked eyebrows and instantly vanished. "More to the point I would have thought is that your previous husband is keeping you under his wing three weeks after you were widowed.'' She turned to Patrick. ''How's your jade collection these days?''

''Fighting fit,'' said Patrick, but warily. Maggie had obviously been reading up on the newspaper accounts of Peter's death and the last thing he wanted was a long, informed interrogation on his collection from an interior designer.

CHAPTER 5

Halfway through dinner I started to become uneasy. Even though we'd left the Marines behind in Devon we were still on the same island. It must have occurred to Patrick of course and I could understand that he would prefer to be in a crowd, even if this presented him with different problems.

We had gone to an Indian restaurant lavishly decorated with ornate screens and little fountains with coloured lights inside. It takes a lot of concentrated worry to prevent me enjoying Tandoori chicken but as the day continued to unfold itself like an episode of *Dallas* I grew more and more miserable. I could be at home now, I kept telling myself, up in my cool writing room, Radio Three ready and waiting to ease moments of mental stagnation.

Maggie and Patrick seemed to have hit it off and Maggie was making the most of it. I nearly threw a dish of rice at her. Ye gods, he was positively the last man you could dig chummily in the ribs but she was getting away with it. Then he gave her one of his onion bhajis when I knew he could easily eat it and actually whispered something in her ear. I was determined to remain outwardly calm. Once I let go it would be like Krakatoa all over again. Besides, I possessed the enormous advantage of ten years' experience of marriage to the man.

Therefore I joined in the laughter when Maggie made a joke, the latest of several when the wine began to take away her commonsense. Never could remain sensible after a few drinks, could Maggie. And I watched Patrick fill up her glass and regard her solemnly when she draped an arm around his shoulders at one point to illustrate an anecdote. Over guavas and fresh cream she had got to the stage where she was weaving a fine scheme to exclude me from after dinner amusement, giving him her come to bed eyes and, I'm prepared to swear in court, a wink. Just after that, without saying a word, he froze her off, an operation that took all of five seconds and got the message across as thoroughly as if he'd dumped her on the floor with her legs in the air.

She took it all in good part. Girls like Maggie have very thick skins; they have to, to survive their lifestyle. In the same short period of time she was smiling at him to show that she didn't mind and he smiled back to tell her that he knew she wasn't really a tart. The fascinated witness went on quietly eating her guavas, brain at the double.

We returned to Maggie's flat for coffee whereupon she produced a bottle of Drambuie. An hour later we let ourselves out, leaving her snoring gently on the sofa. The wolfhound watched us go, eyes sad.

If I'd known that the evening had worse in store, I'd never have let Patrick in for his last prowl of the day around the security arrangements. He came, staggering slightly.

"You're drunk," I said.

"Only the legs," he informed me. "The rest of it's stone cold sober." He checked the room and then meandered into the bathroom which he proceeded to use.

"Minders use their own loos," I said, adding, "and adjust their clothing before leaving" as he came out doing up his zip.

He sat on the bed. "Time to talk."

"Good night," I said.

For answer he patted the bed and beckoned.

"Good night," I repeated. No, it was monstrous, I had been his wife and had gone to him in response to the same gesture for love. I had gone to him for love on our wedding night when I had been twenty-one, an otherwise old-fashioned girl who had gone to that generous source of love since she was fifteen and he eighteen on a potent afternoon when we had both cried out as we lost our virginity together.

"Talk first, sleep afterwards," he said, laconic as always when tired.

I sat primly on the bed, well away from him, and then jumped up fast.

I was too slow. He lunged and caught me by one arm. Effortlessly, he hauled me close enough to feel the heat from his body. I struggled wildly.

"Further to our previous touching on the subject . . ." he said, not out of breath when he had pinioned both of my wrists in his left hand, leaving the right free. This commenced to travel.

"You can play it silly or you can play it straight," he continued. "You can believe me or call me a liar but if we're going to work together let's get one thing clear. I don't want you. I don't want anyone . . . ever. Do you understand?"

No, I didn't. He'd undone the top of my dress, buttoned under frills to the waist, and was fondling my breasts through the lacy black bra, a front fastening one that soon yielded to dexterity.

"Stop it," I said.

What followed can't be described as assault. He removed the matching black panties despite my entreaties, watched me as I lay there loathing that wretched, treacherous inch of me that was providing so abundantly for assuagement and took me all the way, uninvolved and uncaring with those long remembered artist's fingers.

I rolled away from him. There was no answer to selflessly inflicted pleasure, nothing that offered the right brand of soothing balm to my damaged ego.

He had made sure that the message was well and truly across, damn him. "Does that save hours of discussion and argument as to my hopes, fears and general attitude?"

My own hopes and fears, either for him or myself, didn't seem to come into it.

"We were once married," his voice went on somewhere above me. "Now, because of a series of happenings that I'll call fate to save any further arguement, we've been thrown together again. Please say whether you'll accept the terms."

I got off the bed, retrieved one small garment and went into the bathroom to rearrange myself. I didn't look in the mirror.

In every possible way but one he was the same man. He sat on the bed, eloquent, suave and logical, never using long words if short ones would suffice, the twenty-four carat army officer telling the cadets how to cut someone's throat without making a mess on the carpet.

"I accept," I said. I stood quite still as he rose to his feet, wincing as his legs took his weight. He crossed the room to the door and opened it.

"Good night," he said, closing it soundlessly behind him.

The cynic within me wanted to applaud. After all it had been a breathtaking performance, the most perfect revenge a man could take on a woman who wanted him back. I did want him back, I wanted to do all those things that would make a women's libber sneer for a week, but to take him back would be to gain the gingerbread without the gilt.

In the morning, over breakfast, I broke the news about the visit to Alan.

"What time?" Patrick said.

"Ten," I told him. "But I want to be late . . . he sulked when I said you were going to be there as well."

His eyebrows rose a fraction but he made no comment and went away to arrange the hire of a car. At a little after nine I found myself at the wheel of a Sierra, the same as mine at home.

"Sorry the colour's different," he said, rummaging in the glove compartment. "This map's no damn good. Is there a stationer's in the main road?"

"Yes," I said. "But I'd prefer to know why you need one first."

"Theory number two," Patrick replied without hesitation. "I was going to tell you anyway. It concerns a man called Carlos Savedra. Before the war ended for me, we captured a member of 16 Commando, proper Argentinian soldiers not at all like the miserable little conscripts. Savedra turned out to be a real bonus and when I got him talking it was difficult to get him to stop. He told me just about everything I had been ordered to find out, information that may have even shortened the war a bit and saved lives. Well, to cut a long story short, Charlie's over here, skipped, says that the Argentinian Secret Police are after him. He also says he's got some dirt on one of the discredited Generals and this character has friends in this country who might try to shut him up."

"But how was he allowed to leave Argentina?" I asked.

"Oh, you can drive a ruddy tank through the holes in his story," Patrick said. "Given that the country was in a terrible mess after the surrender he wouldn't have just been able to walk on to a cargo boat and work his passage here after being arrested and interrogated, as he says he was, before being discharged. I don't think anyone knew he'd given us the information—we'd have found out most of it anyway—he was sent back with all the ordinary prisoners of war. No, I think he's trying to buy a future for himself in G.B. Special Branch are keeping him at one of their safe houses until the Home Office decides what to do with him.''

''Perhaps a nasty little traitor should be sent home,'' I said.

He shrugged. ''His fiancée was one of the thousands who disappeared, and his mother was Welsh. I don't think that he feels too guilty.''

''Patrick, I still don't understand what this has to do with you in your flat in Plymouth.''

''It's Daws being ultra-careful. Savedra could be lying on other counts, too. He could be part of a plot to pay back Britain for having such a successful fighting machine, get some of the undercover commanders out into the open and then kill them. He might have told his secret police everything, including my description. What I did to him to get him to talk wouldn't exactly have had them purring at the Geneva Convention either.''

I said, ''So we're going to check if he's sticking to his story.''

''To check on him generally. Daws voiced some concern.''

''But you said that Special Branch were looking for him.'

''They are,'' he said. ''Don't be so bloody naive.''

I drove, parked somewhere nearly legal and walked the quarter of a mile to the shops. I bought his street map, a pound of home-made fudge, two pounds of apples and, almost, a white kitten in a pet shop window. When I got back he'd moved the car into a space vacated by another and was dozing, listening to Fingal's Cave on the radio. He was amused by my armful, helped himself to the map and an apple and became very quiet, perusing it.

We were close enough to Hyde Park to hear the clopping of hooves and I watched a crocodile of riding school ponies with their housewife riders, the instructress mounted on a bay horse worth approximately ten times the value of the others, mostly native crosses that would soon have to be clipped before they went winter hairy. One day, when I hang up my typewriter, I'm going to buy myself a Welsh Cob and explore Dartmoor on my own, up in the sun and rain with the cairns, tors and curlews.

Patrick folded the map after a while and stared into space.

"Where to?" I asked when his eyes swivelled in my direction.

"Ahead to those traffic lights and then turn right," he said. "I'll tell you as we go."

There were several, incredibly convoluted exercises that took us loop de loop toward the river, splashing down potholed alleys behind disused warehouses. Very soon I stopped worrying about deep puddles and someone else's tyres. When he was satisfied, either by this or with shaking off a real or imaginary tail, he lifted us out of the maze and we were on our way.

Right on the other side of the city, a good while later, I said, "If this was a mystery tour I'd want my money back." We had entered a district he had just told me was called Manor Park.

Of the park or the manor there was no sign, just streets and streets of mean little houses.

"Second left," Patrick said. Halfway down the road we turned into, unbelievably named after a poet, he said, "I've seen the one I want. Park over there just past the bus stop."

I prepared to sit and wait but was left in no doubt as to my function when he removed his jacket, unbuckled the shoulder holster, took out the gun and put in in my handbag, giving it back to me. The webbing and straps went under the seat.

"In case of fire cut round dotted line?" I wondered aloud.

"Only if there's danger of my imminent demise."

It was the wrong house. It had to be. The individual who answered the door of number twenty-seven was not one of those wearily handsome young things with five o'clock shadow, Special Branch writ large all over them, but a middle-aged man who reminded me strongly of a lizard. It was the way his chin slithered into his neck and shoulders.

"Joe, I presume," my escort murmured and went in, waving a piece of cardboard encased in plastic.

"Who's this?" Joe said, indicating me with a grubby thumb.

Patrick turned with the tiny polite frown of someone who's had his train of thought shattered. He gestured vaguely as if the whole business was too mundane to explain. Finally, he said impatiently, "He's going to make a statement . . . she's going to take it down. What's your problem?"

"She should have a pass," Joe said stolidly.

"Don't be a fool," Patrick told him sternly. "Since when have stenographers had to carry a pass when they're with Department Twelve operatives?" He carried on through the narrow hall and up the stairs and I was dragged after him purely by the force of his wake.

It was dark in a gloomy neglected way, every inch permeated with the smell of stale food, curry and Chinese take aways, and the other odours of neglect, dirty sinks, greasy dishcloths, stale bedding; a house of men, slumming it.

A younger man with ginger hair travelled precipitately backwards on the landing but whether this was because he observed the cut of Patrick's jib or was assisted by a hand on the chest I never discovered.

Weeks of no exercise, bad food and no fresh air had taken their toll on the third man we found in a locked front bedroom. He lay on the bed on his stomach, the pillow stained with congealed blood. He was conscious and I shall never forget to my dying day the look he gave Patrick when he saw him. It was a look with no name, comprised of hope, fear, hatred, love and overwhelming misery.

Patrick got him to the washbasin just in time. I busied myself looking in a cheap suitcase for clean clothes, shutting my ears to the dreadful retching and other associated sounds.

We worked as a team. I ran both taps to wash away the unspeakable, discovered Vim and a cloth in the bathroom next door and cleaned the basin, refilling it with hot water. Patrick stripped off the filthy shirt and washed the prisoner, with the same cloth and consideration but not a shred of tenderness.

"All right?" he said once, in a manner that he might have used to one of his own men after a slight training accident.

It succeeded, too. The man who must be Carlos Savedra nodded, noticed me for the first time, looked very surprised and tried to smile. He was about thirty, dark and of wiry build, a real live Argentinian. But Savedra was more Celt than Gaucho, with small hands and feet, sharp, agile, rather pleasing features. I wanted to feel angry with him but the anger focussed instead on the ginger-haired man standing in the doorway, trying to hide the hands that had made Savedra's features less than pleasing.

Patrick chose the least squalid of the rooms in which to preside, no other verb could do justice to his demeanour, the downstairs sitting room. A pale sun occasionally peeped from behind heavy clouds to penetrate its grubby net curtains. He asked Joe to carry in three dining chairs for himself, Savedra and I, but made the two Special Branch men sit in the much lower armchairs. Good psychology.

"Timing is the essence of both comedy and interrogation methods," Patrick opened the proceedings, strangely addressing Savedra who, so far, had not spoken.

I perched on the edge of my chair in what I hoped was a business-like pose and took down everything in shorthand, properly, in case I was asked to read it back. Patrick had warned me that I might need a pad and pencil before the day was out.

"Timing," Patrick said again, this time to Joe. "I resent deeply that you've utilised the notification of my visit in this fashion. You knew damn well it would look as though I was trotting in right on cue."

"I'm not paid to be fussy," Joe replied with a heavy glower in the direction of his assistant who had given up trying to keep his bruised knuckles out of sight. "I don't care a damn whether he tells the truth to me or you . . . when he has we can all go home."

Patrick turned to Savedra who had by now progressed from dead white to putty colour. He said, "I hope that neither of them strike you as nominees for an Oscar. If this little pageant of Joe's were with my permission it would continue thus—I would tear them off a strip, take you for a ride round London on a double decker bus to show you Buckingham Palace and Tower Bridge, then conduct you to a quiet pub on the river where you could pour out your heart with every last bit of truth. Right?"

He was way off beam. How could a foreigner penetrate that mixture of idiom and patronising derision directed at no one but Joe?

Savedra looked at him and across to me questioningly, then fixed Joe with a stare of unconcealed hatred. "There's a lady present," he said in perfect unaccented English. "I'm not saying a word."

"It's been done before," Joe said to Patrick.

"I have not done it before," he replied grimly. "I do not mop up your department's failures in a blaze of mock cameraderie."

"You're tearing them off a strip," Savedra said suddenly. "The first stage." His feelings got the better of him at this point and, in his own language, he launched into a tirade directed at all of us that lasted at least two minutes. Afterwards, into a rather stunned silence, he said to Patrick, "Second stage—you get me out of here and take me for that ride round London." He held out both wrists. It was an act of submission but was not abject; proud, rather.

"You can't have him," Joe said, proving his stupidity once and for all. Even the red-haired one looked disgusted.

"I have no intention of further questioning him on these premises or in this company," he was told. "The ultimate responsibility lies with us." Patrick borrowed my pad and pencil, wrote, ripped off a sheet and gave it to Joe. "Send his things to that address."

"We wait until I get clearance," Joe said heavily, manoeuvring his large body into the doorway.

"Then phone," said Patrick. "But make it soon. You know what happened at the Alamo."

Joe was still awaiting instructions over the phone in the hall when we left. His assistant abandoned all ideas of heroism and in the end opened the front door for me, the men following. Savedra was installed in the back seat of the car and then Patrick came round to my window. I wound it down a little.

"No," I said.

He turned to look back at number twenty-seven's peeling paint and grimy windows.

"Don't go back," I said. "Please."

The smile he gave me was part apology, part regret. That's if you didn't look at his eyes. He limped away.

"He won't hurt them much," said Savedra after a minute or two.

I jumped. I had forgotten all about him. "There's been too much violence already."

"Not the words of a stenographer."

I didn't answer him.

"You aren't worried about the old iguana either," he persisted.

"You have iguanas in Argentina," I said brightly.

He clicked his tongue reprovingly and turned to look at the house, his breath hissing as he twisted round.

"I'm sure iguanas come from South America," I said.

"Bloody millions of them," he replied absently, still watching the house. "Come on, man." A rapid glance at me. "A comment on your distant manner, ex–Madam Gillard . . . or can I call you Ingrid?"

"How d'you know?" I said, shocked.

A grin. How these damn men recover. "He told me . . . showed me a photo of you. I showed him one of Francesca." The grin snapped off like a light.

I thought quickly. She was dead and here was I being beastly to him. "I'm sorry," I said. My gaze followed his to the house.

"The real power's in his tongue, you understand," Savedra said, as if I didn't know already.

I said, "Is it all right if I call you Carlos?"

"Charlie . . . the other's too much like the bloody war."

I had a sudden rush of blood to the brain. "You were there when he was injured."

Charlie studied me very carefully for a moment. "Of course," he agreed. He turned back to the house. "Ah, he comes. I'm glad, so glad that he didn't die. It was a miracle . . . we thought he would die right in front of our eyes. A lot of blood. I'm glad, too, that I didn't run away and could help him."

"A Christian thing to do," I said, seeing the silver crucifix on a chain around his neck.

He saw where I was looking and touched it. "What else can one do? I gave it to him and he held it while they put tourniquets on his legs. We both prayed . . . I used a prayer book he had in his top pocket. Terrible things happen in time of war, don't they?"

Some part of me registered Patrick slamming the car door. He drove the car off down the road for me. I managed to take over when we had gone about a half a mile.

CHAPTER 6

I already had enough material for several block-busters. The realisation coincided with the return of the faculties required to drive the car and the realisation that our passenger had run out of adrenalin. Patrick made him eat fudge and gave me road directions. Some time later, around lunch-time, I parked by a riverside public house and gave Patrick back his gun, thinking about irony.

The day had transformed itself with sunshine; real, hot summer sunshine. We chose a picnic table amongst the trees and I was dispatched for Marston's Pedigree and hot food.

He came from tough stock all right. Patrick introduced us formally when I returned with the drinks: Major Carlos Owen Savedra. After two jacket potatoes topped with chilli con carne and another pint of beer, he was unrecognisable as the same man who had nearly fainted in the car.

"Not enough chilli but nevertheless very good," he said, scraping up the last morsels. "Thank you, my friends, for everything."

A hot lunch hadn't done Patrick any harm either. He smiled at me across the table and said, "His English is immaculate, isn't it? That's why he was given the job of disguising himself as a Falkland Islands shepherd and told to discover British troop movements. Not his fault he tripped over us a few miles from Port Stanley."

Charlie whistled through his teeth with great feeling. "I'm not a countryman even though my parents were. This bastard here was born and bred in Devon. He tricked me by calling a ewe a tup. How the hell was I supposed to know?"

56

"What's a tup?" I asked.

"A ram," Patrick explained. "It had the previous summer's lamb running with it, too."

"God almighty they were a rough bunch," Charlie went on, talking to me, his dark eyes sparkling. Not for the first time I came to the conclusion that soldiers are impossible. In the middle of mud, blood, filth and worse they retained this daft sense of humour.

"An old pony kept coming in out of the rain and lying down under the only bit of the roof that didn't leak. They gave up trying to get rid of it in the end and used it as a bed settee. When I was brought in and the blindfold taken off there was this grim Mafioso leaning back against the pony. I was convinced for a moment that they'd killed it to sit on."

Patrick chuckled. They were both remembering good times—fragments, I had to keep reminding myself. Afterwards, fate had turned their lives into such hell that it was possible to think of small episodes in a war as fun.

"He turned you over to the rest?" I said.

Both registered shock at the suggestion.

"If I'd been a private, perhaps, but there was no time for luxury, no time for boots in the ribs and spitting." He shot a sideways look at his one time captor, probing for reaction, but found only bland good humour.

Patrick must have seen my puzzlement. "Good for morale sometimes to turn one of the enemy over for a little softening up," he explained. "In some people's opinion . . . not mine." He went off for more beer and another vodka and orange. I was designated listener.

"I know you think I'm going to use you to talk out my bad memories," Charlie said.

"I don't mind," I told him, glancing over my shoulder. Had this man succeeded in getting his target, the undercover commander, out in the open?

He smiled at me. "It's a crying shame you broke up. He's a good man. In that filthy hut he hurt me a lot but not enough to . . ." He tried again. "Just the two of us, the others sent away. Every one of them knew it was only a matter of time, no one could stand up to him. I could see sympathy in their faces afterwards, not contempt. When it was over they treated me well."

I said, "Why did you come to Britain? Because your mother was Welsh?"

"Where does a traitor go?" he said softly.

"You're not really a traitor."

"Traitor," he repeated. "No, clever Ingrid, say the word. I have, a thousand times. They did, over and over, when I was arrested in Buenos Aires. By the time they had finished with me I didn't care but now I'm here . . . stateless, a displaced person, a deserter, a traitor."

"Go to Wales," I urged. "Find your mother's people."

"Do they understand traitors in Wales?" he queried.

I said what was uppermost in my mind. "It was Patrick who made you a traitor."

"The generals made me a traitor," he corrected. "From the day Francesca disappeared, I disowned my country. Then, in prison, someone said that she was alive and in London."

"London!"

He gave a rueful smile, rubbing a palm over several day's growth of beard. "Like me, she's only half Argentinian. Her mother's British, divorced from her banker husband. The rumour was that she'd bribed someone to let Francesca go and brought her here. I don't believe it now . . . the more I thought about it on the ship the more crazy it seemed. I asked that Joe find out and he said when he'd checked that her mother was dead."

"That doesn't mean . . ." I started to say, but the look on his face forbade optimism. I got up to take the tray from Patrick as he came out of the Saloon Bar entrance of the "Dancing Rat." No motive, not to get away from any awkwardness, just my automatic reaction to seeing his worried frown as he concentrated on not spilling the drinks.

"Will they come after him?" I said to Patrick.

"They might check the address I gave them and find it doesn't exist," he said. "Was any of your stuff valuable?" he asked Charlie.

Charlie told him that he'd be glad to see the back of all of it.

"So all they can do is complain to Daws," Patrick said. "Cheers."

"Not with his blessing then?" I commented. I seemed to be drinking vodka and orange rather quickly and put down my glass.

"He dropped a hint that they were putting on the pressure," Patrick said. "In my book that's permission." He glanced round to find out if anyone could hear but the nearest people, a couple oblivious to everyone but each other, were a good twenty yards away. "Right, Major Savedra," he said in quite a different voice, "talk."

Savedra's overstrung nerves caused him to twitch all over but he used the movement to shift slightly on the bench to face the speaker. "No," he said politely, "I have nothing to say to you."

Patrick prompted him. "You were taken to a safe house instead of a remand centre before deportation for one reason only, your insistance that the secret police tried to stop you boarding the ship. You further said that two members of the same outfit tried to sneak on board just before she sailed but were thrown off by the first mate. On your mother's grave you swore that your fiancée had been brought to London by her mother and would vouch for you and also that the General in question, now on trial in Argentina, had told you personally during your interrogation that he had powerful contacts in Great Britain. This latter, my friend, is a lie. How much of the rest is false?"

"Your police have found out that Francesca's mother is dead," Charlie said defiantly. "I was just telling Ingrid. Ask her."

I nodded when Patrick looked at me.

"It was a rumour," Savedra said. "Desperate men stay alive on rumours."

"Okay," Patrick said slowly. "See if you can explain this. The first mate on the *Rio Salaras*, I spoke to him over the radio telephone at five this morning, couldn't remember repelling boarders or anything about you at all other than that you badly needed a bath."

"He was drunk most of the time," Charlie retorted. "I doubt very much if he could remember his own name."

"Not of the most saintly disposition," Patrick conceded. "But nevertheless quite sure."

"I've nothing else to say," Charlie said. "Take it or leave it."

Patrick drained his glass and put it back on the table with a deliberation I had seen before. "I suggest to you," he said, "that the whole account of your arrest and imprisonment is a lie . . . the authorities were far too busy with the aftermath of the war to bother about one deserter and, knowing you quite well, I don't think you've the bottle to be a spy. You lived rough, made your way to the docks and eventually found a ship sailing for Southampton. Where did you hear the rumour about Francesca . . . in a dockside brothel?"

Weak, tired, ordinary man that he was, Charlie took a wild swing at Patrick and had his flying arm seized by the wrist. With a sense of mild horror that quickly became absolute I saw the grip tighten. Savedra's whole body went rigid.

"Not here," he whispered.

"Because of your bloody fabrications I was ordered to lay low for a month," Patrick said through his teeth. "For the first week I was in hospital so someone else did the worrying. Try it one day . . . try carrying a gun when you're on crutches."

"I haven't lied," Savedra gasped and then bit his lip, his eyelashes suddenly spangled with tears.

Throwing a scene in public has never bothered me. I threw one now, and the remains of Charlie's Pedigree pint all over Patrick. I can vaguely recollect using the expression "cruel bastard" plus a few others of which I'm not particularly proud. Our fellow imbibers, all at once tenfold in number, got a real treat then. Charlie took a backward swipe at Patrick with his free hand and it connected. At this point I dispensed with the company of both of them and went to the car.

"I resign," I announced to the windscreen and several interested parties watching me through it. "Forever," I added as I turned the key in the ignition. What choice was there now that we no longer got on famously in public?

Alan had not become a top literary, TV and film agent by opening his mouth at the wrong moment. He took one look at me, forgot that I was four hours late and gave me the full works, arms flung wide in welcome, an earful of cooing Italian he'd picked up on holiday, a kissed hand, the lot. For once I let him have his head; he knew I was totally immune. But fat cat curiosity got the better of him. He's feline, too, that's why I can handle him.

"The senora is alone?" he murmured, pressing the button that opened his drinks cabinet.

I replied with an un-senora type epithet, thus reducing him to more sympathetic cooing and the offer of a vodka and orange. He threw himself into the vast green leather seat behind his desk, and revolved a couple of times, a thoughtful expression on his round, self-satisfied face.

For someone who is a failed jazz pianist and university drop-out, Alan is a genius. Jack of all trades, master of none, he has used the rudiments of many skills like an artist to paint a glowing canvas. He is honest, widely read and very funny, casting his pearls not exactly at the feet of swine but with generous abandon. His only mistake as far as I was concerned was to invite me to become his mistress.

There was no question of my ever being tempted. He stands an inch or two shorter than I do and measures a good deal more around the middle. Unlike some women and most men I had chosen to remember that I was married, to Patrick at the time, which had introduced further difficulties. I had no wish to witness Alan being slowly spitted on his own collection of African spears. Fat cats and wolves don't mix.

The collection of weapons still adorned the walls of his office, though "suite" would be a more accurate description of his domain. It was all onyx and green buttoned-back leather; a David Shepherd, an original not a print, of an elephant hung on a wall also adorned with a zebra skin, wooden tribal masks and a shrunken head that I had tried in vain to persuade him to put somewhere else on the grounds that it represented another continent. I hated it. It hung by its black hair like a shrivelled grapefruit, with an expression which was understandably highly peeved.

Alan donned his glasses. They had very large dark frames and made him look like an owl. A subconscious choice, perhaps he always put them on when he was going to be serious.

"Trouble with *Moonlake*, too?"

"I've hit a snag. I might re-write the first half."

"You don't mean that, Ingrid."

Confound him. "I've fallen out of love with it," I admitted.

"Since when?"

Since Patrick came back, I thought to myself. "It strikes me as a mite trivial, that's all."

"Trivia sells," he pointed out cruelly.

"Perhaps I've written enough romantic thrillers."

He removed his glasses and tossed them on to the snowy blotter, a sign that I could relax. "Have a holiday," he suggested. "I advised you to do that a couple of weeks ago. No one can carry on working when—"

I carved him up. "It's nothing to do with Peter."

"All right." He spread his podgy hands in a conciliatory gesture. "But when did you last go abroad? When did you last have a rest, lie in the sun? Everyone should have a break sometimes. Go away, my sweet, forget everything. If you finish the novel by Christmas it'll be plenty soon enough."

"To finish it by Christmas I'd have to work twenty-four hours a day starting yesterday," I said acidly.

"That's how it seems to you at the moment," he soothed. "When you've had a break, all will be different. Life will have—"

Again I stopped him mid-sentence. "You're my agent, not a shrink. I don't need shrinks. I might just give up writing. The least that'll happen is that I'll change my style, write stories with a lot more punch and realism."

If Alan had been a budgie he'd have fallen off his perch. "There's only one Dick Francis, darling," he drawled, bitchy streak coming to the fore. The glasses went back, too. "What section of the population represents the most book buyers?"

"Married women in the twenty to forty-five age group," I recited obediently.

"Right. And what do married women want to make them forget their miserable marriages? Romance. Your style of writing fits the needs of the more intelligent. Well researched background, long enough words to make them congratulate themselves that they read the *Daily Telegraph*, a snippet of violence for spice and a couple of pages of mild porn to give them something to fantasise around when their old man makes love to them. Perfect . . . a best seller . . . can't fail."

This cold-blooded commercial breakdown of something so very dear to me and personal, a cherished ability to write stories that other people wanted to read, had never before been uttered in my presence. I could see the words typed on a card, filed under L for Langley in one of his sage green cabinets.

"I don't sit down and write a snippet of this and a couple of pages of that," I protested vehemently. "It happens. It happens and I write it down."

He shrugged, smiling. "However it happens . . ." A thumb rubbed against a forefinger in an unmistakable gesture.

I must, after all, need a holiday. Never in one day had I wanted to push so many people's teeth down their throats. The world was a nasty, greedy, nightmare factory.

Alan still had his glasses on, all the better to see me by. He called his secretary over the desk intercom and asked her to bring in tea for two. There was silence until it arrived. Perhaps Alan spoke and perhaps he refrained, I heard nothing. All I could think of was that again I had witnessed Patrick's darker side. It seemed that with little or no provocation he became transformed into someone whom I had to admit could have killed Peter. Perhaps he had used him as a shield; surely every moment of those years of training would demand such pragmatism. I would re-write my own mental version of what had happened.

"There *were* two other bodies," I said unthinkingly into my cup of Earl Grey.

"When Peter died?" Alan said. "Don't look so surprised, your face is tragedy personified. Both killed with great precision, a bullet through the heart."

"I don't remember reading that," I said.

"My friend on *The Times*," Alan explained. "The only reporter in London who bothered to visit the scene of the crime. The others got it through the usual channels before it was strangled by Whitehall."

"Peter was shot several times in the back," I said.

"With two weapons of a different kind. What are you thinking?"

"Three guns?" I said.

"Not for publication. Nothing for publication but that it was an attempted robbery." His magnified brown eyes grew even larger. "My pet, are you thinking that your Patrick—"

"It was my Peter!" I raved.

He pursed cushioned lips.

"Well? Speak to me!" I shouted at him.

"Men aren't allowed to die for each other these days without generating a few sniggers," said Alan. "The owner of the flat could be regarded as a cripple at the time of the shooting, I understand. I have a picture in my mind of one man throwing himself protectively before another and—"

"How can you sit there and spout such drivel?" I interrupted. "You've been reading too many trashy novels. Why should Peter want to die for my ex-husband? He went out for a drink with him occasionally, for old times' sake, but no matter how much Patrick tries to convince me they were buddies it was me who listened to Peter telling me how much he loathed him. He loathed Patrick for what he did to me."

"Then why pay him a call?"

"He thought he was being followed and wanted Patrick's advice."

"Who said so?"

"Patrick."

"So you believe that but none of the rest."

"I don't necessarily believe any of it."

"Had Peter mentioned anything about it to you?"

"No . . . not a word."

He kept quiet for a moment, chewing one of the ear pieces of his glasses. Then he said, "Your problem is that Patrick has come back into your life under what appeared to be dubious circumstances and won't go away."

"Under orders to keep an eye on me," I said angrily. "Sometimes I wonder if he thinks he's still at war. You hear of soldiers who go a bit barmy."

After more chewing Alan said, "We met once. You brought him to a Foyle's lunch. I was rather impressed."

"You're never impressed by anyone," I snapped.

"He had, in a word, integrity."

"That doesn't exist in your world."

"No," he agreed. "But that doesn't mean to say I don't recognise it when it is presented to me. No, not a man to go barmy. From what you've told me I'd guess that he wants you back."

How could I explain to him that Patrick appeared to want me only for my physical presence and was unable to provide what I had always wanted him for?

Alan said, "Ingrid Langley won't write a word until her personal life is settled."

"I've been writing solidly since Peter died," I said defensively.

"Blotting it out. Waste paper basket fodder. You said so yourself, *Moonlake*'s gone wrong."

I was grateful for one thing. After the love-lorn Italian episode he hadn't launched into any of his usual vaudeville, hadn't presented me with one of his encounters with the moguls of the entertainment industry, Alan the Righteous with his sackful of Top Ten ratings, every one flying the Union Jack, standing bravely and alone against the tide of transatlantic soap that bubbled out of their offices.

"I might write something for television," I said.

He sighed. "Then make it like 'The Long and the Short and the Tall,' dearie, all one set. They haven't any money."

After another argument he relented and spent half an hour explaining how to lay out a TV script then patted my arm and sent me on my way. By this time I was convinced that I had wasted the afternoon for both of us and had spoiled our relationship, albeit a somewhat strained one.

I had no plans, the immediate future seemed to hold no more than a depressing emptiness. There seemed to be nothing else to do but go back to the cottage with my protector and sit it out until all danger was deemed to be past.

The underground car park beneath the hotel was very brightly lit, a refreshing change after others in my experience that had reminded me of the catacombs at Palermo before the fire. I parked and locked up, feeling only mild surprise to notice a hearse gliding through the lines of cars. After all, people did die on holiday.

It circled round and came down the aisle towards me. I stepped into the lee of a Rolls and waited for it to pass.

The hearse stopped and both doors opened, completely blocking my way. Three men got out, two short, the other tall, all as pale as their normal cargo. In their black suits they looked like crows.

A murder of crows.

CHAPTER 7

I fled down the gleaming sides of the Rolls towards an emergency exit. Like most women I can run much better when I'm not wearing high-heeled shoes but there was so much broken glass on the concrete floor I did not dare kick them off. The men were too close to stop.

One of them was right on my heels. I could hear him wheezing as his tar-filled lungs laboured. My suit jacket was grabbed but I slid out of it and tore on, leaving it behind together with my shoulder bag.

He caught me just as I reached some rubbish bins near the exit. It gave him a shock when I stopped dead, twisted round and jabbed at his eyes. I pulled free of his clawing hands. Another of the men ran round the bins with the idea of coming up on me from behind but I was already facing him when he prepared to seize me and the pointed toe of one of my shoes thudded into his groin. He gave a small shriek and ceased to take much interest.

That left the second shorty, as yet unblooded. He played grandmother's footsteps with me around the bins for half a minute or so and then came at me in a rush, pinning my arms to my sides. I kicked his shins until he yelled but he hung on, our faces inches apart, nearly succeeding in knocking me out with his halitosis.

Some sixth sense made me go limp and he nearly dropped me, the blow from behind aimed at my neck taking me on the left shoulder instead. I could see nothing but a sea of grey with floating black blobs in it as pain scythed through my whole body.

When I could see clearly again I was pinioned from behind and the one I'd poked in the eyes was in front of me.

He was raising what looked like a blow pipe and his cheeks were puffed, ready to expel the air in them. Shorty number two really found his vocal cords when my heel hacked back into his shin. He keeled over as something hissed past my left ear, but I was forced upright again, my arms taking the full brunt of his very bad temper.

There was no possibility of the next dart missing me.

None came. I heard a sound like the pop of a champagne cork and then sat down like a puppet with scissored strings. Feet pounded concrete, doors slammed and they were away, tyres squealing.

People don't open bottles of champagne in underground car parks, I was musing when I heard footsteps behind me. I didn't bother to turn round; the halting gait spoke encyclopaedias. A roasting was in the offing.

Picked up—God, I'd know him blindfold in a roomful of thousands—steadied and guided towards the lift, I wasn't stupid enough to try to come the fainting ninny. Inside the lift he gave me a critical once-over, took out his handkerchief, moistened it on his tongue and scrubbed at my cheek. Always the perfectionist. Then he handed me back my jacket and shoulder bag, helped me on with the former and, glancing round quickly as if expecting armed men to burst from the walls, kissed my forehead. He reeked of stale beer.

Never has a woman had to go to pieces more privately. By the time we reached the hotel bar, I was shuddering like a horse with a broken leg. If he'd produced his silenced gun with intention of putting me out of my misery, instead of giving me a vodka and orange, I wouldn't have noticed.

We sat in a corner of the bar and I could only admire the strategy of keeping me in a public place. He lounged opposite me, watching both entrances and waiting for me to recover.

"One of them had yellow eyes," I whispered when I could trust my voice. "Not the whites . . . the irises . . . like a tiger."

Patrick leaned over and took both my hands. "Will you be all right for a minute while I go and phone? Just over there, by the bar."

I said that I would be fine and asked him to bring me back a coffee, I had already consumed far too much alcohol for one day. Practical soul that he is, he ferried back a vast round of turkey and stuffing sandwiches. I offered him one but he declined.

"You look hungry," I said.

"Saving it for later. Daws is taking us out to dinner."

I can always eat. Through a mouthful I said, "Back to theory number one?"

Patrick frowned. "To be honest I wasn't expecting such drastic developments along that line. Think back if you can . . ." Here he studied me closely. "Do you mind? Was Peter himself a few weeks ago? Did he seem distracted or worried in any way? Are you sure that he didn't say something to you—even a few words—that might give a clue as to what he was doing?"

He knew what he was asking me to do. During these past weeks I had resisted the need even to put a mental picture to Peter, to remember him as he was, knowing that it would only mean more hours of the lonely misery usually referred to as mourning.

"Forget I spoke," Patrick said softly, still watching me.

"Daws will pump me later?" I suggested.

"Daws couldn't care a damn . . . Peter's death is a police matter now."

A hint of anger betrayed him. "But you're determined to find whoever killed him."

He gazed at me soberly. There was a small bruise on the side of his jaw. "Is that what you want?"

"Not if it means you losing your job."

That shook him slightly. "I mean it, Ingrid."

"So do I. The police aren't stupid . . . they'll eventually arrest whoever's responsible."

"That might be slightly optimistic."

I finished the sandwiches and then said, "Supposing you were to try to find out more. What would you do?"

"Make the obvious moves: speak to Peter's boss, go home for the weekend . . . I don't mean to Plymouth."

Home was now Hinton Littlemoore, in Somerset. Since his days as curate at Edgecombe, Patrick's father had moved twice, to Brandon Hill, Bristol, and from thence to Somerset.

I said, "That might expose your parents to some risk."

"Wherever we go there's a risk to others. A country parson should be as safe as it's possible to be, even from loonies in a stolen hearse."

I didn't want to see his parents, not because I didn't like them but because of the awkwardness.

"Someone will do a sub for me if you want to get on with the writing," he said, reading exactly what was going on in my mind. "But see what Daws suggests first. That's if you're still game."

I'm an all or nothing person but until the audience with Daws was prepared to postpone my decision as to whether to go on. Right now, a long, hot bath was all I cared about, that and a long, long sleep. And the truth.

I said, "If I'm to work as part of a close knit team there can be no hang-ups. Why did Peter find it so necessary to die for you? I can understand him trying to get you out or even throwing the furniture at them but . . ." I floundered into silence, entering forbidden territory.

"Okay," he said quietly after a moment of silence. "Peter died for me because it was the only thing he could do better. Human nature's unaccountable, isn't it? We were at school together, joined the police together, were in the same rugby team, swam together—and he could never do quite so well as I did. It became a bit of an obsession with him . . . I even had to cut down on the amount I drank so he could drink one more. He never changed, not even after I'd left the police and gone into the army. In the end he married the woman—" this with a worried frown at me—"who'd chucked me out because he wanted to succeed where I'd failed."

"That isn't a friendship," I whispered. The hurt was awful.

"No, not really," Patrick agreed. "But it was the reason why he took the bullets, whether they were meant for me or not."

I fought down an overwhelming need to cry. "He must have known you'd do the same for him."

"No, I don't suppose he assumed anything of the sort. Besides, the situation would never have arisen, he knew that, too."

I felt stupid and ugly, not understanding.

"If you survive army training you don't have to be a martyr," he explained gently. "When he came to me for help it didn't go against the grain because, by this time, we were in different trades. It was a hell of a shock to him to find I could hardly walk but here was his chance . . . to die for me was the one thing he could do better. Put Peter in any situation where my life was at risk and he'd have done the same.''

So I'd been married to a rather kinky hero who had married me for rather kinky reasons. It took a lot of getting used to.

"I promised him I'd look after you," Patrick said.

I forgot to ask him what he had done with Charlie.

Getting ready to go out, I thought about Peter. It was understandable that Patrick should only see the situation from a masculine point of view. In his own way, Peter had loved me I was sure. I remembered his habit of bringing me little surprise gifts. He had nearly always come home with something: a bar of chocolate, a box of chocolates, a polyanthus in a pot; sometimes a joke like a tin of prunes or a black beetle in a match box. After all, he had gone out with me first, when I was fourteen, working towards ''O'' levels at Edgecombe High. Patrick had remained in the background, head boy, remote and serene as a stuffed lammergeyer. ·

Memories and old-fashioned notions like love and self-sacrifice did not belong in this stark new life I was living. I took Peter's photo from the bedside cabinet, had a last look and then buried it at the bottom of my suitcase.

I eschewed false eyelashes and dabbed on a little shimmery shadow. Dressing for what part? There were plenty of mementoes: a deeply bruised shoulder, sundry scratches, arms that felt like boiled noodles.

There was a knock at the door and I went to open it, then remembered.

"Who?" I asked.

"Me," he replied. "Sober Simon."

I let Patrick in, eyes heavenwards. It hadn't occurred to him that no one could imitate that dry voice even if they knew what it sounded like.

Sober Simon wore his sober suit with another white shirt and a sapphire tie. He approved of my dress in the same shade of blue. Ye gods, had he been spying on my clothes, too?

"The right outfit to meet the boss?" I said.

"We're not on parade."

"No? Then why are you so nervous?" This was one method of ruffling his calm, pretending I could see through him to the core.

"I'm not nervous."

"All right, you're not nervous." I sat on the bed and giggled, a failing of mine.

"Ingrid, have you been drinking?" he asked sternly.

I suppose it was a knock-on effect of the day's events. I could only think of a Mess Dinner during which a tiddly Colonel's wife had let off a soda siphon in his direction because she thought he was playing footsie with her under the table. The culprit had turned out to be a brigadier's dog that Patrick had been feeding with rare fillet steak as he hadn't been hungry. Dripping, his face had worn the same expression of injured outrage as it did now.

"I'm not going to balls it up for you," I cackled. Gradually, the helplessness wore off and I sat hugging my aching ribs.

"You've smudged the silver stuff," he pointed out, long-suffering.

I went to the mirror to carry out repairs. "You didn't exactly rush to my rescue . . . another few seconds and I'd have been crammed full of curare."

"I rushed," he affirmed. "Down the stairs from the security officer's room two floors above. All the lifts were busy. Good God, woman!" he exploded. "You don't imagine they illuminate the place like a film set to prevent people sneaking in for a quick screw? I'd been up in that fat slob's smoke-filled den for two hours, trying to stay awake while watching four TV screens at once."

The phone rang and I reached it first. It was the receptionist informing us that Colonel Daws had arrived and would wait for us in the lounge. He hoped we would not be long as our table was booked for half an hour's time.

Patrick swore with some verve. He didn't speak to me again until he made the introductions, and when he asked me what I'd like to drink he gave me a smile that said if I didn't have fruit juice he'd throw me through the window. I said I'd love a vodka and orange.

The Colonel was not going to be a pushover. A ramrod straight youngish fifty, Daws had fair hair fading to grey at the temples.

Every so often it flopped over his eyes and he scooped it back, a mannerism inbued with a lifetime's practice. His eyes were blue, heavily lidded, and tended to snap wide open without warning in a stare of knife sharp intensity. As they did now, on Patrick's retreating back.

Daws turned back to me with a smile that displayed either all his own teeth or some very expensive dentistry. "Ingrid Langley, no less," he said with a small charming bow. "My wife used to read you avidly."

I made a suitable reply.

"She had four," Daws mused. "*The Last Dance, Hilary's Son, Barefoot upon Thorns* and *The Brandy Glass Murder.* I distinctly remember the titles because I gave them to the hospital where she died, together with quite a few others. Stupid to have a lot of stuff gathering dust when it can be of use to others. I want you to know, Miss Langley," he continued, changing the subject without pausing for breath, "that this isn't going to be one of those evenings where the men talk shop over the lady's head. I hope you weren't hurt this afternoon."

I told him that I was all right, adding that I had expected to be required to give descriptions to the police.

"The Major got a good look at them," he said as though my contribution would be of no real importance.

"You're far more interested in who hired them, I suppose," I said. "Wouldn't identification lead to that, or do police investigations mean too much publicity for your department?"

"My dear, it's in several parties' interest to smash my department, a small unit that has just been set up to counter foreign interference within MI5. The Russians alone have a network of about fifty spies in London—the trade mission, Aeroflot . . . they're all involved."

It is a good five years since I last smoked and for a moment I missed being able to find a cigarette in my bag, light it and inhale deeply while I digested this amazing statement and, more importantly, what it implied. So I could only stare at him with what must have been a rather stupid expression on my face.

"Reluctantly," Daws went on, "and in the light of the most recent developments, I'm beginning to think that your husband had smoked out something or someone connected with national security. Now that someone knows that you've been approached concerning joining my department.''

It seemed to me that we were talking about theory number three. I protested, ''Surely that's stretching credibility to the limits.''

''Did the pair of you ever discuss his work?''

''No, but—''

''We're talking about interference from within,'' Daws interrupted. ''It's not too difficult for a personal file to be examined, an operative watched, his movements noted, including with whom he spends his free time . . . old friends, new friends, ex-wives . . .'' He broke off and smiled sadly.

I knew by some sixth sense that recently, perhaps only a couple of hours before, he had had Patrick's file open in front of him. Just then I would have given a small fortune to know what was going on in the man's mind.

I said, ''By 'interference from within' I take it you mean from within MI5 and not within your department.''

Daws nodded. ''Someone has been paid to cause chaos, and dismantle Department Twelve in the process. Threats to ordinary clerical staff—from obscure sources of course—accidents to others, suspicion, whispers . . . all the usual tactics.''

''The source of that information must be a Russian defector,'' I hazarded.

He shrugged disarmingly, not ready to let me into all his secrets.

''Reliable?'' I persisted.

''Extremely,'' Daws muttered.

''I still don't understand how Peter could have become involved.''

''He might not have been,'' Daws said. ''I did say that I was considering the possibility reluctantly. Who knows, his only crime in a certain person's eyes might have been that he was a policeman friend of a security officer, perhaps snooping for him on the side and making police information available? A good ploy to rattle a man, too, gun down an old friend under his nose.''

''How rattled was he?'' I snapped, angered by the slur on Peter's character.

At this he gave me one of his stares but I held the look and he rose to his feet, ostensibly to arrange the chairs to make room for a group of people who had just arrived at the next table.

"He was pretty upset," Daws said, sitting down again.

There seemed little point in starting an argument. "What exactly is my role to be?" I demanded.

"I think you have a fair idea already. Socialising mainly . . . weekend house parties, shooting parties, coffee mornings . . . everything, really, from jumble sales to state banquets. The pair of you will get to know certain people, meet their friends, listen to them. Most of the time you'll be expected to carry on exactly as you are: behaving, dressing and possessing the poise of a successful lady novelist."

I said, "Taking sneaky photos of people, breaking into their hotel rooms and examining their things, brazening it out or pretending to be blind drunk if caught red handed."

"You have a very good idea already," said Daws. "The Major's convinced that you can both work as a team."

"Rubbish," I said. "He wants me so that he has an excuse to keep other women at a distance, to make it seem as though he's normal."

Daws reviewed Patrick's position in the queue at the bar and spoke quickly. "He's not far from normal now. There's enough of one testicle left to keep him masculine and supply the incentive to prove it. That's medical fact. If you work with him then you might be watched when you're least expecting it. Better to allow people to see you doing what comes naturally than blow your cover pandering to a man who's choosing to forget what his privy member's for. Marry him again if you must but—"

"For Patrick's own good?" I interrupted furiously.

He regarded me blandly. "For the good of both of you. There might be cameras."

I realised I was shaking my head. I had not intended to refuse to co-operate quite so early in the proceedings. "If he so chooses then that's how it is," I told him. "If there are psychological problems, there are clinics he can attend." For a moment my anger took hold. "How about a really meaningful kiss-o-gram?"

It very quickly became apparent that Daws was not going to help Patrick carry the drinks so I performed the small service that even the most rudimentary good manners demanded, my cat's whiskers detecting some decidedly odd vibes.

After some desultory conversation Daws announced that we ought to go, adding that the restaurant was only a short distance away and we could walk. I avoided Patrick's eye, knowing that he also had assumed that we would be eating in the hotel restaurant. Pure cowardice forced me to carry on evading it when we arrived at our destination, Daws having set a fast pace. A quick glance at his profile was sufficient. I caught the faint sheen of sweat on his forehead.

I had guessed correctly that Colonel Richard preferred conventional food, placing him, again correctly, as a steak and chips man. Making myself concentrate on the menu I selected the chef's special, turbot en croûte with dill sauce and a green salad.

I risked a glance at Patrick when the waiter came for our order but he was only a slightly frostier version of his usual self, asking for steak au poivre with plenty of black pepper-corns and silently bemoaning the absence of his beloved curries. Out of favour but definitely not down.

When the waiter had departed Daws said, "I'm beginning to wish the *Rio Salaras* had sunk with all hands. Savedra's cost us several thousand pounds already and we can't send him back, on humanitarian grounds."

"He came clean," Patrick said to me. "Just as I thought."

Suddenly I felt very sorry for Charlie. "At the pub?" I asked.

Patrick nodded. "He only headed for this country because of the rumour about Francesca still being alive. If he'd just told the truth instead of deciding to beef up his story everything would have been a lot less complicated."

"Deserves to be deported," Daws said morosely. "I can't say I blame Special Branch for giving him a going over."

"He was still sticking to his story then," Patrick said acidly. "It was Ingrid blowing her top at me that shook him into telling the truth. A bucketful of cold commonsense . . . his words. I wouldn't know, I was the one who got soaked in beer."

I wondered, totally irrelevantly, who would be the next woman to throw beverages over him. It would have to be a woman; no male could expect to survive such an assault.

When our meal arrived it was eaten in a silence of such deathly quality that I began to wish that the Marines would catch up with us after all. Even a perpetual optimist could only come to the conclusion that Daws had just decided to do without our services. After we had plodded through a sweet and were waiting for coffee to be served Daws excused himself, saying he had to make a phone call.

Patrick screwed his napkin into a ball and threw it on to the table. "So if we assume that he's not too chewed up by the loss of a nice little coup with an Argentinian spy, then what's bugging him?"

"What did you do to those Special Branch men?" I asked.

"Gave them a piece of my mind and then barricaded them in the john," Patrick said. "If he's mad with me it can't be about that . . . they're always regarded as fair game."

"What about after I left you with Charlie?"

"Nothing happened. Charlie confessed and we caught a bus to where he'll be looked after without unpleasant interludes. Daws interviewed him when we got there and then I went straight back to the hotel." He chewed his knuckles.

"Perhaps it's my fault," I said. "I refused to seduce you but didn't imagine that everything would hinge on it."

"You refused . . ." His mouth closed slowly when he realised he had left it open.

"Cards on the table," I said. "He gave me a blow by blow account of the latest with your procreation package."

Patrick's tongue slid slowly along his lower lip. His eyes didn't leave my face. "Well?"

"I told him what you did with it was your business. A joke's a joke, Patrick. What happened in my hotel room was probably me trying to pick up the pieces of the fun we used to have between rows. You don't have to explain or give reasons . . . nothing's the same anymore."

"No," he said quietly. "Nothing's the same."

"I don't mind," I said. "I admit that I stuck our marriage for far longer than perhaps I should have done because you were so good in bed. It doesn't matter now . . . I might even have grown up at long last."

Daws was approaching as I uttered these last words and his presence acted like a steel shutter slamming down on the table between us. Coffee and mints were served. When the bill was paid and we were outside on the pavement, he spoke directly to Patrick for the first time that evening.

"We will continue this tomorrow." He stared at Patrick, eyes blazing. "You know St. John's hospital?"

"Yes, sir."

"Be there. On the steps outside, nine sharp, in uniform."

Soldiers never question orders. "Yes, sir," said Patrick.

Daws turned to leave and then halted, facing us again. "Prepare a little speech of apology to those two members of Special Branch whom you almost killed. Make it good. Quite a lot of people will be listening."

CHAPTER 8

We were alone on the chilly pavement, both shivering. I took his hand and he didn't snatch it away.

"God," Patrick whispered. "God help me."

"Am I right in thinking that your uniform's in Plymouth?" I ventured.

"I told them what miserable little bastards they were," he said, no louder. The shiver went all the way to a full-scale shudder.

I tucked my arm through his and piloted him back to the hotel, my heart in my mouth at every moving shadow, every vehicle a black hearse.

Outside my room he said, "I swear to you I didn't hurt them."

Four years ago he would have found no need to protest his innocence of any action that might lower my estimation of him. Four years ago this look of desperation hadn't existed.

"Not even without meaning to?" I asked, prising myself free from his grip.

He groaned softly, looking away. "All right, I banged their heads together. But not hard enough to put them in hospital."

The one with no faith in the numinous then closed her mind to rationality and took charge. It was only a little after ten, the meal had been over very quickly. I issued precise orders and with many a glance over my shoulder, collected the car from the basement car park. Then I picked him up from the front of the hotel and drove several hundred miles as though a fleet of hearses were after me. After slewing to a standstill outside the cottage in the early hours of the morning, I was too weary to do anything but sit at the wheel as Patrick unlocked the barn,

78

changed his clothes where he stood, spent a penny in the garden and then roared off into the darkness on his BMW.

"Go to Hinton Littlemoor," he had said as he got out of the car. "Wait for me there. I'll ring them from the flat. Don't stay here any longer than half an hour." Then he had pecked my cheek and was gone.

I touched my cheek where he had kissed me, a perfectly natural husbandly kiss. How much longer before he cracked under the strain?

Still seeing double from tiredness and the glare of headlights I turned the car so that it faced up the drive, blocking it, and then entered a cold alien house. Pirate appeared from somewhere and rubbed around my legs but she was the last of my worries, she had a cosy bed in the barn. I collected my case from the car, threw everything out and repacked it with clean underwear and a mixture of summer clothes and warm casuals. Then I fetched Patrick's possessions from the car and barn and put them in the living room.

All of this took more than half an hour, nearer three-quarters.

I had to have a drink of hot, strong coffee. Afterwards I was swilling the mug under the tap when the phone rang. To answer it or not? I did.

"Haven't you gone yet?" Spitting the words at me, terse with anger.

"Halfway out of the front door," I told him.

He said, "They're expecting you," and rang off.

There was a hint of dawn outside, the click as I shut the front door an intrusion into silence. I stood still for a few seconds, getting my eyes used to the darkness. A bird twittered sleepily from the beech hedge, the car a darker outline. Small reassuring details that were simply insufficient to stem pure, unadulterated panic. There was no logical explanation as to why I remained still and did not run, blind and screaming into the village, nowhere, anywhere.

I stood with my back hard against my own front door and finally convinced myself that the crows weren't waiting for me in the gloom. I went to the car, got in and started the engine and no men with yellow eyes leaped into the illumination from the headlights as I moved off up the drive.

After what was probably about five miles, I stopped sweating.

I had to go almost right into the centre of Exeter before I found an all-night petrol station. The cashier told me, puzzled, that he hadn't sold petrol to anyone driving a hearse. I said brightly that it was my brother I was asking after and that he'd borrowed it to go to a Hunt Ball.

The sun came up on Mendip and I pulled into a layby to watch, only dimly being aware of Taunton, Somerton, Castle Cary and Shepton Mallet in my wake. They had all looked the same with their dead curtained windows and orange street lights.

To me, sunsets are more poignant. At the going down of the sun and in the morning we shall remember them. The Last Post, Union Jack draped coffins, a water filled ditch for a grave in the Falklands, plastic body bags. After the divorce papers had come through, I knew he was going to be killed.

Why this awful guilt? The timing had not been mine but a solicitor's and it was likely that he had not received his notification until well afterwards, when he was in hospital in Aldershot. Now, maimed as well as rejected, he wanted me to take him back. Was he deeply in love with me or insane?

A red glowing sun had almost cleared in the low hills that must be those that bordered Salisbury Plain. More memories: a married quarter in Warminster when we returned from honeymoon and, already bored with housework and army wives' coffee mornings, I had set out to put a few more ideas on paper for another novel, *Hilary's Son*, my first best-seller.

A flock of birds flew high and unassailable across the pink sky. I could no more reach them than make amends for what was past. Perhaps it was futile, possibly we were both doomed to failure, but maimed, insane or whatever, a very insistent conscience demanded that I take Patrick back.

Hinton Littlemoor sat, fair and square, in a shallow valley four miles east of Bath, once a strawberry and cream tea venue in the days of steam train excursions. No one came here nowadays. Motorways channelled the foreigners to Stratford on Avon and elsewhere, leaving the village to sleep out its history. It was a creation out of Alison Uttley: teapot-shaped thatched cottages with hollyhocks brushing the eaves; roses drooping, heavy-scented, while bumblebees floundered golden-dusted in their centres. Tapestry gardens edged with shells and chips of coloured marble, rosemary hedges six inches high encasing marjoram, thyme and basil. A Post Office, a village store, the Ring O'Bells and, of course, the church where Patrick and I had been married.

The rectory stood right next door to it, built of the same soft yellow limestone. Elspeth Gillard had planted her garden accordingly, varigated spindle on the walls of the house, green and white foliage with vivid orange berries in the autumn, a Russian Vine, rampant all over an ugly garage, its flowers like rich folds of cream and white lace, and roses, red, orange, white, yellow and cream, set off by a large lawn upon which children were encouraged to play.

Elspeth came out of the front door when she heard the car. Like everything about a family where nothing or nobody was permitted to be second-rate, she was exactly as I remembered her: a slim, pretty, fashionable woman in her late fifties.

There had never been one word of recrimination from Elspeth and this made it easy for me to return her embrace and apologise for the sudden visit.

"I knew it wasn't right when he said you would be here in time for breakfast," she said, smiling.

I apologised again, feeling guilty. She had almost certainly had eggs and bacon ready for me.

Eyes as grey as her eldest son's scrutinized me. "My dear, I'm so very sorry about Peter."

Patrick's father had phoned as soon as they heard, warming, consoling words from a man who knew me to be an unbeliever. They had sent flowers and a letter, penned by Elspeth, the right expressions of sympathy from someone who had had plenty of practice. This was not cynicism on my part. She had once told me herself that the ability to write letters of condolence was of paramount importance to a churchman's wife.

"He hated the idea of mourning," I said. "He once made me promise never to wear black if he died. Life on this planet was only a part of existence, according to Peter. He thought that we journeyed on, not necessarily with the loved ones of this life."

"Only children often feel like that," Elspeth said thoughtfully. "They spend most of their childhood on their own, relying on no one for what John insists upon calling 'the fruits of human company.' They see no reason why it shouldn't be like that in the hereafter, too." She took my case from me. "Poor Ingrid, you look so tired. Has he been treating you badly?"

It was the measure of the woman that she seemed to find nothing strange in the fact that her favourite child had taken up again with his ex-wife. We entered the house and she asked me no further questions and offered no comment. I was shown to the spare bedroom, the blue and white one with a single bed, and left there while she went to see to the lunch.

I stripped and washed, rubbing cologne around my temples in an effort to combat a huge headache. It was nearly one o'clock. By now Patrick had limped up the steps of the hospital. I could imagine the rest but preferred not to. Daws had already ensured that the guilty one would stand out, scarlet and buff in a world of pallor and green.

I wanted to believe Patrick and it was not difficult to do so when one accepted that, when wildly angry, he didn't know his own strength. If he had banged their heads together in the mood he was in when he went back to the house, it was conceivable they would end up needing hospital treatment. But, argued the small inner voice that appeared to have appointed itself to argue his case, if he had barricaded them in the bathroom of number twenty-seven, it suggests they were annoyed and mobile.

"D'you mind eating in here?" Elspeth popped her head around the kitchen door as I approached.

Only a gigantic snob would object to eating in Elspeth's kitchen. Not for her the blue wooden shelves and greasy lino supplied by the Church Commissioners. No, Elspeth had a little money of her own and had used it to brighten what had been the most depressing room in a cold, inconvenient and old-fashioned house. She might continue to turn a blind eye to anaglypta wallpaper painted in sombre shades in the rest of their home but in here there was a stripped pine dresser and oblong table, pine shelves filled with her mother's Spode dinner service, red tiles on the walls and floor, red check curtains and tea towels. Everywhere the evidence of her green fingers flourished, vegetation soared on the window ledge, bristled on the table and swooned from the dresser.

"He sounded a bit strange on the phone," Elspeth said, giving me a large slice of mushroom and sweet corn quiche. "Oh—

I forgot to tell you . . . John's gone to a Synod meeting. He asked me to give you his love and said he'd see you at dinner.''

"Patrick must have rung you at a horrible hour," I said. How much could I tell her?

She laughed. "Just after three. Don't worry, we're both used to him after all these years . . . He's rung us up from all sorts of weird and wonderful places at all hours of the day and night.''

"But not from Plymouth surely," I said wryly.

"Plymouth? His flat you mean?" She laughed again and sat down. "You wait until I see him. Had you been to a party?''

I ate a mouthful of quiche and came to a decision. "We were taken out to dinner by his new boss.''

"Colonel Daws? How nice.''

"Not so nice," I told her. "He told Patrick to meet him at nine this morning in uniform. His uniform was in Plymouth.''

"Deliberately." A statement, not a question.

"There seems to be some justification," I said guardedly.

"You mean he's in trouble.''

"Yes.''

"So that's what it was," she mused. "That would explain quite a few things. What is he supposed to have done?''

"Duffed up a couple of Special Branch men.''

Elspeth laid down her knife and fork. "And has he?''

"It looks like it.''

"Were you there?''

"I saw him go into the house where they were and come out again a few minutes later. He's assured me that all he did was knock their heads together and lock them in the loo. Now they're both in hospital.''

Frowning, Elspeth ate another morsel of quiche. "I wouldn't have thought him fit enough to duff anyone up.''

"Oh yes," I said, wishing otherwise. "Only a couple of days ago he took care of seven Royal Marines . . . six with his fists and then their officer wisely got out of range.''

"Did he lose his temper?''

"Yes," I said. "And paid horribly afterwards." After a short silence I added, "I think they had orders not really to hurt him.''

"Idiots!" Elspeth spoke with more violence that I imagined her capable of. "Humiliation was the name of the game, was it? Daws again, I suppose. One of those who tests hallmarked gold.''

A close knit tribe, the Gillards. If the worth of one member were questioned, you doubted them all.

After we had eaten, Elspeth insisted that I rest. I didn't need to be told twice and slept dreamlessly for four hours. When I woke up, the late afternoon sun glimmered through the shadows of leaves on the wall. Outside, crunching the gravel, engine purring softly, was a motorbike.

I bounced up and went to the window. Not entirely dressed in black this time, he wore jeans instead of the leather trousers. He looked around, still with the helmet on, and then rode the bike over to the old stable and dismounted stiffly. Elspeth came out to greet him as he kicked down the stand and lifted the bike on to it and I heard her exclaim when the helmet was removed and she was confronted by a complete stranger.

Charlie was explaining when I arrived on the scene. He flashed me a smile. Patrick was too tired to trust himself with the bike so was coming by train, and would I meet him at Bath from the seven-thirty?

I introduced him to Elspeth, telling her exactly who he was. She was fascinated, sweeping him indoors and to the little bar in the lounge. She loved a glass of sherry before dinner and visitors gave her a better excuse.

"But, good lady, I cannot stay in your house," he was protesting when I caught up with them.

"What nonsense," Elspeth said. "Of course you can. Besides, my son's already invited you." And with this irrefutable piece of logic she went into the kitchen to fetch him a can of lager.

"To draw the enemy's fire?" I said quickly. To judge from his appearance a detention centre was a haven after his previous habitation.

Charlie nodded. "He gave me the details. It was the least I could do after clipping his jaw." A small shrug. "He signed for me, you understand . . ."

"You clipped his jaw after extreme provocation," I said.

He smiled nervously. "Sometimes he hates me a little. He remembers . . ."

"The war." It made sense.

"Always the damn war," he muttered, and looked away.

Before very long Elspeth had prised out of Charlie most of his story and was making helpful suggestions as to how he could try to trace Francesca. I was grateful that she made no mention of the problem of battered members of Special Branch although she must have suspected that Patrick had spoken with Charlie of the outcome of the meeting. There seemed very little chance of my getting him alone again to tackle him on that subject.

At a quarter to seven John Gillard returned and welcomed the additions to his household with characteristic calm, shaking Charlie warmly by the hand and kissing my cheek. He was a tall, spare man who worked too hard and, like all of his calling, seemed tinged with other-worldliness. I had never been able to bridge the chasm between us.

"Take off your dog collar for dinner," Elspeth encouraged him, aware that he always preferred to don comfortable but ancient sweaters when not on duty. She had always been convinced that his official garb made non-churchgoers feel awkward and her very awareness had made me more jittery than ever in their company.

Now, for some strange reason, I was quite relaxed.

"I can't stay in this house," Charlie said when we were alone.

I guessed what was on his mind. "It's not your fault," I told him. "The Gillards are the very last people on earth to hold Patrick's injuries against you. Blame all your beastly Generals."

He sat, miserably staring at the floor.

"Look," I said. "He's a soldier, too. He's killed and maimed . . . it doesn't need me to tell you that. Neither is Patrick a popular man. Quite a few people would give their back teeth to do what was achieved by an act of war. For as long as I can remember he's been domineering, a bully in some respects."

Charlie was shaking his head as I spoke.

"He's their blue-eyed boy," I continued. "But they were the only ones not to tell me how awful I was for putting him out of my life."

"There's no middle course," Charlie said. "You either love him or loathe him."

Thus have eccentric Englishmen conquered the ingenuous. I said, "Let him use you if it makes you feel better, but don't be too dazzled."

Strange how I can always give others advice but never follow it myself. I thought it over in the car, driving to the station, perhaps my first insight as to what had gone wrong with our marriage. Had I been too dazzled?

I always ignore what has been inflicted upon the city of Bath in the name of progress and steep myself in its treasures. I deliberately drove a route that took me past the Abbey and the Orange Grove, as usual a mass of flowers, and then to the station, resplendent with newly cleaned stone and graceful dark blue wrought iron pillars.

Patrick was sitting in the booking hall, waiting for me, stoned out of his mind.

"You can't go home like that," I said. With a sinking feeling I realized that if Charlie had had good news, he would not have hesitated to tell it.

"They've seen me like this before."

"Have they?" I barked, making the ticket collector smile behind his hand.

He concentrated deeply and stood up. With the amount of alcohol he had inside him he deserved a medal for that alone.

I got him to the car and piled him in. Tried, convicted and sentenced. To what?

"Patrick, you must promise me one thing." From the way he was looking at me, I knew he was seeing double.

"What?"

"Charlie feels very guilty about what happened to you in the Falklands. Please don't let your tongue run away with you at dinner and—"

"It's because they don't play cricket at school," he interrupted, laying a hand winningly on my arm. "Never teach the little sods how to throw straight."

"Please Patrick!" How did you sober people up fast?

In the end I admitted defeat and drove him home, asleep, dreading our arrival more than I had ever dreaded anything before.

Woken roughly, by now I had run out of patience. Patrick walked into his mother's kitchen, having not seen her, I suppose, for a couple of months. She was putting the finishing touches to some seafood cocktails, a favourite of his and only, she had been at pains to point out, enjoyed on very rare occasions. He kissed her cheek and as all mothers will, she held him at arm's length to look at him. His breath must have given him away a thousand times but she didn't bat an eyelid. Then his father came in the door behind me and paused. Patrick turned, saw him, and came across, hand outstretched.

I bit the tip of my tongue hard. He was hardly limping. The drink? A skinful of painkillers? Was he in fact drunk or merely fit to drop from exhaustion? I hadn't bothered to kiss him after all.

None of these things?

No, it was most of these things. He was exhausted, drunk, being brave and they had accepted that he sometimes needed to behave like this. What I had forgotten was that the system would not regard it as a lapse.

CHAPTER 9

The odds were against it but the meal was not a disaster. I remembered just in time that grace would be said; the only one, to my shame, to lapse.

Charlie proved to be an amusing raconteur, skillfully steering away from any subject that might prove to have sensitive overtones. Where he had found such loquaciousness after his earlier discomfort I could not fathom but, watching him, I began to understand. Deliberately, he drew Patrick into the conversation. As he ate what must have been his first proper meal of the day, and the alcohol worked its way out of his system, he began to come alive. True, he drank the Soave his father gave him but lost that silly fuddled look and the tendency to lose control of his speech. The only bad moment for me was when cricket was mentioned.

"I see Somerset lost to Yorkshire on their own ground," the rector said disgustedly. "Threw it away . . . disgraceful fielding."

"Someone dropped three catches," Charlie said. "I sympathised, I would have done the same."

"They don't play enough cricket in Argentina," Patrick commented. "Mostly football." He turned to Charlie. "Are you good at football to make up for it?"

"Not that either," Charlie admitted, looking slightly offended. "I race motorbikes . . . or, at least, I used to."

"Of course you do," Patrick recalled. "That's why I asked you to ride the bike down. You also play polo."

"Polo!" cried Elspeth. "How lovely."

"Only a small local team with ordinary ponies," Charlie

explained. "Nothing like your Royal Family play. Rough and ready. Really rough . . . people using their sticks on each other. There's a sin bin for those who are rough with their ponies, the referee's a retired bishop's wife . . . she has the loudest voice I've ever heard in a woman. I thought you'd like that," he said smugly when the loud laughter had died down.

I helped Elspeth clear away the dishes and there was an unspoken mutual satisfaction in the way everything had gone.

Measuring out ground coffee she said, "You always used to worry tremendously about the way Patrick behaved here when you were married. It doesn't matter you know, we know what he's really like, you don't have to feel responsible."

I could think of nothing intelligent to say.

She went on, "But I'm going to ask him about this spot of bother he's in. He expected me to bring up the subject earlier, over dinner, but it won't hurt him to stew for a bit."

"He doesn't know I told you," I pointed out.

"He's guessed you have . . . I can always tell when he's in hot water by the way he gives me a sheepish kiss."

"Elspeth . . ." My hesitation wasn't a question of getting used to my new status as Patrick's ex-wife so much as never having engaged with her in any meaningful conversation.

She took my hand. "Ingrid, you've no idea how pleased I am that you've taken it upon yourself to—"

I had to stop this train of thought. "No," I broke in, "It's not like that at all. I don't want you to think I've taken anything upon myself. He's done that. He promised Peter he'd look after me."

"Well, he would, wouldn't he?" she said matter-of-factly, "Patrick's like that. You can't expect him to obey a piece of paper. Now," she continued briskly, "what were you going to say?"

I had originally filed for divorce on the grounds of his mental cruelty, not strictly true, and my solicitor had guided us into separation for reasons of breakdown of marriage, a lot less bother and with a considerable reduction of bad feeling. I said lamely, "Must you tackle Patrick about this business tonight?"

"No, of course not, not if you don't want me to."

"There's a lot more going on than we all know about and he's under terrific pressure. Perhaps . . ."

There was no need for me to stumble on with any more reasons, Elspeth had patted my arm and turned to busy herself with the coffee. It was a relief but I still had to remain calm and outwardly relaxed while the coffee was drunk and through an hour of somewhat stilted family conversation. At last the Gillards went to bed, Elspeth taking Charlie upstairs to show him his room after she had explained the new sleeping arrangements; Charlie in the single room, I was now in Patrick's, and he was on the camp bed in the box room.

I thought that Patrick had fallen asleep already but almost as soon as the door closed behind Elspeth he spoke.

"Joe is in intensive care . . . in a coma with head injuries, a broken arm, ruptured spleen and multiple bruising. He might die."

"And the other one?" I enquired, having to remember to breathe.

"He has a fractured skull. He woke up while I was there."

We might have been discussing the weather, such was his calm.

"They were released from where I had put them about ten minutes after I left by men who proceeded to set about them with pick-axe handles, fists and feet. From the vague description he was able to give it seems that they were the same three who tried to kidnap you in the car park."

I made myself stay in the chair and not rush over and hug him.

"Joe's oppo has a thick skull," Patrick continued. "The medics seem to think it was intended that he should never wake up. He was very surprised to see me and his first reaction was that it was still going on. He cried out to me for help so I held his hand and told him it was all over. I didn't dare look at Daws. He'd wheeled in half the Metropolitan Police to hear me apologise."

I said, "The idea was to make sure you got the blame."

"Seems like it."

"Then this was what Daws was telling me about . . . some plot to discredit and therefore disband his department. Why didn't you mention it to me before?"

Still inert and seemingly half asleep, Patrick nevertheless smiled. "You hadn't agreed to join us then."

"I'm not sure that I have now," I snorted. "All this makes your original excuse for coming to protect me seem very thin . . . it gets less and less to do with Peter all the time."

"No," he replied thoughtfully after a short silence. "Daws is speculating that Peter was assumed to be sleuthing for me on the side."

"So he said."

"Think," said Patrick.

"Think for me," I told him. "I'm tired."

"If whoever it is has been paid by a foreign power to cause chaos, what better way than to murder a bloke's friend, make it look as though he'd done it, and all this with the choice little advantage of knowing that the bloke was originally married to the victim's wife?"

I said, "Has it occurred to you that if we work together I'm likely to be in far more danger than I've ever been in my life?"

Patrick didn't answer, just reached for the whisky bottle.

The box room was the kind of antiquated store house where children of imagination might play murder in the dark. It was unheated and damp with only a small, rusting iron-framed window that had never opened in the sloping ceiling. You hit your head everywhere you wanted to be, your hair mopping up the cobwebs.

It smelt musty and of mothballs, this latter emanating from three thin blankets on the camp bed, the legs of which wobbled badly. The woman was crazy if she thought I was going to let him sleep in here.

I had just come from his own room with its ten tog quilt covering a king-sized bed and the contrast could not be more stark: posters of tigers and tanks, the mobile of early Second World War planes he had made as a boy, some rosettes he had won at a local gymkhana, a gull's wing, a stuffed owl. The box room had memories, too, but they were of the less pleasant variety: a tailor's dummy like a corpse with no head, dusty suitcases, a nightmare abstract painting that Elspeth had won at a jumble sale raffle. If he slept in here he'd wake with the screaming shakes.

I moved in as quietly as possible, taking only those things that I would need in the morning. Patrick would never notice. By the time he had finished drinking he would automatically head for his own room or stay right where he was, downstairs.

Some time later I heard him come up the stairs and he made straight for where I shivered under the thin blankets before turning aside to enter the bathroom. I buried my head under the covers and a long time elapsed. When it seemed that he had almost certainly fallen asleep in the bath the door opened and the light was switched on.

"You're in your own room," I said from where I was. "Good night."

There was a short pause and then fastidious fingers twitched away the blankets from my head. I could feel his eyes boring into the back of my neck but stayed still, feigning sleepiness.

"I lied," he said.

"You're drunk," I mumbled. Heaven preserve me, he had cracked.

"Two glasses of wine with dinner and a nip of whisky just now," he said. "I refuse to be held responsible for Daws buying me a few drinks."

He was speaking normally but I knew precisely what I was going to see. Yes, he had showered, shaved and was quite naked, magnificently ready.

"I'm going to apologise in advance," Patrick said. "For raping you or loving you, your choice, and making a complete hash of it." With that he picked me up as if I was a sack of feathers and carried me into his room.

One doesn't cry havoc in a country parsonage at one o'clock in the morning without excellent reason. Dumped into the middle of the bed I came to several startling conclusions. He had decided to get drunk in order to give himself courage, and then had failed to find the courage to achieve even that.

The inevitable took place very quickly. He came down upon me heavily, his mouth on mine to keep me quiet. With soldier's science I was positioned and penetrated and he was already ejaculating when he brought us together. I could do nothing but be a vessel to a raging tumultuous release. Of pleasure there seemed to be very little, the spasms that shook him wrung small whimpers from his throat and caused him to clutch at me, shuddering.

I rejected half a dozen possible reactions and lay still.

"I'm sorry," he mumbled into my hair when he could speak. "God, I'm so sorry."

"It would serve you right if I screamed the house down," I hissed. "Am I really so unapproachable that you couldn't share a problem?" I was saying the things he would expect me to say but in intimate warm contact, every smallest movement of his body against mine was a blessing. His former studied artistry might be gone forever but technique was not all.

"There's been no one else," he said. "Just machines that gave me electric shocks and totted up the sperm count. It was hell."

So he needed a lot more practice. I pulled his head down close and commenced to give his mouth something else to do, using him unashamedly for my pleasure. The golden advantage was still in his possession, the ability to retain his erection for some time afterwards. The dumbhead got the message after a while that because he might not now be perfect in bed, it didn't mean I no longer wanted him.

I had my pleasure, softly muted as always after abstinence, and then, a little later, roused him from drowsiness, slipping up my nightdress to my waist and showing myself to him, anything to feel him inside me again. This time his outraged nerve ends gave him a lot less hell and considerably more pleasure and he had the nightdress ready to muffle me as I sang out my ecstasy. Then we both giggled because he'd remembered.

"Thank you," was all he said before he fell asleep.

CHAPTER 10

"Tea," Patrick's voice said.

I instinctively buried myself but was sought and found, his laughter vibrating all the way down his arm.

"Your mother came in?" I breathed.

"Came in, saw and approved," he reported. "You didn't honestly imagine she intended anyone to sleep in the box room?"

Over breakfast a slightly puzzled John told us that he had passed the time of day with a man who looked like a hiker, leaning on the churchyard wall, and had been asked if he wanted the grass cut. Grass cutting volunteers for churchyards being as common as bald yaks in January, the good rector had praised his Maker and rushed for mower and shears.

"Well spoken and tidy," he assured us as though he would have forbidden entry to hallowed ground if the accent had been on the rough side.

"University graduate," Patrick informed him with a smile. "Name of Terry Meadows . . . wizard with explosives and unarmed combat."

The rector choked in his tea. When he had finished mopping he said, "One of your mob."

"He works for me," Patrick amended with another smile, passing me the toast. "Ingrid and I are going out," he continued. "Charlie is on nobody's hit list so when he gets up he can give Terry a hand. Any funerals today?"

"It's weddings on Saturdays or had you forgotten?" his father said. "Why?"

"The ungodly have been known to borrow a hearse," he was informed. "I should hate it if Terry bombed the wrong one."

Elspeth did not like the idea of Charlie being thus detailed off.

Patrick said, "He's an illegal alien, no entry visa, no permission of any kind. I had to sign for him to bring him here for a couple of days, otherwise he'd have stayed in the remand centre. Quite comfortable and with a better library that the one in the village but, nevertheless, prison."

"It seems so unfair when you think that he's the same rank as you," she protested.

"On the losing side," Patrick pointed out. "My guess is that he'll be allowed to stay. It shouldn't be too difficult for him to adopt British citizenship . . . his mother was Welsh."

"I take it he's a deserter," John said heavily.

"From the army not *your* commanding officer," Patrick retorted, leaving the table. "I don't think I could stomach a military set-up that shoots its conscripts in the feet to make them stay in the trenches."

I wanted to shout at this blind man of God that his son was newly made and whole but had to stay silent, munching toast.

Elspeth, however, was taking keen pleasure that her stratagem had worked. "Man was made for woman," she said softly over the washing up. "You've bloomed, Ingrid, and so has he. It broke my heart when you split up."

I was unable to refrain from glancing at myself in a small mirror behind the kitchen door. Everything seemed to be exactly the same.

Elspeth said, "Sexual frustration isn't a thing to which many men will admit. John used to have his bother about Lent until I put my foot down. It was driving everyone crazy . . . he was impossible to live with." She swished a hand around the bowl, hunting for tea spoons. "I watched Patrick get better and then had to watch him get worse. He brought girls home on a couple of occasions and there were no midnight excursions. I knew why—it beats me why neither John nor Patrick realised that the doctors had told me exactly the same—that the psychological side of things might control the physical for a time. How extraordinary men are. He hadn't even the nerve to give himself Dutch courage."

I was experiencing a keen curiosity as to the identity of the girls who had failed to lure him out of his difficulty. Perhaps they hadn't tried, huffily dismissing him as incapable. If so, how amazingly stupid of them.

"I hope you'll stay with him, Ingrid," Elspeth was saying.

"It doesn't have to be me," I demurred.

She tipped away the water. "Then who? He's a bit old to find someone else."

"He's a very attractive man," I declared stoutly.

"And an organised woman's idea of hell." She ticked off on her fingers. "Youngsters are out . . . can you imagine him with a bit of jangly fluff teetering on his arm? No. An older attractive woman with no ties or children? They don't exist. One who does it for money or because she's bored? He wouldn't touch that sort with a bargepole. That leaves you."

I was still grinning over that "jangly fluff." "There are plenty of older attractive women with no ties or children," I said. "I would count myself among them."

"You have your writing," she told me. "That's a tie. You're quite independent, too . . . I'm talking of older attractive women actively looking for a man and worth having."

She had underlined the last three words and, generally, I was inclined to agree with her. Personal experience with friends such as Maggie strengthened such an argument. I wouldn't wish any man to be inflicted with an egocentric interior designer. But Elspeth was being just the slightest bit whimsical.

"Yes, I write," I said. "I have my own house and I don't want to sell it. Can you see him coming to live with me?"

"He did before."

"He was an ordinary soldier in those days." Even before arrival in this house I had made up my mind to keep quiet about any involvement I might have with Daws' department. "Ordinary in the sense that he went on fairly regular tours of duty," I explained. "I get the impression that life will be erratic for him from now on."

"He won't notice," she said, picking up a wine glass left over from the evening before to dry it. It fell from her hand to smash on the terrazzo tiles and, horrified, I saw the tea cloth flood with crimson. I snatched it to stem the flow, yelling for Patrick.

The entire rim of the glass had sheered off, cutting a finger almost to the bone. Patrick arrived, observed and went away again at a limping run. I sat Elspeth down, assuming he had gone for the doctor who lived opposite, but he returned immediately with a first aid box, presumably from one of the panniers of his bike.

"It needs stitching," I said.

He sat down and set up shop on the kitchen table. "Morphine in the backside or bite a bullet?" he grinned.

"Neither if you don't mind," Elspeth replied, adding, "No doubt you've hundreds with you."

"Mostly shells for the howitzer this trip," he replied, working quickly.

It was a very comprehensive first aid box. The whole hand was swabbed with a clear blue pleasant-smelling solution from a plastic bottle and the bleeding ceased almost straight away. He prepared a suture needle and Elspeth quailed.

I put the kettle on. At least two of us would need hot sweet tea.

Patrick said, "I haven't a clue what to do about Ingrid."

Elspeth flashed me a grin. "Such a typically male remark. The girl's fallen in love with you."

I noted the twisted smile he gave her. "For the first time?" he said.

"Would you like me to leave the room?" I said.

"You of all people should know that," Elspeth said to him.

"All right . . . for the first time. Don't watch the needle and you won't feel it. Ingrid in love might prove to be an even bigger pain in the neck than Ingrid plastered in woad."

"Patrick!"

"I've been through it all," he continued wearily. "Going out together, holding hands, engaged, mild fornication in the back of Dad's car. Then the wedding, honeymoon, rows, silences, separation, divorce. All the misery." He carefully snipped the thread of the first suture. "Now the silly cow's fallen in love with me."

"Peter was a substitute," Elspeth told him firmly.

"Of course he was. All husbands are substitutes for something or the other."

"That's very cynical. No, you're wrong. Peter was a substitute for you." Elspeth winked at me, asking me not to mind.

"Look at me, don't watch the needle," her son ordered. "He was a far nicer guy than I am."

"True," she agreed, flinching for the first time.

"Sorry. He stayed around too . . . didn't leave her in the lurch all the time."

"I don't think that matters if the marriage is sound. How many more?"

"Keep still. I'm too perfect for her." He glanced up. "The insufferable Gillards. Vicars of Little Puking since the Civil War."

"Oh dear," said Elspeth. "Are we really like that?"

The tiny scissors paused in mid-air. "Of course not. A capable competent family with a pile of capable competent ancestors."

"But that's the same, only put more politely."

It was time I made myself heard. "I was fighting mad with him when I said that."

"But it's true," Elspeth exclaimed. "John's always waffling on about his great-great-great-uncle Bertram who fought—where was it?—with Gordon at Khartoum, and another miserable old bore who married the Duke of Bridgewater's daughter and collected moths. I'd never realised how ghastly we are . . . living in the past and with no real conversation."

"I didn't mean it like that, Elspeth," I said, louder, inwardly cursing him.

Elspeth inspected the provision of a neat bandage. When it was finished she said, "Well, it's coming to an end, today." She surveyed us both. "My goodness, when you think about it the entire house is like a museum. I'm going to get rid of it, throw out all the dusty old tat." A triumphant nod. "Even the picture of John shaking hands with George the Sixth, everything, all of it!" She swept towards the door. "I shall buy a scarlet leotard and take up yoga, fill the walls with lovely posters of sunsets and horses. I've wanted to do it for ages. Good . . . wonderful . . . splendid," she concluded, and could still be heard talking about paint and wallpaper as she went down the hall.

I said, "I realise that you had to provide some kind of anaesthetic but did it have to be quite like that?"

He looked up from packing away his doctor outfit. "Ingrid, you are quite unique insofar as your insults, however obscenely rendered, are steeped in a good measure of truth. I've been trying to blow down a few cobwebs every time I come home but progress is painfully slow. The garden and kitchen are a dream because my mother organised them but she hasn't had the nerve as yet to tackle the rest. By tradition rectories are gloomy and without charm.''

''Patrick, she *was* tongue in check.''

''I know. And enjoying it all tremendously, having a dig at both of us. She'll do it.''

I sat down by him. ''Doctor, your prescriptions are little short of miraculous. Is there really a dark bad world out there with madmen and drugged darts?''

''Yes,'' he said quietly. ''Are you still taking the medicine?''

Why did I love him so much then that I was bereft of speech? He leaned over, tilted up my chin and kissed me for a long, long moment, a cool, practised kiss like of old.

''We must go out into the world again,'' he said. ''If things go wrong there might be blood and mayhem. One day, if I'm alive and in honest employment, will you consider me for general tidying up and emptying your wastepaper basket?''

He was proposing to me for the second time.

''Yes,'' I said. ''I'll have you to grace my heart and my hearth even if you're broken and old and just out of prison.''

Which was why, when Charlie came in, he went out again quickly.

A short while later Patrick came in through the door that led to the garden and dropped a kit bag on the floor.

''Put these on. I'll see you outside in ten minutes.''

''These,'' turned out to be what looked like a woolly romper suit. It was not very clean. I climbed into it, leaving on my own thin cotton jeans and sweater. At the bottom of the kit bag were thick yellow waterproofs, spattered with oil and mud. Convinced by the smell that the previous incumbent had been a large incontinent dog, I rebelled.

Outside, adjusting the bike, Patrick said, ''Yellow perils always get rolled up wet,'' in a manner that suggested it was one of the unwritten rules of the universe.

''That's haddock,'' I said.

''I jest, fair maid,'' he groaned. ''Put them on.''

''They stink.''

''Sprinkle some perfume on the inside, use some of my after shave if you like.'' He was utterly disinterested, frowning over a minute spanner.

''Patrick, I'm not going on that thing.''

A few minutes later, smelling like a brothel after a sewer had been diverted through it, I was fitted into helmet and boots, the latter Elspeth's gardening ones and rather tight. It was true that he washed the mud off first but only because they would be touching the foot rests. Even the man called Terry stopped mowing to watch the sight I made.

Patrick beckoned him over and it was plain when he arrived that they were both from the same stable, that indefinable and high octane presence that could only very loosely be described as training.

Young Terry had brown curly hair, broad shoulders, and shook my hand with exactly the right shade of deference towards the officer and his lady. His next remark slew it dead as mutton.

"At least there's no danger of her being arrested for soliciting in that rig, sir."

Patrick appeared to give it serious thought. "For those who like a challenge, perhaps . . ." he murmured with a theatrical shrug. "What would you do," he continued without a pause, "if I told you that a man was ten yards behind you with what looks like a gun in his hand?"

Every vestige of air left my lungs as Terry shatteringly shoulder-charged me to the ground, the helmet hitting the gravel with a crunch. Instinctively I rolled toward the wall of the outbuildings, some three yards away. When I got there I yanked the helmet straight in time to see Terry flat on his stomach and facing in the opposite direction to that which I had previously seen him, gripping a gun in both hands, the courtyard otherwise empty.

"Behind you!" Patrick shouted, coming from nowhere.

Before Meadows could react the gun was kicked from his grasp. He rolled away, dodged another kick and leapt up.

"Failed!" his tormentor admonished and neatly bloodied his nose for him.

The test of security extended, I suppose, to five minutes during which Terry's reflexes sharpened considerably but never, it seemed, quite enough. In return for obvious considerations he was permitted to vent any chagrin, Patrick ducking or taking what was offered on leather clad shoulders or chest. At no time did I want to avert my eyes and at no time did what I was watching become more than reasonably good-natured controlled warfare. It ended, suddenly, when the one who had instigated playing with fire burnt his fingers.

A feint that was all too successful and what amounted to cross-purposes sent Patrick full tilt backwards into the side of the water butt. It was an oak cask nearly as tall as I was and full to the brim. His back took the full impact and then he slid sideways and down.

To his credit and my surprise, Terry did not leap on to the bike, gibbering with terror, and depart for the Foreign Legion. He wiped the blood from his nose with his cuff, gave me a wry grimace and went to resurrect his immediate superior, who lolled inert.

Sitting like an oversized traffic cone, I held my breath. As one who had been taught as a child to approach dead adders only if armed with a stout stick, I could see Nemesis stalking Meadows, licking her lips. An inch too close and it was over, a savage kick to the knees and then silence as they both took the consequences.

"That's a tenner you owe me," Patrick said, first up. "Best of five . . . my three to your two. I'll have it now if you don't mind. There might not be a cash card machine this side of running out of petrol."

Which proved that he treated the whole of humanity in the same manner, I thought, as I gingerly sat astride the machine. Taught, cajoled, bullied, charmed, punished and caressed to get his own way; plotted and planned for the betterment of everyone with the stipulation that they obeyed him to the letter. Every situation was milked of maximum advantage to further an efficient world. We left Elspeth thrusting family mementoes into the back of a cupboard, and Meadows ten pounds the poorer and with a couple of bruises but unlikely to die because of succumbing again to bucolic inattention in a country churchyard. I understood all this but was not at all happy.

To be fair Patrick proceeded very sedately to begin with but, as when one first gallops a horse, the scenery flashed past with terrifying speed. When we arrived at a petrol station, would you believe it at the other end of the village, a large loop around the countryside later, I was glad to dismount.

"You always play God with people," I complained.

"I'll apologise tomorrow," he said, grinning. "Where are you going?"

"To the loo."

"Woman, we've only just started out!"

"Only you were aware of it," I said, presenting him with the helmet.

When I rejoined him he said, "If I'd known you were going to be so long I'd have arranged to have the bike serviced."

"It's not as easy as for men," I replied, coloratura, a style of address that has been known to make some members of my own family cringe. "All you have to do is unzip and find it."

To a chorus of muffled sniggers from customers and staff alike he placed the helmet upon my head as if covering a parrot's cage and invited me to embark.

"Are you sure you're fit?" I enquired belligerently from inside my mixing bowl. Meadows was built like an adolescent bull and with fists in proportion.

"Surely you don't think we were hitting each other for real?" he growled.

I mounted the bike.

I fully expected, when we set off, that our destination was Plymouth for an interview with Detective Inspector James Hudson, Peter's boss. But, hitting each other for real or not, Patrick had walked into a hell of a piledriver from Meadows, cannoning into English oak with a force that would make anyone see stars.

We went no further than Bath where I visited a small grocers to buy a French loaf, cream cheese, fruit and a bottle of chilled Muscadet. We took it to Landsdown Hill and had a picnic near the racecourse.

"It's a known fact that winter starts a full two weeks earlier up here," said Patrick, full-length in the sweet grass and wild flowers.

I had thankfully shed the yellow perils and romper suit, the former of which hung inside out on a bush like two halves of a deflated Mr. Michelin. I said, "I'm glad we didn't go any further today."

He scanned my face, eyes slitted against the bright light.

"You won't like Hudson," I said. "Not the type of bloke to meet after a long bike ride."

"You mean, and keep my temper."

That was precisely what I meant. "He steamrollers people rather . . . won't be reasoned with. And if you turn up looking like that he'll immediately assume you're a Hell's Angel. He loathes bikers whoever they are.''

''Remind me to drape myself in luminous skulls,'' Patrick said. ''Where did you meet him, at one of those Police Balls?''

''He came to dinner with his wife. I felt sorry for her. He dominated the conversation the entire evening and I only found out afterwards that she's quite a well-known local landscape painter. But he's good at his job, gets results and isn't slow to give praise where it's due, according to Peter.''

''Peter didn't like him either.''

Patrick was painting a picture of his own, a portrait to hang in his mental gallery. I said, ''Not really, but Peter was such an easy going person he could overlook personality and get on with the job.''

''It was Hudson to whom Peter took his suspicions about being followed.''

''I presume so.''

''I haven't completely ditched the other theory,'' Patrick murmured. ''That's why I want to see Hudson. It's not impossible that the ungodly at this end hired some thugs from Peter's patch to do the dirty work . . . people that he knew about.''

''Haven't they been identified yet?''

''Dawson won't say . . . he insists that it's a police matter. He's sticking to the idea that Peter was only followed and shot in order to get at me, much the same as the attack on the Special Branch men.''

''Daws has forbidden you to investigate further, hasn't he?''

''Sort of,'' Patrick agreed blithely. ''But I'm still going to ask Hudson quite a few questions. Ingrid, I can't get over the fact that Peter said nothing to you about being followed.''

''He wouldn't, he never liked to worry me, especially when I was writing.''

He grunted. ''It must have been a pleasant change.''

''How come?'' I asked blankly.

''From the times I used to come home and relate every second of my day or try out a new combat hold when you weren't looking.''

Marriage to Patrick had been a very physical experience. ''Early days those,'' I reminded him. ''I went jogging to improve my stamina.''

He sat up. "You didn't!"

"You were asking me about Peter," I said.

Patrick subsided again. After thinking for a moment he said, "Did he ever mention a hit and run?"

"The policewoman, you mean?"

"I don't know . . . you tell me."

I bit into an apple. "The hit and run Peter mentioned to you was almost certainly when Morag Wilson was killed. That was in all the papers, too."

"Probably when I was on the operating table," Patrick said. "Peter said something about a black Rolls."

"Black or dark blue . . . the only witness was a girl of ten. All the local cars fitting the description have been checked and rechecked. There aren't very many of them and by and large they belong to Lord Mayors and car hire firms."

"A black Rolls and a black hearse," Patrick mused.

"She was working in Peter's team . . . the one investigating cattle thefts."

"Was she begorra! Where did it happen?"

"At North Hill, Tavistock Road," I told him. "Before you get to the shops at Mutley there's a zebra crossing. She was halfway across when the car came up the hill doing about sixty. No chance. Killed outright."

"Was she in uniform? On duty?"

"Neither. Just off to meet her boyfriend for a Chinese meal. She lived with her parents in the next road to the hospital." I thought of that night when Peter had come home after working until nearly midnight. "He cried," I said. It was the first time I had ever seen a man cry. "She was only twenty, lovely, blonde, like a heroine from a Nordic Saga."

A skylark soared, pouring out its song.

"Please don't try to avenge Peter's death," I said. "He wouldn't have wanted it."

Patrick's eyes glittered. "They gunned him down like vermin. That made it very easy for me to regard them as the cardboard cut-outs we use for shooting practice. Somewhere in this country there's another one . . . perhaps two."

"That's a dangerous attitude."

"I don't expect that kind of trite bigotry from you," he

snapped. "I'm trained to live with attitudes that are dangerous to most people." A pause. "I know what I'm doing."

I began to make a daisy chain. A short while later I was offered three buttercups and a poppy.

"Sorry."

"It's so hard to take," I said. "Being on the other side of the barrier that makes you different."

"That was the worst part of our marriage, wasn't it? While I was out doing exciting things you stayed at home, washed my socks and wrote about the exciting lives of fictional people. While other wives were holding coffee mornings and saying 'Ooh' and 'Aah' sitting in tanks on opened days, you wanted to be crawling through water-filled drain pipes and learning to fire a pistol."

I madly gathered daisies.

"I only realised when it was too late," Patrick continued. "It all came back to me when you kicked that bloke in the goolies and tried to gouge the other one's eyes out."

"Any woman would have done the same," I said, lapping it up.

"Not so," he said emphatically. "If Daws wants me to have a partner, female, it has to be you. Besides, I wouldn't have the patience with anyone else."

"Patience?" I said.

"Training," he answered. "Some of it from me, most from other people."

I looked at him askance.

"No longer on the other side of the barrier and all that it entails," he elaborated. "You'll have to be able to run a mile in boots, know how to climb and abseil, be able to give first aid, including mouth to mouth resuscitation, and injections, also learn how to inject yourself."

This latter to someone whom he knew if she ever developed diabetes would rather die than have to administer insulin to herself every day.

"You'll have to be able to use a gun, kill with a knife fairly tidily and map read accurately because other people's lives might depend on it. I hope to God you never have to use any of it."

This is what you've always secretly wanted, I told myself firmly, the feeling of panic will soon fade.

Patrick was still talking. "But before that you and I will be seen together again. Gossip columnists will receive a few titbits such as our weekend here, a holiday in Wales in a few weeks' time. Questions will be asked as to whether, now that I'm invalided out of the army, you have taken me under your wing. It will be discovered that I have been given a desk job and spend most of my time head-banging the wall. Word will get around that I've flipped and been carted off to a nursing home. At that point you come to the rescue and take me to live with you. Then we start work.''

"The word 'sometimes' was mentioned initially," I said.

"Sometimes we work. In reality most of the time I live in my locker just off Gower Street and weekend in Plymouth and you make money writing. All the world will think of us in cosy abandon in your cottage, happy ending for Falklands hero. Occasionally we emerge from our retreat to attend various social gatherings for Daws and country. Dear girl, you'll end up with masses of material.''

"Plus a small remuneration," I said.

"About twelve K a year."

"Twelve thousand!"

"Paid in sacks of spuds and things like that . . . no records kept.''

"That's an awful lot for not doing very much."

By now he was in his super-informative mood. "I get even more, plus my army pay. If the ones we're watching get wise there's a chance of trouble, even a skirmish, where someone might get hurt. The money's insurance. Once we go below the efficiency line, for whatever reason, we're out forever.''

I lay back in the grass. "Tell me about mouth to mouth resuscitation.''

CHAPTER 11

When I awoke the next morning the sun was high and I was alone. I washed and dressed slowly, deciding on white cotton jeans with a navy blue and white top and matching scarf. I brushed my hair in the rather suave style it will condescend to hold just before it needs washing, applied a little more perfume and make-up than on a week day and went downstairs. A psychiatrist would have filled three notebooks and then scampered away to write a paper on my behaviour. For I knew where Patrick was.

Elspeth welcomed me distractedly into her little kingdom, surrounded by cookery books and bunches of wilting fresh herbs, rosemary, bay and thyme, dying in fragrant abundance.

"D'you mind burning your own toast?" she said, looking at me over the top of her glasses. "The doctor's wife has just given me three chickens to casserole and freeze."

I laughed. Elspeth also forgets toast under the grill. "I thought you'd be in church," I said.

She thumbed quickly through one of the books. "The ten-fifteen's a bit too much of a song and dance for me. I like it quiet with no hymns and processions. Not a word to John . . . he thinks I go to the eight o'clock because it's more devout to take Communion before breakfast. So do I, but I get terrible tummy rumbles during the sermon if I wait any longer."

I made my dark brown toast, poured us both coffee from the pot on the heated stand and sat down where Elspeth had cleared a space for me. There was farm butter, local honey, home-made marmalade, and all of a sudden I was not hungry.

"Is something wrong, Ingrid?" said Elspeth.

I told her no, stirring my coffee.

"The nub of the Gillards being so insufferable," she said after a full minute's silence. "He was very cruel to quote your words to me like that, but unintentionally so. Something that we all take for granted is totally alien to you. I only wish there was a way I could help."

"You always help," I said, smiling up at her concern. "But this time I can't take the easy way out."

"He loves you very much . . . you know that, don't you?"

"Yes," I said.

I drank my coffee and went out into the sunshine of an English Sunday morning. On the seventh day thou shalt be miserable. Not a hundred yards away was the cause of my misery, mossy and lichened, the church. Between this and the rectory garden lay the graveyard. Beyond, fields extended along the valley for as far as I could see in the direction of Stroud.

I found myself watching a car that was slowing to a stand-still in front of the lych gate, a large black Mercedes.

It wasn't possible.

Terry was in the stable, dubiously sniffing the contents of a small metal can. "Meths," he said. "Do you know where they keep the oil for the two-stroke mix?"

"There's a big black Merc out there."

He put down the can and came to look. "Better not take any chances. Get him out of there. Go through the graveyard and walk, don't run. Bring him out through the vestry door . . . I'll go round the front."

I walked, my knees feeling very peculiar. Out of the corner of one eye I could see the car. It had stopped a little further along from where I had first noticed it. Terry had come out of the front gate of the rectory and was sauntering with deceptively long strides towards the lych gate, carrying a pair of shears.

The enormous oak door was open. I entered the porch and pushed open another door. Within, a blur of colour, a host of strangers lit by dusty sunbeams. They moved about, toing and froing to the sonorous presence of the organ.

Where was he? At the front, idiot, in the family pew. I went forward, wanting to call out his name but one didn't, not in this place. Then I nearly did when my wrist was seized in a vice-like grip.

An old woman pulled me towards a strong smell of liniment and wide gummy mouth. "Doesn't matter, girl. You go on up. Better to come late than not at all."

"I'm looking for the rector's son," I whispered.

An even wider toothless grin. "I know who you'm are. I was sitting here the day you'm were married. Go and be with your man."

I made to leave her but she held on.

"The best wedding this parish has seen for sixty odd years," she said. "We had special prayers for him when he was hurt out in the fighting. You look after him now, girl, he's a wonderful man."

"We're not married anymore," I said, before recalling the "now." I pulled myself free.

"No," she said, blinking up at me like a large mother toad. "And I'm the Queen of Sheba."

Patrick was in the front pew, kneeling and quite incommunicable. So as not to attract unwelcome attention to myself, I also knelt and a little eternity went by. Murder, death and mayhem might be stalking us but for a moment I trespassed in an alien land. Before me, John Gillard, in green and white robes, moved along the altar rail administering sips of wine to his kneeling parishioners.

Patrick stirred and saw me.

"Possible trouble," I said. "Terry says to leave by the vestry door."

He rejected my helping hand simply because it was not strong enough and levered himself to his feet with both arms, teeth in situ in his lower lip. How many times are you expected to kneel during a church service? was the thought that tripped inconsequentially across my mind.

Dusty hassocks, empty cassocks, stacked chairs, a roll of carpet. He closed the door, long familiarity having made leading me down two steps and a dark passage easy enough to be achieved in silence.

"There's a blak Merc outside, sort of lurking," I said, suddenly feeling extremely stupid, a little girl in the grown-ups' world, smelling the Communion wine on his breath.

"Where is Terry now?"

"He's gone round the front."

"Stay here." He drew his gun.

I sat on an oak bench. The opening notes of a hymn I had sung at school came, muffled, through the door. O God our help in ages past.

I was in. For better or for worse.

It was worse. There were four of them this time and they wore the same black undertaker's suits. At the precise moment that I rounded the corner of a buttress one of them blew a dart at Patrick as he went towards them with his odd hopping, scrambling run. He swerved frantically and then his right leg seemed to buckle and he went down, sprawling. Then I saw why he hadn't fired. Two of them held Terry, limply unconscious, a gun at his temple.

The blow-pipe hissed again and at that range it couldn't miss. The dart hit his neck and he tore it out mouthing, struggled for a moment and then became still.

I knew I was screaming, threats, insults, nonsense . . . Terry was thrown to one side and I ran to him. They ignored me, dragging Patrick away by the arms. I ran at them, kicked, bit, fought, scratched. It meant not a thing when I felt a tiny sting in my cheek. One of them had me by the arm and was twisting it agonisingly. Somewhere, a man shouted.

The whole world tilted and hit me sideways. Strangely, the mind remained sentient and in a kind of grey fog I was carried to the car, with no sensation of lifting arms. I floated, a captive bubble. Dominating everything was the terror that I would slither through their fingers and burst like a jellyfish on the gravel.

The bubble somehow stayed intact in the back of the car. The vehicle remained motionless while a silent film of endlessly passing scenery was projected on a screen in front of it. I told myself that this was impossible but there was nothing to convince me otherwise, no sound, no sensation. The crows did not move, two in the front, one on each side of me. I occupied some indefinable space between them, a balloon on a string.

Someone was missing.

After a while I began to be aware of my head lolling on the back of the seat, legs wide apart and arms tucked tightly into those of the crows. My knees seemed to be higher than they should be.

Soon, a hum of tyres vibrated through the nape of my neck and slowly, as it was returned to my control, I closed my mouth and swallowed the saliva swilling around my back teeth. There was a wetness over my chin and neck where it had dribbled out. I could not move my body on the seat to discover if there were any corresponding horrors.

I closed my eyes, breathing as deeply as possible without it being noticeable. It was what they told you to do in hospital to get rid of the residues of anaesthetic. I had my feet on something soft that moved. Patrick . . .

Contact with a hard, cold floor. I pushed a hand under my face and lifted myself up a few inches so I could cough up what was trying to choke me. My limbs had no bones and I floundered, coughing excruciatingly. A bitter fluid gushed into my mouth and when it presented itself for the second time I spat it out. A foot jabbed me in the ribs.

A cellar, bright, clean and tidy. Patrick and I on the floor and four pairs of legs and feet standing above us. What followed was neither the mildly brutal one-upmanship in the rectory yard with Terry or even the bloody mauling of three men in the barn on the moor. This was something else, that tore at your stomach until you vomited, something that should never happen to anyone.

He kept quiet while they beat him with what looked like a police truncheon, managing, despite their efforts to kick him over on to his back, to keep his face towards the floor, protecting his head with his arms. All the while I yelled and swore at them and was almost glad when my insults claimed their attention. They hit me twice and then turned their attentions back to Patrick. Pain flared across my back.

The proceedings had a certain similarity with sessions in Hut Ten on Salisbury Plain during the course when Patrick had been chosen for duty in an undercover unit. He had recounted some of it, the patterns that were followed in order to break people down. It's asking for trouble to hit back, the instructor had warned, throwing a bucket of water over a gasping volunteer. Unless you have the ability to cripple, save your energy.

Patrick had that ability. We were lying quite close by this time and when one of the crows casually burned me with his cigarette, his nose promptly flowered against his face in a profusion of scarlet. He tottered away, red, black and white. Shortly afterwards I was sick.

A lull, during which a door opened and closed. I was picked up and sat in a chair then my chin was wrenched up.

Everyone's bank manager gazed down at me, a frown creasing his goodnatured brow. He let go of my chin and seemed surprised when it didn't drop down again. A casual gesture and Patrick was hefted into another chair by my side. Then they all walked out.

There was no need for me to be told. Five minutes' respite to think and whimper and lick our wounds.

"Next, the questions," Patrick said. He breathed in gasps, holding his side. "If they start on you, I'll try to knock you cold. Can you move your chair a bit nearer?"

I tried, mostly for his sake. I knew that the blow, if it came, would be merciful and annihilating. Several sweating moments narrowed the gap by a distance of precisely one inch.

"Forget it," he said harshly. "I thought it was just me that couldn't move their legs. Plan two: get them really mad so they lose their cool and finish it. Gets it over quicker and we aren't reduced to begging for mercy. With a lot of luck they'll dump us at the side of the road and come home."

It was a nightmare solution. I said, "Someone might have followed the car. If they phoned the police quickly—"

"Wishful thinking," he butted in. "They'd never find us down here."

We lapsed into silence, there was nothing else to say. During the short time that was left to us I tried to get some life back into my legs but they remained heavy and useless, sensation returning slowly as when the circulation has been cut off.

The men returned.

Patrick said, startlingly clearly, "This is where I make a lot of rude wise cracks and you start hitting me again. Page forty-seven, paragraph three."

The man in charge said nothing. He took the truncheon from one of the others and brought it down across Patrick's shins.

Patrick screamed.

"This is where you talk," the man said when the sound had ceased. He used the truncheon twice more, setting it going again.

"Why did Clyde go to you?" he asked, swinging the truncheon.

Blood trickled down Patrick's chin where he had bitten into his lower lip. He said, speaking in jerks, "I used to be in a special unit . . . he thought I could help him."

"Why did he want your help?"

"You know why . . . you were having him followed."

Everyone's bank manager took a stroll down the cellar and back again. "I think that it was a pre-arranged meeting."

Patrick's head jerked downwards as he momentarily lost consciousness.

"Speak," the man said.

"No," Patrick said.

"You're lying. You were using him to obtain information."

"No," Patrick said again.

He considered for a couple of seconds and then hit Patrick twice more, quickly, without any warning. The ghastly sound went on and on.

I yelled, "It should be obvious to anyone but a half-wit that Peter hadn't seen Patrick for months. Patrick had been in hospital for ages . . . or isn't your inside information as good as you appear to be making out."

The mild blue eyes transferred to me, seeming to see me for the first time. "I can't imagine why you should be recruited if your late husband wasn't up to his neck already. How would you know anything of the last conversation he had with this man?"

"Patrick was convinced that I'd think he'd killed Peter out of jealousy. So he told me every detail of their last meeting together to clear himself. I wrote it down, every word. I'm sure he's telling you the truth," I babbled. "I was married to him for ten years, wasn't I?"

"Your husband never discussed his work with you?"

"No."

The truncheon was lifted.

"Sometimes," I corrected quickly. "If it was amusing, if he'd interviewed anyone interesting . . . but not details of crimes or suspects. It wasn't allowed."

"You offend me," he murmured. "We might not be talking of crime or suspects."

"What else?" I retorted without thinking, one small burn and aching ribs clouding my judgement. "You killed Peter. Vermin clearance is the responsibility of the council."

Men don't hit women really hard, I thought when it was too late. The truncheon cracked into the side of my skull with a detonation that felt like a bullet. The floor came up to meet me and they left me there. I heard one of them laugh and offer to rape me to encourage Patrick to talk.

"They gave you a medal," the good-natured voice continued a long way away. "Was it for bravery?"

"No, you stupid bastard," said Patrick. "For cooking the best boiled rat."

The wretch made as if to hit him and then laughed when Patrick cried out in anticipation.

"Choose the most sordid death a soldier can die."

"Shoot me in the back while I'm running away," Patrick suggested quietly, so quietly that I had to concentrate hard to understand. He sounded sleepy. Then he was beaten until he passed out. Mercifully, it did not take very long.

I played possum when they came for me but there was no rape, just a hoisting on to someone's shoulder. Tumbled head-long into the back of a vehicle, a Land-Rover this time, I could not move before Patrick was thrown face down on top of me. A tarpaulin was thrown over us and the engine started. I wriggled and heaved, sick, aching and terrified that he had suffocated. In a hot, lurching nightmare I felt for a heartbeat and found one, racing and thready. I held on to him tightly for the rest of the journey to stop him rolling and crashing about.

What did it matter? They were going to kill us.

CHAPTER 12

The vehicle had slowed, bumping over ruts in a rough track, and there was the scrape of twigs against the bodywork as it came to a standstill. When the tarpaulin was pulled off I thought I was blind but a torch shone into my face shocked me out of the sick torpor. It was night time.

Hauled out, dragged, shoved, my legs wooden and useless, I was then half thrown into the passenger seat at the front. Moments later they came back with Patrick and he was slung in alongside me behind the wheel. Fumbling and brutal with haste, they then made us swallow neat gin.

This was the very worst. They began with Patrick who, as soon as they forced the neck of the bottle between his teeth and up-ended it, choked, the spirit gushing out of his mouth, and turned into a madman. He fought them, grimly, murderously and quite uselessly. They clubbed him semi-senseless with one of the torches and resumed their task, one of them holding his head back by the hair, another tilting up the bottle.

When they came to me I didn't struggle. By now they were in a mood to smash my front teeth rather than suffer any more delay. One filthy hand grasped my nose, another prised opened my jaws. I bit him for good measure, tasting his blood, and he swore and slapped me stunningly. After that resistance became impossible; it was drink it or drown. Frantic, they did not notice that most of the gin ran out of my mouth and when they deemed the amount sufficient they tossed the bottle into the back of the vehicle and ran to the Mercedes, parked nearby with its engine running.

Sobbing and retching I saw what they were planning to do.

The big black car reversed a little way down the road and then came forward again, lights suddenly blazing, straight towards the Land-Rover standing on a slope by a hedge. An awful jolting bang and then everything turned upside down.

Someone screamed. Was it me? Then, metal and wood and glass hit me all over and I lay in a leaden silence, broken only by the sound of the Mercedes' engine. It stopped. They had not gone away.

I groped for Patrick and found a shoe with a foot in it. I felt up the leg and reached a warm stickiness and a knee. He groaned, like an animal in pain, then, as will an animal wounded in its lair, became quiet when he heard approaching footsteps.

I smelt petrol at the same moment as he did and our reaction was the same: escape! But there was none. In the dim light I could see that the vehicle had come to rest on its side, the rear end in the hedge—there was no getting out that way—and the windscreen unbroken. That left the doors, one of which had burst partly open on impact and was jammed into the ground, the other now letting in light above our heads.

Somehow, I pulled myself towards it, finding handholds where I least expected them and hitting myself on other unforeseen obstacles. The window was wound down and I could see the dark outline of trees and a thin crescent moon. Standing on the edge of the driver's seat, I managed to look out.

One of the crows was shaking the last few drops out of the petrol can. He dropped it on the grass and took something small from his pocket. I knew it was a box of matches. While he was fumbling with it something so extraordinary occurred that for quite a while I thought I had died in the blaze that would result when he succeeded, finally, in striking the match and was experiencing some kind of afterlife.

Later I was informed that the phenomenon was only the Honourable Secretary of Bovington Car Club, Lance Corporal David Beath, who had come up on the now darkened Mercedes with some speed, swerved and driven himself, his navigator and his brand new Toyota MR2 Sports with all-independent suspension, including MacPherson struts and two rear spoilers, right through the hedge.

Even in the state I was in I could appreciate his style. Beath came back through the gap he'd made, on foot, shedding twigs, as angry as any man who had achieved the same whilst not at the controls of a tank. He loped a long, dangerous lope and the crows took one look at him and fled, almost leaving behind the one with the matches. Matches, can and all went in the scramble to escape, the car nearly hitting a huge red painted sign post at the road junction.

By this time Beath's navigator had seen the Land-Rover and was running over, shouting. He saw me and scented the spilt fuel at about the same moment. Leaping up he wrenched opened the door, felt for and grabbed a handle, the belt of my jeans, and lifted me up and out.

I can't remember whether I told them that Patrick was still inside or if they found him themselves. I was drinking in their wholesomeness, anger, disgust and outrage. There was disbelief too, a suspicion that what appeared to be atrocity might only be a hoax to disrupt the treasure hunt. When they began to think a little more clearly and listened to what was being said by the man they were easing with all possible speed from the wrecked vehicle, loud warning bells began to ring in their brains.

Their car had travelling rugs and we were wrapped in them, Patrick by now quite unconscious. Beath's friend wrapped himself around me as well, long arms cradling me protectively. He carried me into the Casualty Department of the hospital himself, proudly, like a man bearing a great treasure. In the bright lights I opened my eyes and looked up into an ordinary face, short brown hair and brown eyes, an everyday face. Just like Peter's.

There was really nothing remarkable about the rest of that night. I slept, diligently dosed, clean once again, warm and soothed by two Malayan nurses who removed my filthy clothes as carefully as if these alone were responsible for my appalling state.

During the night I was moved from the open ward into a small sunny room with its own toilet and shower. Flowers were the first thing I saw on waking, roses, and carnations tied with huge ribbon bows, chrysanthemums in pots and mimosa dropping its scented yellow pompoms.

And my mother.

"Elspeth is here," was her opening remark as if announcing the end of the world.

The aches, stiffness and soreness were unbelievable but my

mother was not about to be made aware of them. Since I was twelve she has remained in total ignorance of my real feelings and general health. One of the main reasons being that she immediately passes on all information, no matter how delicate its nature, to the rest of humanity.

"What on earth were you doing having a car accident in Dorset?" she began. "The last time I spoke to you on the phone you said you were staying at home to write."

My mother is short, plump and in her middle sixties. She keeps up with the fashion tastes of an age group thirty years her junior and is prone to wearing chucky plastic jewellery in primary colours.

"Alan sent you the roses and carnations—he's such a nice young man. The papers are full of it, darling: well-known writer in car crash. It gave me quite a thrill to read about you like that."

With heavy deliberation I picked up my watch from the bedside cabinet and looked at it. Tuesday, July sixteenth. I had slept a day away.

"I haven't seen you since the funeral," my mother rattled on. "What an awful wet day that was . . . I had to give the black hat to Oxfam afterwards, it was no good for anything." She picked at a loose end on the bedcover. "I can't come down to look after you, dear, the decorators are coming to do the front bedroom."

I would ask Elspeth about Patrick. In casualty I had caught a final frightening glimpse of him in the next cubicle. There was a tube up his nose and a doctor was coaxing another thicker one down his throat. The rest of him had been screened by other people working on his legs.

My mother said, "The newspaper said you had a companion with you in the car. Do you have a young man already? Don't you think you should have waited a bit longer? I mean, I don't mind—what you do is your affair—but . . ."

"Is there something to drink?" I croaked.

She looked inside the cabinet. "No dear, not a bottle in sight."

"Water," I told her. "There's usually a jug and beaker."

Finally, I persuaded her to ask a nurse. The nurse found a sister who predicted what would happen when I drank. Under close supervision I was permitted half a tumbler of water and when it bounced back with spectacular results, increasing tenfold in volume, my mother left the room.

For what seemed a lifetime I choked and retched, regurgitating the fluid that the immobilising drug had deposited in my stomach and lungs. When it was nearly over and I slumped against my pillows, Elspeth was allowed in to comfort me and, if necessary, hold the bowl.

"Don't try to talk, just listen," she said. "Taking everything into consideration he's not too bad. They knew what the drug was in advance because of young Terry . . . he's in the Royal United, Bath. They had to removed the fluid from Patrick's lungs and stomach because he's so weak he can't cough but there's no danger of any of you getting pneumonia now, although they might have to drain Patrick once more."

"You've seen him," I gasped between retches.

She helped me sit up for another use of the bowl. "Just for a minute or so. His father's with him now. No, dear," she added hastily when she recognised incipient panic, "just sitting at his side, talking to him. He can't answer because of the tubes and the respirator helping him to breathe with cracked ribs."

I asked her where we were and she told me Dorchester. We had been found not far from Sherbourne at a cross-roads. The red-painted sign post was famous, one of several that marked the site of former gibbets.

Prompted by Elspeth, I recounted some of our ordeal, knowing that she was frightened for my mental state if I bottled it up. I left out the more distressing details. These could only be spoken of with the one with whom I had shared them.

"I hope that Lance Corporal comes to see Patrick," Elspeth said as she was leaving. "I'd like to meet him."

I was sure Beath would. Promotion wasn't usually to be found, ready like ripe fruit for the plucking in the lanes of Dorset.

That afternoon they took me in a wheelchair to see Patrick. All the pictures I had built up in my mind were wrong. If I hadn't been guided and his name clearly printed on a band around his wrist, I would have gone right past without recognising him. In the intensive care unit, his face the same colour as the pillow upon which his head rested, he was just an object sprouting nameless plastic apparatus.

His chest rose and fell in obedience to a machine that wheezed softly at the side of the bed and, on a screen, his heartbeat blipped and flashed. I did not dare touch him for fear of awakening some ghastly dormant agony. What could he be thinking of, immobilised, encased and impaled, or had a merciful dose of drugs rendered thought and imagination impossible?

A nurse touched his arm and when he opened his eyes pointed towards me.

For a moment or two he frowned in perplexity, scanning his visitor. Then his eyes widened and he reached for my hand. His strong warm grip shook slightly, unmistakably. When I got back to my room, I asked to be taken to the mirror. Sure enough, he had been laughing and I could see why.

Another two days passed with more visits from Elspeth, using the police as a scapegoat for her worry because they had peremptorily taken Charlie back to the remand centre, and Terry, blaming himself for carelessness and still very pale. Whether this was a result of his having come straight from hospital or his commander's bedside I was not sure but his brief was to stay with me until ordered otherwise. I asked him if this meant he had to sleep across the door but the pathetic attempt at humour failed for he shrugged and went away again.

Daws arrived, saw for himself that I was sound in mind if somewhat shaky in limb, and departed, having warned me to tell the police everything I knew but to leave his name out of it. For a while I made him a scapegoat for my own misery but then saw what seemed to be his unsympathetic attitude in another light: he was the real target, the one they'd meant to break.

A police constable who introduced herself as Anne Cooper took down my account, and if my talent as a story-teller got the better of me I put it down to weakness for by the time I had finished we were both in tears and her notebook smudged. I could not help but think of her as one of Peter's colleagues and told her how he had died.

She shut her notebook with a snap. "We'll get them."

"This all started in Devon. Won't Devon Police continue to handle the case?"

"God above knows. Kidnapped in Somerset, taken for a long

drive to a house with a cellar. Then taken for another long drive to Dorset.'' She smiled. ''I see I'm in for a lot of phone calls.''

''The electricity meter had SWEB written on it,'' I said. ''Does that help?''

She whipped out her notebook and wrote it down. ''Most certainly. Can you remember any part of the number?''

But I couldn't, only that the cellar was clean, swept, newly painted and bright, as clean as the man who had beaten us. Afterwards he had probably gone into a bright, clean bathroom and treated himself to a shower.

''The Land-Rover was stolen from a farm near Launceston,'' she said. ''They hadn't missed it because it was kept in a barn and only used once in a blue moon.''

Right on the border with Cornwall. I had already been told that the Merc had been taken from a car hire firm in Exeter on the Sunday morning. No trace had ever been found of the hearse.

Anne said, ''Can the Major talk yet? I'd like to ask him if he's remembered any more.''

No, I told her, Patrick was on the respirator until tomorrow night at the earliest. However, he was permitted to communicate by writing on a pad kept by him for that purpose.

No one, not a soul, had mentioned his legs. These were encased in protective tunnels that lifted off the weight of the bedding. I hadn't even dared to ask Elspeth.

On the third morning I made myself get up, showered and washed my hair. Every last inch of me was smarting, aching and sore, a lump like a guinea fowl egg on the side of my head and, of course, the two lovely black eyes. I was drying my hair with a dryer borrowed from the nurses when Elspeth arrived with Terry and another taciturn individual who remained outside the door.

Elspeth shooed Terry out, too. ''I've brought your red slacks and sweater,'' she said triumphantly. ''You can come home with me but you've to stay in bed for another two days. Shall I go away while you dress?''

I hugged her and told her not to be silly. Then, on an afterthought I said, ''It seems an awful imposition . . . I don't want to cause trouble for you.''

''It's your home, too. No really,'' she insisted. ''It always has been. John was a bit worried about the security angle but the local police have assured us of round the clock protection and we've got Terry, too. Besides, where else would you go?''

Not to my mother, Elspeth was the first to be aware of that. ''Why aren't all people like you?'' I said, kissing her cheek.

''What a bore the world would be,'' she replied, laughing. ''If this wasn't so awful I'd be really happy.'' She went on talking in her pleasant, chatty way while I got ready—about some heifers getting into the garden and making a terrible mess but not eating anything precious, how a woman in the village had produced triplets after fertility drug treatment, a flower show date clashing with the next village's gymkhana—about anything that would keep my mind off other things.

At last I could stand it no longer. ''Please tell me the worst,'' I said.

She sat on the bed, all pretence gone. ''He was taken to Aldershot late last night. We got a phone call this morning and all the woman would say was that he's to see the surgeon who performed all the other operations on his legs. It was what I was dreading in a way . . . the Army taking him back.''

''There must have been X-rays done here first,'' I said, wanting to reassure her.

She took a deep breath. ''No one is saying very much but there must be damage. A doctor I spoke to said there were a couple of small fractures near the pins in his right leg. It sounds disastrous to me . . . I don't think he realised how touch and go it was in the first place.'' Her lips quivered.

It sounded disastrous to me, too, and my cursed imagination paraded all the melodrama of a thousand penny-dreadful novels: the crutches, the sticks and the wheelchair, even the wedding in the Register Office before we went back to Devon to live quite comfortably on my earnings while I coped with an embittered man.

''I suppose it's not the end of the world,'' Elspeth sighed.

''It is if he's a cripple,'' I muttered.

''I've lived with the idea of that for a very long time,'' she said, ''He nearly had to have his right leg amputated when he came home.'' She picked up the bag she had brought my clothes in. ''Terry was with him just before he was taken away. He might have a bit more news.''

I asked the nurses to find homes for the flowers except for

Alan's roses and carnations which I took for Elspeth. We were in the car, the silent watchdog driving, Elspeth at his side, when I received a conspiratorial wink from a visibly more cheerful Terry. Suddenly the streets of the lovely old Dorset town no longer seemed so grey and dingy. He dug in his inside breast pocket and held out a folded piece of paper.

Patrick has always refused, under any circumstances, to write letters in ball point pen. He must surely have commandeered Sister's or Matron's or the Consultant's Sheaffer. The writing was as sprawling and legible as ever although not too straight on the paper, as if someone had held it for him at the wrong angle.

"Dear Black Eyes, whatever happens remember Landsdown. It is no longer for me to tell you what to do but advise following whatever Daws and the police suggest. If there are contradictions, favour Daws. Terry has the key to the cottage if you should want it. Yours, Patrick."

The first sentence set the tears pricking my eyelids. He had thought of that, our smooching in the grass, when most men would have referred to it last. But perhaps a chemically impaired intelligence was to blame. I had my own key, in the handbag Elspeth had brought from home.

CHAPTER 13

For the next six weeks I wrote in order to stay sane. I had accepted Elspeth's hospitality for three days and then gone home, taking Terry with me. There, he was augmented by several plain clothes policemen who came and went in turn, cleaned the windows, dug the garden and photographed birds from a hide by the river. What the village thought of my harem I never bothered to find out, I was too busy writing.

Terry and I met for meals and without any discussion on the subject fell into the routine of him cooking and cleaning, fetching the shopping, changing his bed and using the washing machine while I organised my own washing of clothes and ironed his shirts. I definitely had the best of the bargain for he was an imaginative cook when given more money than he was used to, and I only prepared food at weekends to give him a rest.

It seemed a dreadful life for a young man but he never complained, just devoured the contents of my bookshelf in steady gulps or watched television. To me he remained polite, if a little distant, and I could see him obeying official doctrine on the handling of lone women. In other words, leave well alone and don't kiss them goodnight.

I wrote, hoping guiltily that the tapping of my typewriter wasn't driving him insane. Even with all the doors closed, including the one at the bottom of the spiral staircase, the sound penetrated. When I needed a break I made us both tea or coffee and we ate at pre-arranged hours. I tried to make the weekend meals slightly special with a bottle of wine but he would never take more than a single glass with the result that by the end of each meal I was slightly sozzled.

I wrote, tossing *Moonlake* into a drawer on the first morning back. No, this next book was to be different, I had ideas to get my teeth into now. I took out the reconstruction of Peter's death, changed the names and several details and turned it into the first chapter of *A Man Called Celeste.*

I wrote and the postman came and went, bringing bills, get well cards, a few lovely letters from fans, a letter from my mother bemoaning the mess that the painters had made and was I going to stay with her at Christmas? That went into the In Tray with the rest. No, no, a million times no.

I wrote several letters to Patrick after Elspeth had given me the address. He didn't reply. I could understand his feeling too ill to write but just a few words whispered over the telephone would have put my mind at rest. When I spoke to Elspeth she admitted that he had not written to her either and phone calls to the army hospital had elicited the information that he was progressing normally. At this I saw red and phoned Daws' life or death number given to me by Terry.

My tirade died in my throat when a female voice answered. Of course, his secretary. People like Daws were cushioned from their own shortcomings. I told her who I was and what I wanted, explaining that I regarded it as basic human charity that I be given some information. She asked me to hold the line.

Daws came on. "I must remind you that this number is only to be used in emergencies," he said.

"This *is* an emergency," I informed him. "If I'm not told what's happening to him, I'll go clean out of my mind."

He hurrumphed. "I'm only respecting his wishes."

"You mean he wants his mother to have a nervous break-down?" I stormed.

"Mrs. Gillard was told the same as you: that his right leg has been amputated below the knee and he's had two operations on the left one. He's progressing normally. Are you still there?" he said when I didn't speak.

"I'm still here," I said faintly.

"He doesn't want visitors," Daws continued. "Don't worry, he's in no danger now."

I put down the phone and then picked it up again and dialled the Gillards' number. Thankfully, the rector answered and I was able to break the news of the communications breakdown matter-of-factly.

Terry didn't appear to mind too much when I sobbed on his shoulder and took the reason for it calmly.

"He doesn't want anyone to see him," I said, trying to restore his own composure.

"Doesn't want a lot of women drenching his nightie," said Terry. "I'll take you out for lunch at the pub."

And he did.

On the Wednesday of the seventh week one of my Galahads draped himself around the front door and said that Detective Inspector James Hudson would like the pleasure of my company for a short chat.

"Can't he come and see me?" I enquired. "I'm rather busy."

If I was going to Plymouth, shopping, during the next few days that would be fine. Just pick up the phone to arrange a time.

I looked at Terry. His dismissive shrug pointed out exactly the differences between those who loafed on the peripherals and one who stayed out of the rain with a gun tucked neatly under his arm. The policeman bared his teeth in a humourless smile.

We went that afternoon. I can never settle to writing if even a dental appointment lurks over the horizon. It was a good day for a drive and I let the Sierra have its head going over Blackdown on the long swoop down into Mary Tavy. We banged over the cattle grid, slowed to obey the law and headed for Tavistock. Then past Yelverton with the moor high, wide and handsome and I floored the accelerator for a sweet short distance past the war-time runways. After that I behaved myself all the way down into the city. The Sound glittered between the arms of Rame Head and Mountbatten. It would have been a good day for a sail.

"You're quite a driver," Terry said.

The warm glow that most women of the non-libber variety experience upon receiving praise from a man coursed through my veins, but in this case a libber would have been right to fume: I had passed my Advanced Driver's Test and saw no reason to withold the fact from him.

He grunted.

"His lordship doesn't know either," I said. It just slipped out, I had promised myself that I would not mention and thus be reminded of him. If there were to be no letters, phone calls or news and I was to carry on working then a door had to be locked and the key thrown away.

"There's no need for you to stay with me when I go see Hudson," I said, concentrating on retaining the car's paintwork at Charles Church roundabout. "If I can't be safe with him then there's no hope for this country. Have two hours off to do what you like and I'll wait for you inside."

He was only too pleased to be let off the leash but dutifully escorted me right to the enquiry desk, departing chewing imaginary gum and with a swagger that suggested the clinking of spurs. Lacking a sense of humour, the duty sergeant went pink with anger. Word had got around.

Hudson fished me out of the aquarium of a waiting room himself and his office shook my hand, saying he was sorry he had not been able to attend Peter's funeral and would I take a seat, all very correct and impersonal.

"I thought you might like to see how we're progressing," he said when he'd offered me a cigarette and I had declined. He lit up without asking if I minded. I did.

"So there are developments?" I said as some comment appeared to be required of me.

He flipped open a file in front of him on the desk and sighed, world weary.

"I realise what a crashing bore it must be to be landed yet another case with Major Gillard as principle witness," I said crisply.

Hudson carried on reading. By some women's standards he was a good-looking man. He had waving fair hair and the habit of leaving a couple of tufts of hair on his cheekbones when he shaved, his high colour and very slightly too close together blue eyes always put me in mind of a Victorian gamekeeper.

"To take first things first," he began as if I hadn't spoken. "The two who followed your husband and were killed by the Major have been identified as Seamus and Patrick O'Neill, thugs. We can't discover why they did it."

"Irish thugs," I said.

"Secondly," he went on, without looking up, "the Rolls that killed Morag Wilson has been found in York. No connection."

"How is there no connection?" I asked.

Again he did not look up. "Rich yobbo borrowed the old man's car while he was in hospital. Drove down here to impress other rich yobbos, got himself high on drink and drugs, and bang, didn't see her until it was too late. Wilson's blood and hair were on the radiator grille."

"Less complications for you," I said.

"Not for him. Two deaths. The shock finished off his old Dad."

I took it on the chin. "What about the bunch that abducted us?"

"Good descriptions," he said, reaching for another file. He read aloud in his best courtroom manner, "Four men all dressed as undertakers. Good quality suits and shoes. One man short to medium height, thirties, fair thinning hair, at a guess an East Ender, bouncer type; the second tall, dark, early twenties, could be a junkie, looked bombed out. The third might have been a retired boxer, short, powerfully built, early fifties, possibly punch drunk, his nose got broken agiain." He dragged his gaze from the file. "Do those three descriptions fit the men who tried to kidnap you in the car park?"

"Perfectly," I said. "The first one also had yellow eyes and bad breath."

"Jaundice?" Hudson asked, writing it down.

"No, the irises . . . just like a tiger."

He shook his head minutely but carried on writing. Then he said, "The fourth man—the one who turned up on the Sunday—he's described as a middle-aged pervert, greasy red hair, medium height, scar on his chin. He's almost certainly got a record for something nasty. How does that that fit in with what you can remember?"

The one who had watched and enjoyed. Small forgotten details came back to haunt me and I felt sick. "I can't add to that. How did Major Gillard manage to give you all these details if he couldn't speak?"

"Wrote it down," Hudson said, surprised. "When he came round, the first night he was in hospital. It took him quite a while, I understand."

I savagely repressed the images this conjured up. "What did he say about the other one, the man whose house it was?"

"How do you know it was his house?"

I had never questioned in my mind that it was not. "There was a proprietorial air about him."

He made a note of this and then cleared this throat. "Heavily censored," he continued, "he is thus . . . tall, thin, and probably in his early sixties. Very well dressed, like a banker, grey hair beginning to thin, pale blue eyes, clear complexion. Left-handed and wears a signet ring on the little finger of that hand, a tiger's eye set in gold, clawed setting. Grey suit, white shirt with a thin grey stripe, silver grey tie. Black leather shoes, hand made, laced." Hudson closed the file slowly. "If a third of my people had memories like that the crime rate in this city would be just about zero."

"He had plenty of time to study him," I pointed out. "He paraded himself in front of us with all the confidence of a man who's confronting the already dead . . . What happens to truncheons when they're no longer required?"

"There's no control over them like firearms," Hudson replied. "I hope that you're not about to make allegations that you were—"

"We were beaten with an item of equipment normally issued to police officers," I interrupted. "Pardon my curiosity."

"You can buy old ones in junk shops," he said, colouring even more deeply. "One of my men bought an antique one because he prefers the feel of it."

"So what happens to those no longer required?" I persisted, picturing Plymouth Argyle fans being tidied up with Edwardian bric-a-brac.

"It's probably in a cupboard somewhere. I really don't see—"

"I'd like to see one."

"Mrs. Clyde, I see no point in—"

"They must vary over the years," I persevered.

Hudson jammed a finger into his desk intercom as though it had done him a personal injury and made his request known. The desk sergeant brought it in and I took it from him. Identical, even to the leather loop that looked as if it had been chewed by a dog. It was smooth and polished and clean.

"Is this yours?" I asked the sergeant.

He told me it was a spare, kept in a locker.

Terry searching in the old stable, the smell of meths . . . This smelt of meths, too. "Do the cleaners polish everything in the cupboards?" I queried.

Both men regarded me as though I had taken leave of my senses.

"Obviously not," I said. "But this has none of the greasy dusty residue that one would expect to find on an item just slung into a cupboard."

"Mrs. Clyde—" Hudson said angrily, but I cut him dead.

"Just what someone might do if there was the least likelihood of it being a suspect weapon," I said. "I'm not even suggesting it was this one. All I'm saying is that it's too clean, it reeks of meths which is ideal for removing fingerprints, blood . . ." I gave it back and the door closing behind the sergeant was an island in a sea of silence.

"This has all been a bit too much for you," said Hudson, not unkindly.

"No," I said. "During the past few weeks I've written more than half the rough draft of a novel. When I'm working my brain goes into a hyper-alert state with enormous powers of concentration. Someone knew when Peter was being given an escort to work and also, it seems, his every movement. Has it occurred to you that one of the cleaners might be moonlighting?"

Hudson swallowed all this down and then choked. "Mrs. Clyde . . ." He steepled his fingers, resting the tips on the bridge of his nose. It made him look as though he was praying.

"We were questioned about Peter," I said. "That suggests to me that this man lives in the area and thinks that you might be on to his activities." I put a brake on my tongue as my brain galloped ahead, producing other suppositions. If everyone's bank manager really was the one employed to throw a spanner in MI5's works and had suspected that a member of the police force was relaying information to one of Daws' operatives, then Hudson should not necessarily be made aware of it.

"It's not inconceivable that an attempt's being made to implicate you, bring a slur on the police," I said wearily.

"All right," he said quietly. "It's wildly improbable but I'll bear it in mind."

"Will you have this examined by forensic?" I indicated the truncheon lying on his desk.

He opened and closed his mouth a couple of times and then said, "OK, if it'll put your mind at rest. You'll have to give us your fingerprints on the way out. Remember though, that if that match had been struck no one would have known you'd been beaten with anything." He leaned forward, elbows on his desk. "Do me a great favour, Mrs. Clyde, and leave the county for as long as possible. If this sounds callous then I'm sorry, but when my men aren't tied up with looking after you, and things have settled down again, I've far more chance of getting results. Disappear, good lady, and I might just catch them."

Perhaps my defences were exhausted after launching into him or perhaps he took me by surprise. All I could achieve when he finished speaking was stunned immobility. He had summoned me for no other reason.

"Have a little holiday," he suggested, and one could not fault his friendly manner.

"Holidays are miserable on your own," I said.

Hudson spread his arms expansively. "Why don't you ask Colonel Daws where Major Gillard is convalescing? He might be only too glad of a little company."

He was treating me like a child now. I gritted my teeth and wished him good afternoon.

Terry drove home. It was the sight of his big capable hands spanning the wheel, relaxed and confident, that brought some kind of light into my black despair.

"Terry, what shall I do? Hudson wants me to go away for a while."

"Didn't he put it all in the note?"

"Who? What note?"

"The Major. The note he wrote that I gave you. They'd just taken out the tubes and he couldn't really talk but he got me to understand that it was up to you what you did . . . the option was there. I don't know, Mrs. Clyde, I didn't read it."

I tipped my handbag out on to my lap, the same one, my favourite red leather shoulder bag. A confetti of shopping lists, car park tickets, train and bus tickets from years ago fluttered around the dashboard and down to the floor. I undid my seat belt and scrabbled.

What I was looking for was creased and had a roughed out plan for chapter seven of *A Man Called Celeste* written on the reverse. I'd been hunting for that everywhere. I smoothed it out.

A restored, rested intellect cut through all the dewy-eyed sentimentality with which I had endowed it at the first and only reading. "Remember Landsdown." Of course, the breakdown of his future he had given me there. On Landsdown he had said that word would get about that he had suffered a mental breakdown. He was already in hospital so was this removal from duty going to be utilised instead to save time?

I said, "So if he wasn't half daft with painkillers after all, which key do you have if I want it?"

It came out of the same pocket of the same jacket as the note, confound him. I glanced at the address on the tattered label but had already remembered more of the proposed plans. It was the key to the Gillard's Gwynedd coast holiday cottage, where we had spent our honeymoon.

"Why didn't you give me this before?"

"You didn't ask me for it."

"But you never said a bloody word!" I bellowed at him.

"I didn't know what was in the note, did I?" he responded, all sweet reasonableness.

I counted slowly up to ten. "Is he in any state to be taken there?"

"Search me," said Terry. "No one tells me anything."

When we arrived home my sister Sally was on the doorstep, being thoroughly checked over by the bird-watching Galahad. She looked even more surprised when she saw Terry but, wonderfully sensible creature that she is, was soon all smiles at the explanations.

"I'm not going to be a nuisance and stay," she hastened to say. "I'm on my way to see a school friend in Truro."

Of course she had to stay; expeditions on this scale for her entailed endless lists for Derek to remind him when to feed the dog and collect the children from school, days of work filling the freezer with food even an absent-minded husband would be unable to ruin.

"He's staying at home to delve into Hadrian," she yawned over tea. "Isn't it absolutely exhausting doing nothing?"

Sally and I have always drawn great comfort from one another's company. Although, of necessity, virtually submerged in domesticity, she has never allowed it to rule her life. Her three children have a huge play area in the converted loft where they can make as much noise and mess as they like and are only allowed in the living room if clean and quiet. Derek's study is totally out of bounds to them. When I first started to write I used her as a sounding board for plots, characters and ideas and she proved so useful that when *Hilary's Son* was accepted I dedicated it to her and gave her a share of the advanced royalty.

Clear-sighted enough to see the hours of slog while the sun is shining that writing means, and applying the same insight to Patrick's chosen career—mud, sweat and boredom behind the glamour—Sally nevertheless always took a keen interest in what the pair of us had been up to. I exchanged the information gladly for hints on how to achieve a clean house in half an hour and recipes for dishes that took no longer than that but gave guests the impression that one had been cherishing the thing for hours.

"It was Patrick you were with in the crash, wasn't it?" she said when we had cleared away and Terry was cleaning the car in the yard.

"He's had his right leg amputated," I said. "It doesn't sound as if the left one's much use."

She stared at me, horrified. Then she said, "Have you been to see him?"

"He doesn't want visitors," I said. "That makes me fear the worst. Despite a note he wrote giving me the key to Plas Gwynn. That was before."

"Before what? Before the crash?"

"Before his leg was removed."

Another scion of the Langley tribe applied herself to the problem. "Phone," she said suddenly. "Ring up and see if he's there."

"I haven't got the number," I said, shrinking from the idea.

"I have," she said. "We've stayed there several times."

"It's not as easy as that," I said when she had found her address book and was flipping through it. "Sally . . . he might not want . . ."

"He gave you the key," she pointed out ruthlessly.

"That was before," I repeated.

She has never had any patience with me when I fail to be

practical. "Surely he must have known when he wrote it that the worst might happen."

"Please don't phone," I begged.

"Don't worry, I'll pretend I'm a friend of Elspeth's."

It was useless to explain that Patrick had everyone's voice recorded inside his head ready for instant checking because I knew she wouldn't listen; Sally never does when she gets a bee in her bonnet.

Patrick wasn't at the cottage. I went limp with relief as Sally had quite a long conversation with the person who was, his brother Larry with his wife and two children. Both were named after saints whose respective lives the brothers until recently had seemed to emulate. Saint Lawrence had lost out and been grilled medium rare over a gridiron, Larry's fate with his wife, Shirley.

Sally came back and sat down. "Larry was staying another week but the weather's awful, the loo won't flush, and Shirley found a dead mouse in the butter dish so they're going home tomorrow."

I decided there and then to travel to Wales on the following Monday.

CHAPTER 14

I missed Terry. Not just because I was driving alone on the journey north after nearly two months of having him by my side at all times when I was outdoors, it was more subtle than that. Terry and I had got on well. We were birds of a feather, both private people, and this had meant that when in one another's company we were comfortable and had not felt that we ought to chat in polite fashion. The stuff of which good marriages are made. Once or twice I had caught myself observing his broad shoulders and glossy brown hair and had then gone away to do myself a little mental violence. One day this twenty-four year old would lose his beguiling innocence, but not to me.

On the Saturday a sealed envelope had arrived for Terry, brought by special messenger. Orders for both of us from Daws. I had asked the messenger to wait and rapidly typed my intentions together with a résumé of my interview with Hudson, told him how impressed I was with Terry's conduct, signed it and handed it over. Seconds later the army car had sped out of the yard.

I was to leave the south of England for a destination given only to Daws. When he knew where that was to be he would arrange protection. It was vital that I telephone him when I got there but only to say that the parcel had arrived. The address was to be put in writing and given to the messenger. Daws had gone on to explain that due to the same need for security, Patrick's present whereabouts could not be discussed over the phone.

This cryptic statement was intriguing for it sounded as if Daws no longer knew where he was. I doubted it but the nearer I got

135

to Machynlleth the more I wondered if a bored and immobile hospital patient had found an ally and had himself taken off into the blue. Who the hell else knew that Shirley became hysterical at the very mention of mice and had a fetish about clean toilets?

Nothing was clear in my mind. Sally would suit Patrick so much better than me, I told myself, while I made the acquaintance of the school friend in Truro. Sally would not flinch at the prospect of crutches and specially adapted cars. Perhaps the job was to be adapted, too, if he could cope with the socialising, a drink in one hand, stick in the other.

I love the Dovey estuary. It basked in hot September sunshine, sparkling water, green meadows and a myriad of water birds. Larry had chosen the wrong week.

No vehicles were parked outside Plas Gwynn but someone had recently weeded the window boxes, planted with trailing lobelia and petunias, and tidied the handkerchief-sized front garden. A pile of grass and dandelions lay wilting on the path. Not the work of Larry or Shirley, who both loathed gardening and lived in a flat.

I tried the key in the lock and it fitted and turned, thus proving that no one was in to leave a key on the other side. Late afternoon sunlight entered with me, illuminating a hallway slightly dusty and with a sprinkling of sand on the carpet near the door.

I was an intruder and this was not the cottage I remembered. It seemed lighter and more spacious, the staircase now a spiral one and the kitchen, always the first room to be investigated by a woman, painted crimson and white, polka dot red and white wallpaper, curtains to match. One unwashed china mug, white with small red hearts, was in the sink, the only sign of human habitation. There was hardly any food, half a carton of semi-skimmed milk in the fridge together with an opened pack of butter and one wholemeal bread roll, stale. In one of the wall cupboards I found half a jar of marmalade and a box of meusli with about a tablespoonful left in the bottom. The rest of the cupboard space was taken up with china, glass and saucepans, all different from those I remembered.

I wandered into the tiny dining cum sitting room. Personal belongings lay scattered around, a Canon camera still in its box, a grey leather jacket, also new, loose change, a pair of swimming trunks drying over the back of a dining chair that took all my willpower not to remove and hang in the kitchen, a pair of walking boots . . .

The coward in me locked the front door again gladly while at the same time I cursed my stupidity for not checking with Elspeth first. The cottage was hardly ever empty as it was let or lent to any friend or parishioner who promised to leave it clean. I had driven a long way for nothing.

What could I tell Daws? Not the address of a nearby hotel for security reasons. And if I couldn't give him an address then he couldn't provide me with protection. Neither could I return home. The only possible way out was to leave the country entirely, drive to the nearest airport and catch a plane to . . . where?

Choosing the seafront café with the prettiest curtains I went in and munched my way through a cream tea, not because I really wanted it but to kill time while I decided what to do. The hundreds of calories I was consuming were of no concern. My size twelve skirt had been swilling around my waist all day. Gaunt was the word that had come to mind upon noticing myself in the mirror that morning, gaunt and pale and with hair that badly needed a trim.

When I left the café a chill breeze was gusting from the sea, the sun setting, a great glowing orb sending long shadows across the rippled sand. People walking dogs, a man kicking a beach ball, all looked like the moving hands of clocks.

I huddled into my thin anorak and descended the stone steps on to the sand. A lolling-tongue, soaking wet German Shepherd passed me by with a grin and then went back to chasing seagulls. I strolled into the sun, trying to ignore the cold, thinking of nothing at all.

The horizon took a small slice from the sun and the old choking feeling of a day dying caught at my throat. Then I laughed aloud; it was too easy to become maudlin. But the sun blazed on, brighter and redder as it slowly sank and my laugh was stilled and had to be prevented from turning into a whimper.

Against the light, the man kicking the beach ball sent it bobbing over the wet wave patterns in my direction. I botched kicking it back to him and had to retrieve it from a shallow pool, soaking my shoes. He watched me, hands on hips, a dark outline against brilliant light. When I sent the ball back, quite accurately this time, he ran to field it and fell flat on his face.

I went closer, right up to him, beholding a track-suit dark with sea water as he laboriously regained his feet.

"I never flirt with strange men on the beach," I said.

"I'm glad to hear it."

I collected the ball from where it was being nudged by the incoming tide and he came and took it from me, walking tall and graceful, the merest eccentricity to his gait.

He said, "God, woman, you're like a broomstick with the wood scraped off." He dropped the ball to feel for himself, pinching my arms.

He was fit, tanned and had put on weight.

I said, "I wrote four letters."

Patrick said, "I took them to the States. Sorry, I wasn't allowed to reply. I did write though . . . brought them all back with me. Have you been to the cottage? I left them on the bed for you to read when you came."

"I didn't go upstairs," I said. "I didn't think walking boots could possibly be yours."

He held me close then. "The most intensive crash course in history. Come on, you're shivering."

We walked and, covertly, I watched him. Not a limp certainly but there was something mechanical in the way his right foot was placed on the ground.

He read my thoughts; not difficult, considering. "It was never a success. The pins were breaking away . . . bloody agony all the time. It could have killed me."

"Because it was so weak?"

"The crows would never have taken us if I hadn't fallen like that."

"Does Elspeth know you're back?"

"I gave her a surprise . . . disobeyed orders and phoned her from Heathrow last week."

It hurt.

"You had to come of your own free will," Patrick said. "Not because of sympathy or misplaced nostalgia or whatever else you women call it."

Like love for instance, I thought savagely. "You're not sure of me," I said.

"I am . . . Daws isn't. But only because you've been so knocked about."

I changed the subject, too tired to think about Daws. "Did you go to the States to be fitted with your new leg?"

He showed me, there and then. Below his own knee was a complicated, lightweight, definitely not cosmetic contraption of alloy and flexible plastic.

"The shin was where it gave out," Patrick explained, tapping the spot where it had been. "A cool two thousand quids' worth, best in the world and courtesy of Her Majesty's Government."

I asked him about his other leg and he told me that when the bruising had healed the surgeon had discovered nothing wrong but had decided to operate to repair tendons that had been damaged in the original injury, this being regarded as part of the ongoing treatment. Now that he no longer had to put so much of his weight on it and could be given exercises to do, it was very much stronger.

"I have to walk a mile a day at least and kick a ball around gently to get the business of balance sorted out," he said, tucking his arm in mine. "As you saw, I'm not too clever at that yet."

I voiced what was uppermost in my mind. "Daws insisted you pay this price for carrying on."

Patrick said, "It isn't a price, it's freedom. It should have happened in the first place. I no longer have to take small white pills three times a day in order to function sanely."

I stopped walking and grasped his arm. "Did he ask you? Did he say that if you wanted to carry on the money would be forthcoming for an artificial leg?"

He stared at me quizically for a moment. "No, not Daws. Someone more senior."

Daws, then, had not known where Patrick was. I ignored some of the implications of this, content for the moment that he had been fairly honest with me.

Patrick said, "You're tired, and this thoughtless bastard hasn't even asked you how you are."

"I'm all right," I said, and we walked back to the car. How do you mention nightmares without seeming feeble?

There was a small corner grocer's shop near the cottage that stayed open late and I bought tea and coffee, although I later discovered that he had both with an electric kettle in the bed-room, more milk, biscuits and chocolate. I would not be doing any cooking. When I got back he was mooning around, tossing the beach ball one-handed.

"Hitting a pub heavily, I presume," I said, laying the armful down.

"Are you staying?" he asked lightly, obviously not listening.

"I might," I said. I made tea, brain marking time.

"There's a nice little pub further along the coast," he said, heading the ball into a cupboard. "I propose a shower and then dinner for two."

I wove a small plot around him carefully. "Better make it a shower, two hours sleep, and then dinner for two."

He nodded sagely, drank his tea and went upstairs. There was the sound of running water and a steamy warm smell mixed with something exotic enough to give ideas to a warthog. I waited, sitting in the living room.

Sure enough, he called down, "Are you having a rest before we go out?"

"No, I'm all right," I said.

"A shower then."

"I might do . . . while you have your sleep."

I could almost hear him grinding his teeth. Not one to give up easily he came down, hopping, I realised with a pang of guilt, on one leg. When he appeared in the doorway our eyes clashed like swords.

I said, "Not because of sympathy or misplaced nostalgia or whatever else you men call it."

He breathed out slowly. Then he said, "When you suggested bed I thought . . ."

"You weren't allowed to write," I said. "Yet you disobeyed orders and rang Elspeth. I seem to recollect accepting a proposal of marriage."

"Surely Daws—"

"Daws said you'd had your leg amputated," I interrupted. "I've been trying to work out how you were going to get your wheelchair through the front door of my cottage." The stump of his leg, I couldn't help but notice, was visible below the hem of his bath robe and although powdered over, seemed raw in places. Somehow I found the courage to continue looking in his direction.

Patrick manoeuvred himself to an armchair and flopped back into it, regarding me with a slight frown. "Do I take it that you want the job but no longer want me?"

"No," I told him. "Is that why you cut yourself off from me all these weeks . . . because you thought I'd regard you as disabled?" Ye Gods, didn't I always want him, in every meaning of the word, when his hair curled damply on his neck like that? "I'm sorry. It was a cruel little trick to play on you."

His eyes left my face and focussed on the ceiling. Moments later he almost succeeded in smothering a chuckle.

I said, "It's strange . . . we used to yell abuse at each other over this sort of thing."

We talked for a little longer and I was telling him about *A Man Called Celeste* when he fell asleep.

The barmaid at the small seafront inn made her disappointment plain when she saw that Patrick had company so I now knew where he had been going for meals. She was wearing a very low-cut black satin blouse and a tight black skirt with a slit that revealed more than the backs of her knees. The hoyden had the temerity to pout and glower at me from under her false eyelashes but concentrated on serving drinks after I had given her the look that had once caused Alan to spill coffee all over his green leather and onyx.

We were later than originally intended because Patrick had slept for over three hours. I had solved the problem this time not by sleeping beauty kisses but by dropping an assortment of items, unbreakable, down the stairs and then cheerfully apologising.

There were hardly any other customers and I made my way to a corner table, ducking under trailing fishing nets festooned with plastic crabs and lobsters. Ship's wheels hung parallel to the ceiling and were fitted with small electric lamps that imitated candles and flickered. Portholes in the walls contained real water and treasure, junk shop jewellery, not the kind of stuff that Davy Jones would burst out of his locker for.

"The food's better than the decor," Patrick said, bringing the drinks.

"You don't like vodka," I said, observing two identical glasses.

"Mine's just orange." He grinned smugly and I deemed myself forgiven.

"Very droll," I commented.

He got his own back by asking Jezebel for menus and when she brought them took a good slow look at everything on offer.

"Her name's bound to be Tracy," I said under my breath when she had returned to the bar. "She's old enough to be your daughter."

His gaze dwelt briefly on my primly buttoned cream silk blouse and then he was all owl-like innocence, studying the menu.

It was not the kind of establishment where beef curry would be other than a puddle of mince with curry powder stirred in at the last moment, so on Patrick's recommendation we both had steak with melon to follow. It transpired that he was merely banned from drinking spirits while on a course of tablets so we shared a bottle of house white wine, eighty percent to me.

"Hudson ran me out of town," I said, over coffee.

Patrick came out of his reverie. He had phoned Daws from the cottage to tell him that the parcel had arrived and had endeavoured to answer the barked questions from the other end of the line. "Bum's rush?"

"Not quite." I related everything that had taken place during that interview.

"He won't find them," Patrick said when I had stopped talking. "Are you now prepared to get more involved? To play the part we discussed in Bath?"

I said, "I'm not fit."

"Who the hell is?" he retorted.

"I mean . . ." I lowered my voice. "Look, I blabbed when they wanted us to talk. I'd have told them anything to stop it."

"No, you wouldn't. Not once did you mention Daws or what was planned for both of us. If you'd been privy to information the giving of which would have risked peoples' lives, you wouldn't have blabbed it." He saw that I was far from convinced. "You shouted rubbish, just the kind of thing a frightened woman would yell out to stop someone hurting her. It was very convincing."

"I wasn't acting," I insisted.

"Neither did you snivel and whine. There are techniques that help overcome the trauma of being taking apart but I'm damned if I'm going to explain them now."

Something urged me on and it was more than not wanting to be alone again, ever. I nodded and signed the small buff form that already had Daws' signature on it as witness. It went back into Patrick's wallet.

"We can't talk here," he decided suddenly, surveying the cigarette smoke and people who had seemingly sprung out of the floor.

We sat in the car on the seafront and watched the waves, me wondering what difference writing my name on a piece of paper could make.

"There's a maggot in the apple all right," Patrick began, staring out to sea. "But until he tried to kill us nothing was known about him or his helpers. I looked through a hell of a lot of mugshots while I was in hospital, just to be on the safe side, to eliminate the purely criminal element. Then I went through hundreds of others that didn't represent members of the underworld. That's where I found our smartly dressed friend."

"Government servants?" I said.

He nodded. "Mine was there, too. Gillard, Patrick Justin, Major. Army for the use of."

He was making a joke of it to keep memories at bay.

"Chief maggot or raving lunatic," he continued, "was an Arts student at St. John's College, Cambridge, did his National Service right at the end of the war and naturally came out unscathed having turned down a commission. Went back to university and read law, then accountancy, and then somehow drifted into MI5. All Daws can find out is that he's involved with Eastern European affairs and is as untouchable as a leper.

"There's no proof. I'm sure he's the one who gave me the biggest hiding of my life but we're going to need more than my word for it because I'm only whitebait in a world of great white sharks.

"As you might imagine Daws has steam emanating from every nozzle. The attack on us is the culmination of months of what can only be described as a smear campaign conducted from within, to smash his little group before it gets off the ground."

"Am I to be allowed to know who this bastard is?"

"Code name Trelawney . . . he lives there."

"Near Polruan? Across the river from Fowey?"

"Your geography's incredible," Patrick said. "I hadn't even heard of it. It looks as though he orchestrated everything, had the Special Branch done over to get me the blame, found out he'd failed and went out for destruction."

"How on earth did Peter find out about him?"

"I don't know how Peter fits into all this. Now that the hit and run's been ruled out we must fall back on the theory that Peter was killed because Trelawney thought he was tied up with Department Twelve."

I said, "I hope you're going to be allowed to arrest him."

"Not yet."

The moon came out from behind a cloud, gilding a path across water that now covered the sand we had walked on in the afternoon.

Patrick said, "We'll stay here for the rest of the week and then it's back to work."

"With this lunatic prowling around?"

"Trelawney is in Greece, for a holiday. On the fifth of October he's invited to a certain gentleman's weekend shooting party and so are we. Cheer up," he added.

"When the cat's away the mice do play," I said, but only to myself. I thought over what had been said, not really noticing when Patrick started the car and drove us carefully back to the cottage. When he had parked, a trifle raggedly, I said, "I'm fairly sure Hudson's clean. Peter used to say that he had an almost pathological hatred of crime."

"Don't become obsessed that it was the same truncheon," Patrick warned, getting out of the car.

"It was the same one," I said when we were indoors. "The leather loop had been chewed by a dog. How many—"

"Police truncheons in the West Country have been chewed by teething puppies?" he finished. "Bloody dozens."

I went upstairs. Arguments like that had been known to get out of hand. Coming out of the bathroom a few minutes later I turned the wrong way and found myself in the main bedroom. On the bed were the letters, held together with a rubber band. I sat down.

It was a tale that any publisher would have accepted, a closely detailed account of a man surprised to find himself still alive. It was all there, waking up to see his father and thinking for a moment that he was being given some kind of last rites, the days spent with tubes down his throat wondering if he was going to lose both legs. A phenomenal memory had recorded every detail right through to the flight to the U.S.A., a millionaire's clinic, swimming in a sea water pool to heal his legs, the first tottering steps with the artificial one, stringent workouts in the gymnasium to regain bodily fitness.

But above all the account was addressed to me. Love letters. "My darling Ingrid," the first began, followed by an explanation that he had been forbidden to post any mail, or telephone, but hoped that I would be able to read them at a later date.

There stood the author, waiting for me to say something.

In the event I was saved from voicing any reaction for someone rang the doorbell and it was Charlie, absconded from his remand centre.

Patrick did not, to my relief, phone Elspeth there and then and give her a verbal withering. Instead he gave Charlie a fairly imaginative breakdown of his own reaction and after listening for the first few moments I left them to put the kettle on, not that my presence seemed to be cramping his style in the slightest. Exactly how long he held out in the face of evidence of further weeks of confinement and poor nourishment I do not know but when I returned with mugs of coffee and biscuits for Charlie the stage was bare but for an uncomfortable silence. It was not to last for long.

"Your lady mother is not to blame," said Charlie.

With the speed of a striking snake Patrick had him by the front of his shirt, up out of the chair and quivering on the end of a ramrod arm. "My lady mother? You speak just as good colloquial English as I do but we're being treated to the cringing Gaucho bit now. You didn't give me that crap when I took you apart in the South Atlantic." A small shake. "What's the matter, Charlie, reverted to type?"

Charlie didn't reply and was flung back into the chair.

It seemed utterly callous, of course. Charlie had made one thoughtless lapse after weeks when he could have muttered all day to himself in Mandarin for all anyone cared—that would have been most people's reaction to his remark. To me, one of the initiated, it was apparent that Patrick's anger had nipped in the bud an imminent, if temporary, breakdown.

Charlie accepted coffee and a biscuit.

"Elspeth is to blame," Patrick said as if nothing had occurred. "She might have unwittingly got you into more trouble than you are already."

"*You* are his legal guardian," I reminded him.

"But I haven't signed for him this time," Patrick replied. "No one bloody has." He threw up his arms in a gesture of defeat and went to the phone in the hall.

"He'll fix it," I said to Charlie.

Patrick fixed it but by the time he had done so and had given Charlie a sleeping bag and shown him to the spare bedroom, I was in bed and asleep. When I surfaced, very late the next morning, he had been up for hours, one of which had been spent kicking the beach ball around on the sand. This much I learned when he put his head round the door, surprisingly still speaking to me.

"Is Charlie still asleep?" I asked.

Patrick came right in, shut the door and peeled off his track suit. "Like the *General Belgrano*."

"You didn't used to go in for tasteless jokes," I admonished. There was no doubt that the month in the States had done him the world of good, the increased weight appeared to be all muscle and the tan was entire, a detail he had just confirmed by removing his underpants.

"Are you by any chance . . . ?" I started to say but stopped speaking when the question became superfluous. Quite simply, in the most earthly fashion, he was showing me what was available.

"We're not married yet," I said, taking off my nightdress and throwing it on the floor.

He stood there, blatantly teasing me.

"Nothing to do with an offer of marriage," he remarked and pulled off all the bedclothes. "We'll discuss our relationship later."

What came next I would never attempt to set down on paper and use in one of my novels. They aren't that kind of literature.

Later, we discussed everything but our relationship, the sexually replete have nothing to discuss. Over the finest cooked breakfast I've had in years, in a transport café not fifty yards from the cottage, we talked mainly about Charlie.

"I had the whole story," Patrick said. "The place had no real security, he walked out rather than escaped. There's a reason."

"Don't tell me he's heard something about Francesca."

"Better than that, or worse really, poor bugger. A priest who visited the centre did some detective work and what the police failed to do he managed to achieve. Charlie knew that the girl's mother was a partner in a fashion firm and that her maiden name had been Simmonds, she'd been divorced from Francesca's father in Argentina. Father Paul literally bashed through miles of Yellow Pages and phoned all the possibles. He ran it down in Leyton, East London, a rather sleazy rag trade workshop turning out stuff, believe it or not, for South America. You know the kind of thing, cheap copies of real fashion with pseudo fancy labels.

"The dead woman's partner wouldn't tell the priest anything over the phone other than that Francesca was safe and working for her as a trainee manager. So Charlie wrote to her."

"Oh dear," I said. "A massive brush-off?"

"Too right. So he went there the day before yesterday and she threatened to call the police. What would she want with a deserter, a man disgraced, when London was teeming with rich elegible young men?" Patrick mopped up egg yolk with a piece of bread. "What am I going to do with him, Ingrid?"

"Will he be allowed to stay?"

"It's quite likely . . . on humanitarian grounds if nothing else. The Home Office is contacting his mother's family in Cardiff."

"Can't we . . . ?"

"Adopt him?" he said, brimming with sarcasm.

"No, but . . ."

"Sell him to Elspeth as a home help?"

"I'm serious. I like him."

"That's one of the reasons he broke out. He knows a soft touch when he sees it."

"There's a limit to the time that an innocent person should be locked up."

"He'll have to go back when we return to London."

"We can afford to feed him," I wheedled.

"He can go running with you to get some fresh air and fitness," Patrick said, smiling. "Half a stone off him and on to you."

Which is exactly what happened.

CHAPTER 15

At our next meeting with Colonel Daws he had the grace to apologise to me for his unsympathetic demeanour at the hospital. Sand and sunshine were now far behind; Charlie, puffing and panting beside me on our daily runs, a memory blown away by the first autumn gales and driving rain. The sun had shone all the rest of that wonderful week, on picnics, on our swimming, on the kiss that my running companion had stolen when safely out of sight of our stern mentor, a thank you for what he knew to be my part in his being permitted to stay with us for a short while.

Now I discovered that Daws was the jade collector of those fabricated newspaper reports as he held out for me to take a small figure of a lion. His favourite I was given to understand. It was like a fat green worry bead with a built-in snarl, smooth with handling. But not cute, nothing out of Disney, this was ferocity in miniature. Dutifully admiring I gave it back and his right hand closed over it possessively.

Patrick anticipated the question. "Fully fit, sir."

"Can you run?"

"When a rabid dog's after me."

Daws gave him a smile so small that the only visible evidence was the extremities of his moustache lifting approximately one millimetre. Then he called his secretary over the intercom and asked her to make us coffee. While we waited he prowled.

I am not prone to biting my nails but at this moment would gladly have exchanged Daws prowling for Daws giving his impersonation of a glacier falling into the sea. He came to rest facing us in front of the window so we had no choice but to look at him.

"Hudson's got a lead," he said.

"We know who we're after," Patrick said.

"Evidence is the watchword," Daws told him with less venom than I might have expected. "Much as he loathes having to keep me informed he gave the go-ahead that you should sit in, as it were, on following it up. I'm quite happy with that."

"Do you know any details?" I asked.

"He assured me that it would be in the post before lunch. No, nothing else, not over the phone. He's a good sort," Daws reflected. "I like his manner, co-operative but not afraid of letting me know I'm making life difficult for him. Quite right, I can't stand obsequious people."

I filed away this insight for future reference. Daws gave away very little about his true feelings. He spared another of his microscopic smiles to his secretary when she bought in the coffee and then sat at his desk, not in any hurry to pour it out. There were four cups on the tray, the time a little after ten forty-five.

The time was not important, of course, it was just that I was looking at my watch when the reason for the fourth cup was admitted, a man who was introduced to us as Clive Haydock. He apologised for being a little late and sat down, suavely, in the manner afforded by those who have Number 10 as a working address.

He looked as though he was paid to be a sceptic. He sniffed his coffee as if suspicious that it might be instant and gave us an all-embracing glance. Flick, flick, flick, from face to face.

"I hope we've survived the mud slinging," said Daws, chin jutting.

Haydock sipped his coffee. "Difficult to say which is worse," he murmured. "The fact that mud was slung or the direction from whence you insist it came. Personally, I can't help but favour the latter." He glanced at Patrick. "If the Major is convinced then naturally, that's how it is." He gave his full attention to Daws. "But neat, Richard, very neat, if I might say so. There are others who quibble at such expenditure on a new department and you just happen to have picked the one near the top of the heap."

Daws munched at his moustache. "Major Gillard possesses

the kind of conviction that comes from having acquired an artificial leg as a result of an encounter with someone upon whom the sun of official favour has never set. Blind favour, the old boy network, precisely the kind of stupidity that his department has been set up to do away with."

"Kindly do not lecture me, Richard," Haydock sniffed.

"How many Bettaneys will it take to convince you?" Daws growled. "What I want from you," he continued when Haydock, understandably, didn't reply, "is an assurance that I have the full support of the P.M."

"Oh, you have it," Haydock observed, brushing an invisible speck of dust from an immaculate trouser leg. "I have the feeling that it would take more than rumours to get you out." He rose, smiling bleakly. "But a warning to you, Richard. Stir up the press into further wild clamourings against us by ill considered action and I cannot answer for your future security." He left, begging another appointment, his coffee virtually untouched on one corner of Daws' desk.

"Grrr," said Patrick.

"That was addressed directly to you." Daws said. "Go in for any spectacular shoot-outs and you'll be digging drains for the new airport in the Falklands." He turned to me. "Ingrid, my dear, you've had no training but I'd like you to accompany the Major here as support. Keep in the background on this occasion, report to me immediately anything goes wrong . . ." He paused and turned to gaze out of the window. "Logistics. Keep the front line functioning smoothly." We were dismissed.

I was steered out into the corridor.

"He couldn't look me in the eye and say that," I raved.

Patrick put his hands on my shoulders. "That was training. He'll treat you like that until he's made sure that you won't flounce off and leave him in the lurch. He's terrified of professional women. Don't rise to the bait—underneath he quite likes you."

"Perhaps I should ask Alan to find me a job scrubbing floors."

"We'll navvy together." He led off and we travelled ever downwards: corridors with fly blown notices pinned to the walls, occasional glimpses into offices with the regulation doormat under the desk and wooden hatstand, a proper carpet for the privileged, all the decor pre-Beatles era.

"That's a sinister squeak you have," I observed during the second lift journey.

"Not properly run in yet," he replied, grinning. "I'm down for weapons assessment. Care to watch?"

No, it wasn't a coal mine into which we emerged, merely the lowest level of an underground complex. My brand new identity disc was checked by a soldier at a security checkpoint and then we walked what seemed to be halfway across London down yet more corridors, all illuminated with the red lighting I had once seen when invited aboard a nuclear submarine.

Patrick shoved me through a door. "You'll need overalls. It's dusty as hell down here. Meet you in five minutes."

A changing room of sorts, racks of overalls, boots, ear defenders, sweaters, all presided over by a WRAC reading not a love story magazine but a NATO publication on tank warfare. She found nothing strange in kitting me out and giving me the key to a locker in which to stow my pink suede trouser suit and matching high-heeled shoes. I thanked her and she returned to annihilation tactics.

"Any comments on the rosebud in your button hole?" I enquired outside, referring to the small theft from an arrangement in the hotel foyer.

"I was asked if I wanted it put in water," he replied, unrepentant. "The sort of army you're thinking of doesn't exist anymore."

Perhaps it didn't. What became apparent to me in this tiny corner of the national security network was that Patrick was recognised; a brisk salute here, a wave from others, similarly attired, there.

I said, "For a new boy you know a lot of people."

Patrick pointed to a flight of iron steps that led upwards. "I used to be one of the instructors," he said, and disappeared through a massive pair of sound-proofed doors.

I climbed the steps, opened a door at the top and entered what looked like a control room with winking coloured lights, closed circuit TV screens. My first impression was that I had strayed into forbidden territory.

"Welcome and pray be seated," said the denizen of a large instrumentation panel, spinning a swivel chair on castors in my direction. "My name is Ken, and I've shares in all the laundries within a ten mile radius of this building."

I captured the chair, swivelled it lower and sat down to gaze through thick curving glass at an unbelievable scene below. It reminded me of a science fiction film set; an indoor assault course fitted into a room the size of a small warehouse; adventure-land crossed with pantomime, imagination the only limit.

Ken was in the region of thirty years old, had hair like a full blown marigold and, from what I could see of him in the subdued lighting, was a gangling fellow devourer of nervous energy.

"Mad Paddy's alter ego," he said with a broad grin. "I knew as soon as you walked in. You look like him."

I surmised that the term was an accolade and not familiarity and gave my attention to what was going on below. In the corner furthest away from me was a construction loosely resembling a fun fair helter-skelter, a towering edifice of rocks, presumably made of fibre glass, with camouflage netting and dead branches. What appeared to be sheets of hardboard, shiny side up, had been arranged to form a slide down one of the steep sides. Anyone fortunate enough not to land head first had then to do some fairly nifty footwork as they were decanted into a small area covered with cobble-sized beach pebbles.

"Watch the first one go through and I'll explain," said Ken, reaching for a mike clipped to a stand. "Number one gentleman if you please. This morning we are on Red Alert programme . . . repeat, Red Alert. All targets not hit fatally will be assumed to have fired back and hit you. You have three lives." He switched off the mike. "Good luck to all of them . . . I'm in a killing mood today. Get those ear defenders on."

I had barely done so when the first candidate appeared at the top of the rocks. On my right Ken donned a head set and then his hands hovered over the keys of the control panel. A finger selected and stabbed down and there was a bang as the man on the rocks took a shot at a cardboard cut-out of a gunman as it jack-in-the-boxed up on his left. He then slithered down the slide with a panache born of long practice, skimmed over the rocks, taking care of another target Ken gave him, and went from sight into a labyrinth of piled tea chests and cardboard boxes.

"Screen two," Ken snapped.

The corridor in a disused warehouse, a partly demolished block of flats, a tunnel, a sewer, it could be any of these. The camera was placed so that one had a view, as it were, over the shoulder of the man going through, realistic enough to make me jump when a target suddenly popped up in front of him. He shot it in the centre of the heart.

"If you're talking to me I can't hear you," Ken said. "You're on your honour not to tell a soul that there are mikes all over the set so I can hear them swearing. Not sadism on my part . . . it helps in the assessment. Watch."

A jet of water hit the unfortunate gunman, who slipped, fell flat and missed the next target.

"You're dead," Ken said over the tannoy, the disembodied voice metallic and derisive. "Two more lives permitted." He switched off the mike and chuckled as a reaction was made known to him. "Water pipes sometimes get hit by bullets," he said.

The next section was constructed of the same materials but not roofed over so I caught occasional glimpses of a set of khaki overalls. On number three screen was pictured a maze, at ground level totally confusing, but through the glass viewed from above simplicity itself, a passage leading off to both left and right, the left fork a cul-de-sac, the right with a bogeyman waiting.

The candidate glanced into the left-hand passage, gun ready, dived in and then out again, jinked into the right, saw the target, ignored it and tore straight on. A thunderflash went off, almost right in his face, and he jerked to a standstill as boxes toppled into his path. Back into the right, shot the target slightly off centre but still within the black circle, and dived for cover into a pile of cartons.

Another chuckle from Ken.

Below, furtive movement. Cardboard teetering, he crawled out, coughing on the thick dust that had been spread around lovingly, and then fell victim to another missed target.

"One life remaining," Ken told him. "Also running out of time." He switched off the mike again. "We change it slightly every week or so . . . I'm working on having a few small electric shocks to hand but the hierarchy aren't happy because of all the water." He moved quickly to press another button and even though I saw this the bang made me jump again. Electronics further assisted the fall of a tall stack of boxes, causing the luckless one to lose his cool and shoot blindly. I began to see the necessity for bullet proof glass.

"What must be realised is that he's one of the best," said Ken. "Down there it's different. I know, I try them out after I've designed them. At Christmas I let them build one for me. Always very interesting."

The first candidate had now entered the lowest level, a wide ditch partly roofed over with railway sleepers. He could either wriggle through it beneath the sleepers and climb out the other end, or cross the sleepers, thus gaining immediate access to the final stage, a crazy Beau Geste fort in full view of the control room window.

Ken said, "There's a time limit of one hundred and eighty seconds and unless he's not careful . . ."

He wriggled through the ditch, took no notice of sound effects of gunfire, shot the target that presented itself on the rim of the ditch and went up the rope at the end of it like a scalded cat.

Another target was taken out that had leaped unnervingly in front of him as he mounted the exterior staircase. He reached the top and I was close enough to see a pulse beating in his throat and hands slippery with sweat. After Ken had told him that it was finished he relaxed and walked across a gantry that led to another door in the room where Ken and I were.

It was a troubled warrior who joined us, still breathing hard, a little damp on the brow and very wet everywhere else.

"Did you enjoy that, squire?" asked Ken with a wink at me. "Second volunteer ready if you please," he said into the microphone.

"No," said the first sourly.

"Then enjoy this," Ken chuckled. "Your conceited colleague, Robert."

"Bob's all right," came the immediate reply.

"And due for a bullet unless he stops behaving as though he's Christ Almighty."

There was a short delay while Ken's assistants put the course to rights and then conceited Robert made his entrance. He got off to a good start, shot the first target as soon as it appeared and then a second and yet a third that Ken sneaked in when he stumbled running across the beach cobbles.

The master of ceremonies considered his man. Then, a soupçon of gadgetry nudged a pile of boxes, which swayed. Bob got soaked, waiting for them to descend on him and only managed to shoot the target in the arm.

"Dead and buried," called the inexorable voice. "For you that was a complete balls up." Ken clipped the mike back on the stand. "Conceited but soon disconcerted."

"You're a bastard," said the first victim but without heat. "Just you wait a few months . . . we'll bloody kill you."

"No doubt," Ken said quietly.

The one below was in more trouble. He trotted into the right hand fork of the maze, shot the target, reloaded, got a thunder-flash and bolted right to the end of the cul-de-sac.

Ken's lip curled into the mike. "It's mined old love. Two lives down . . . one to go."

I held my breath while a decision was made to go for death or glory. He ran, jinking, the reason for this apparent when a whole section of boxes leapt at him sideways. He flung himself away from them, decided against the safety of dust laden card-board and successfully destroyed the next target. Two people breathed out.

Ken caused the apparently solid sleepers to collapse as soon as weight was put on them but his prey jumped and gained the lowest step of the stairway. Still going for glory he raced up it, blasted at another two targets and gained the roof. He was so busy giving Ken a two-fingered salute that he failed to notice the sandbag on a rope and it hit him, right between the shoulder blades.

"Grenade," Ken yelled. "You're dead." He waited until the one to whom he was speaking detonated through the door. "The one you shot last wasn't dead. Shot in the shoulder, my son, he threw a grenade at you with the other arm."

Was there an axe in a glass case? I wondered, in event of aggrieved clients breaking glass. I left Bob to master his temper and gazed through the screen. One more to go of the first group, Ken was saying. The second consisted only of Patrick. One more before I had to watch him being humiliated.

Five minutes later the last gentleman of the first group bobbed up on the pinnacle of rocks. He shot the target cold bloodedly in the head, slid cautiously, found his feet at the bottom, judging it nicely so that he was crouching comfortably when the second target was presented.

Ken gave him another, by way of interest, as he crossed the pebbles, wary but not running, and then frowned when it was neatly terminated. "They've changed places," he muttered.

No one had so much as coughed, me included.

Patrick was already in the tunnel, standing like a statue, listening.

Ken removed his headset and gave it to me without speaking. I was left with no choice but to eavesdrop and braced myself to learn a few new phrases.

Patrick was given two thunderflashes but all Ken received for his trouble was the sight of a man ducking down fast. A collapsing pile of boxes shooed him along no further than a yard and when Ken turned on the water Patrick curled away, turning his back to it, killed the target and made for dry ground.

The shots came very loud over the headphones but I reasoned that there must be a device to deaden the sound or else I would never be able to hear him breathing over and above it. He sounded remarkably calm.

He had reached the maze already. Another thunderflash nudged him towards the blind alley but he looked first and reversed, climbing over some boxes with which Ken had tried to block him in. Unerringly he took out two more targets, paused to reload and then lost concentration sufficiently to try to avoid a jet of water. It missed but Patrick lost his footing and was buried by a stack of tea chests that Ken toppled over him.

"Take care," I whispered.

Ken tapped my arm and I lifted one side of the headset. "Too true, lady, he's sent one into this screen before now."

Patrick fought his way out from under the boxes, killed another two targets and a spot lamp and went to ground in the dust laden boxes.

Dust swirled and seethed and there was no other movement.

I had just come to the conclusion that Ken's microphones were not working when I heard a sneeze, followed by another. Patrick inched his way out of the boxes on his stomach, coughing, and whilst in this position shot another target, getting it in the side with the first bullet and in the stomach with the second. Messy.

None of the contestants had attempted to attain the fort by

any route other than the staircase, adhering, I assumed, to un-written rules. Patrick was no exception and I didn't blame him. The only other possible way up was to climb some supporting scaffolding and from there swing across to the gantry, a good thirty feet above the ground.

I knew that he wouldn't make a bid for the ditch and he didn't but was not expecting the sleepers to give way under him. I bit down on a thumb hard as he catapulted into the very bottom of the ditch in a somersault that seemed to go wrong. As I removed the headset to protest to Ken a shot ricochetted off something close by and everyone involuntarily ducked.

"Missed the target though, laddie," Ken purred over the tan-noy. "Two lives to go."

He red-flagged the bull with another cardboard cut-out and it was holed precisely in the centre. "But how to get out of there with a tin leg, eh?" he went on, fizzing with glee.

Then the cover of leaning sleepers gave up its fugitive and, with a fast crawl, Patrick reached the end of the rope and used it to haul himself up. The knots were useless to his feet but he didn't require them, went up hand over hand to the top, his good leg feeling for a hold.

"Blimey," said the man who had gone first.

It was plain by the way that Patrick carried on using his hands to pull himself up the staircase that it was not to his liking but he was alert enough to take out another would-be terrorist half-way up. When he reached the top he nearly had Bob in tears by crouching again quickly so that a well timed sandbag only ruf-fled his hair. Then he lay on his back and took aim at the slowly penduluming rope.

Ken sighed and clipped the microphone back into its holder.

Patrick fired, the rope parted and the sandbag soared over the chipboard ramparts to thud into the top tea chest of a swaying tower. The whole lot went down like a factory chimney, smashed into part of the maze which set off a dominoes effect, demolish-ing most of it. The sandbag progressed with its destruction, its weight ripping out hoses and producing a passable imitation of the Fountains of Trevi. Somewhere a fuse blew, several thun-derflashes exploded and all the lights on the assault course went out.

Through the screen we heard a braying laugh.

I was smiling my own relief when the door opened and I was seized by a breathless apparition covered in dust, hurtled out through the other door, down the iron steps, through the double doors, along a kind of backstage corridor and up a ladder. Then I was on the top of the rocks.

Half the lights were working and someone had turned off the water.

"I'll get you, Gillard," came a manic cackle over a loud-speaker.

My horoscope that morning had warned of personal affairs suffering a downward trend but had mentioned nothing about a slalom and a crazy fibre glass rockery.

"Down!" shouted Patrick, and down I went only because he provided impetus with a violent shove. By the time I had decided to steer with my feet I was at the bottom and sprawling on the cobbles which was just as well as he was right behind me. His gun cracked, appallingly loud without ear defenders. I had no illusions about him giving me his. If you forgot your kit you took the consequences.

I couldn't believe we were in the same setting. It was real, not cardboard, plywood and plastics but a pitiless landscape of rocks and dead trees. There were caverns, looming shadows and tunnels with eyes. Another target leapt in front of me, not a shape made of pressed board but an ugly scowling form armed with a sub-machine gun. Patrick grabbed my elbow and fired right by my shoulder but there was no time to see if the bullet hit the heart, I was running.

At the entrance to the tunnel I was halted by a powerful grip on the loose material of the seat of my overalls. Patrick pushed past and went on ahead, signalling to me to keep quiet. I could picture Ken, listening intently, watching us on the screens. But it was likely, with illumination down to a fraction of what it should be, that his view was nothing more than a grey fuzz.

There, in the gloom, Patrick gave me his gun, slipping it into my hand as we stood at the side of the tunnel. I was terrified of guns and was damned if I was going to keep it under those circumstances. Precious seconds were wasted while he utilised uncharacteristically humane methods of persuading me otherwise and then total war was declared as one of Ken's assistants leapt on Patrick from behind. The three of us went down in a heap, a fierce jet of water hitting me in the face as I fell. I crawled away and as I did so my knee nudged the gun which skittered along the floor and hit something unseen with a clunk. I went for it, found it, and as if that was the signal the lights went out again.

Silence. Then, behind me, a dragging scuffing sound. I crouched, holding the gun in both hands.

Above me, a light bulb glimmered, dimmed again and then became fully bright. The tunnel was quite empty. I went all the way back to the bottom of the rock slide but there was no sign of Patrick, not even a pair of boots, horizontal, sticking out from beneath one of the boulders. Damn all men.

All right, I thought, I'll play, just this once.

Ken's masterpiece had not recovered from the damage inflicted upon it. Water hissed somewhere to my right and there was an unnerving sizzling sound as moisture sprayed over bare wires. Then, quite clearly, a click as some mechanism prepared to do something nasty. I shied away from the sound just in time to escape cascading boxes. There was no going back. The whole of the roof of the tunnel had fallen in.

The passage was peopled with shadows, one of which tilted like a falling corpse as I went past. Only a carton. I stamped it flat. When one of the cardboard horrors jumped up from nowhere it was fear that made me take aim, squeeze the trigger and shoot the beastly thing right in the middle. The noise and jar to my wrists made me want to throw the weapon down but on I went, into the maze.

"We're all friends here," I consoled myself out loud, and with that someone took a shot at me that banged like an angry wasp into a tea chest a foot above my head. I bolted.

Not the left-hand passage, take the right and kill the target—but a grim reaper waited in the central one. I braked hard, slipped, and cannoned into the edge of the dividing wall. A thunderflash later I'd forgotten where I was, huddled with my hands over my ears, gun on the floor. Another bullet from above snicked into the woodwork inches from my head.

There was only one person present who could shoot like that.

I pretended that the leering target in the central passage was him, risked a one-handed shot, missed completely, swore, half-crying, a real snivelling mess, and got it in the guts at the second attempt. Then I ran like a hare for the safety of the sleepers.

Only it wasn't safe, they were still in a semi-collapsed position and fell all the way into the ditch as I reached it. Another very real bullet thudded into the pitch-scented wood. I skipped over the tops of the sleepers and into the ditch, far deeper than it had looked from above, a good four foot drop even though I was halfway down already.

For someone who was quite useless at gym in school I had great success with the rope, tucking the gun into the belt of the overalls, pulling myself up and using my feet to walk up the wooden side of the trench. I gained the bottom of the stairs and began to climb. There was no hand rail and the whole device was rickety, staple-gunned together for ease of dismantling.

The overalls were heavily soaked; one of the too long legs that I had tucked into my boots had come out and was threatening to trip me at every step. I glanced round, put down the gun and rammed the offending cloth back where it belonged. Up popped another target and I would have been theoretically dead but for a whirlwind of activity that arrived from above, snatched up the gun and used it to full effect.

Those bloody, wiry fingers closed over my wrist in a grip that made me squeak in protest and dragged me willy-nilly to the top where I had sufficient sense to dive flat under the embattlements. The gun cracked twice more and then, ye gods, the lights went out again.

"Do we carry on until you've demolished the whole damn caboodle?" I asked.

In the dark, teeth nibbled my ear.

"We got round without losing a life," said that well remembered voice.

"More by luck than judgment," I snorted.

"No, Ken's a fine shot."

"Will you buy him a pint for not killing me?"

For answer he flattened me to the floor and seconds later a thunderflash went off, seemingly, a yard from where we were lying.

"You're outnumbered," someone called. "Surrender at the count of five."

"Let me see that I'm outnumbered," Patrick shouted back.

The lights were switched on.

"The whole lot," Patrick muttered. "The Wizard of Oz, his two remaining technicians and the three from the first team. Curl up in a ball, hands over ears, mouth open."

A swift movement, a grunt of effort and his whole weight hit me hard. Whether the instructions were obeyed or not remains conjecture, the following moments were a puzzle always. I was told afterwards that it was a stun grenade that he had appropriated from Ken's secret cupboard of surprises. All I know is that it made my ears ring for hours, knocked two men cold, stunned another two and was instrumental in making the one who had thrown it miss his footing on the staircase so that he fell into the ditch and rendered himself senseless for ten minutes.

At some time during the ministrations to the wounded, a medical orderly gave me a cup of tea.

I said, "If you want to know who's my next of kin he's over there, with a lump on his head the size of an egg."

We had been married at nine-fifteen that morning.

CHAPTER 16

The ceremony had been quiet to the point of funereal in an over-heated room decorated in fetching shades of sepia and peasoup green. The pot plants on the window ledges, hapless Busy Lizzies and Partridge-Breasted Aloes, were visibly bracing themselves for another day of suffocation from fumes from the gas fire and the Registrar's pipe. Both witnesses had coughed with such resonance that I had found myself wondering if they would survive to the end without oxygen.

"I don't feel married," I had said on the steps outside, into the teeth of a gale.

"I don't feel married," I whispered to myself later, driving into the teeth of the same gale somewhere on the A30 with a passenger who had ceased bothering to stifle his groans every time we went over a bump in the road.

"You will show off," I complained. "And your leg's absolutely raw." I had not the courage yet to talk of stumps.

"Fifty quid," he said with great economy of breath. "Fifty quid I couldn't climb the fort the wrong way without penalty." He gave me his wallet, fat with new five pound notes.

"Where the hell did Ken get all this money?"

"Not Ken . . . Daws. Two months ago, in hospital. He ordered Ken to find out if you were gun shy to shorten the odds in his favour. Half of it's yours, Mrs. Gillard." He chuckled, regretted it, and slept through the remainder of the journey to Devon.

It seemed indecent to be married so soon after Peter's death but I kept telling myself that Patrick had promised he would look after me. I was being looked after magnificently.

"Alleluia," said Patrick when the car stopped. "Terry should be here. Kindly sound the horn briefly to let him know that I have no intention of testing his security arrangements."

I fretted, gripping the wheel tightly, during the minute or so it took for the young man in question to make an appearance. He came over the ridge of the barn roof, swiftly slithered down the slates and thence to the ground via a drain pipe. He could so easily have been a quiet dead huddle in a quiet dark corner.

"Can I kiss the bride?" he asked.

"If you find it absolutely vital," Patrick said as he went indoors.

"Fell in the moat," I explained, after a bear hug and a more than passable kiss, amused that he now regarded me as safe to approach in this manner.

"I know."

"How the hell do you know?"

"He phoned me, told me to lay in some plonk."

"There's plonk under the stairs."

"No champagne. Not *the* moat?"

"*The* moat."

"For the bet?"

"Daws lost," I said, thus concluding our peculiar conversation.

"Daws lost," Terry observed inside, calculating whether it was worth it as Patrick squinted at him through his headache. Whatever conclusion he reached he kept to himself but he did take the champagne outside to open it.

I said, "I hope you're going to give him some."

"Of course," said my husband.

In the end it was split three ways. When the bottle was empty I reimbursed Terry most of Patrick's share of the money and he went back on watch, serenely wishing us a night of unremitting passion.

I giggled.

"He who laughs last laughs worst," said Patrick.

There remained an unfortunate tendency to snigger on my part and also other feelings that would need to be firmly quelled. Later, I leaned over to kiss him good night and then wanted him enough to take the law into my own hands.

"Ingrid, I've a terrible headache," he said plaintively, opening his eyes wide as I availed myself of the results of my endeavours. Then he said, dreamily, ''Will you walk a little faster, said a whiting to a snail. There's a porpoise close behind us and he's treading on my tail.''

At a little after four the next morning, Hudson rang. I awoke sufficiently to listen to what he said and then hastened the waking processes with hot tea. I took a mug up to Patrick, finally having to resort to tactics little short of brutal to rouse him from sleep.

''Hudson wants us down at the station at five-thirty.''

''Five-thirty,'' he reiterated woodenly.

''Five-thirty,'' I agreed.

''Is he expecting the place to go up in flames at nine?''

''He tried to get us on the phone last night but the lines were down at Bridestowe.'' I made good my escape then, leaving him to drink tea, swear and commence the intensely personal rituals associated with wearing an artificial limb.

Keeping the front line functioning smoothly entailed making more tea for Terry and giving it to him in his bunker in the barn, together with news of our impending departure. He didn't seem to think that we were crazy.

Thinking through a chapter of *A Man Called Celeste* I washed, dressed, tidied the kitchen and living room, made the bed and then drove us into Plymouth, my initial inspiration only a silent, unshaven profile by my side. It was five-fifteen when we arrived, and just getting light.

We parked in a square marked ''reserved for E.T.,'' and entered the building through a side door with a notice over it that read, ''No entry to members of the public.'' I can be very bloody minded when I wish. The duty sergeant gave us an old-fashioned look and let us out from his side of the desk.

''The price for my name is a cup of coffee,'' said Patrick. ''A bacon sandwich for address and date of birth. You are forgiven for assuming that this is a domestic matter . . . I fell whilst jousting yesterday and hit my head on the drawbridge.''

It was a beautiful bruise, just above his left eye, thankfully mostly hidden under his thick, uncombed, curly hair. It was a slight shock to see quite how grey his beard was. This morning he faced the world looking like a kind of battered Old Testament prophet.

"Inspector Hudson's expecting us," I said, thinking that I ought to enlighten officialdom before we were charged with wasting police time or being drunk and disorderly.

Giving me another penetrating look, the duty sergeant said, "Aren't you Peter Clyde's widow?"

"I was," I replied feeling the heat climbing into my cheeks. "Major Gillard and I were married yesterday." How could he, my husband of only hours, turn out for this first meeting with Peter's boss looking like this: faintly sweaty tracksuit, old trainers and with his muddy old parka thrown over the top?

"Major Gillard you said," the sergeant was saying, writing it down, and I felt myself flush again as I heard the emphasis on the rank.

"That's right."

He opened a drawer and consulted a school exercise book. "There's no record of any appointment. Are you sure you haven't made a mistake? He wouldn't make an appointment for this time of day." He did not add "No one in their right mind would" but his expression did.

"He telephoned me just after four," I told him, embarrassment, anger and resentment threatening to conspire a form a spectacular and unholy trinity. "We were asked to be here at five-thirty. If he phoned from home on impulse, it wouldn't be in your little red book, would it?"

He agreed that it wouldn't and I went to sit in the glassed-in waiting room, alone. My companion—and I preferred to think of him as such as that moment—leaned, brooding darkly, on the edge of the enquiry desk, hardly an advertisement for the beneficial effects of a honeymoon.

Some effort had been made to brighten the waiting room. There was a poster with illustrations of poisonous plants and another depicting, in lurid shades, lethal fungi. I had always held the view that those who nibbled indiscriminately in the countryside got what was coming to them, perhaps the charter of the cowardly and unadventurous.

"Would you tuck into a plateful of fly agaric?" I called through the open doorway.

Patrick had most of his weight on his left leg. He said, "Those bright red ones with white spots? Kids might, they're used a lot in illustrations in story books.''

I toyed with risking a charge of assault and battery and then picked up a magazine, flipping through it unseeing. Another bête noir in our previous marriage but one unlikely to cause argument this time.

Children.

In the days before I had become an established writer and scribbled endlessly while the breakfast dishes remained unwashed, the subject of children, in a very new marriage, had not interested me greatly. We had taken vague precautions when Patrick was at home, which had not been all that often, and had been lucky. Then, a few years later and with a novel coming off the production line about every twelve months, I had detected paternal broodiness, the otherwise grave countenance softening alarmingly as he related the exploits of a colleague's baby son.

Our trouble had its beginnings in the fact that I started taking the pill without telling him, and blossomed into full hostilities some time afterwards when he discovered that he had been making love to me, assiduously and very frequently, for nothing. On reflection the fault lay with both of us. We had never discussed the subject, thus neither had realised the depth of feeling of the other, his yearnings and my antipathy.

I didn't dislike children but loathed untidiness, noise and plain cooking. To me, children represented all those things. Selfish opinions, I knew, and I could be more selfish than that. I had not wanted to swell up like a balloon, be sick in the mornings, fancy kippers with strawberry jam at midnight or any of the other bizarre trappings of motherhood.

Peter had not questioned my wish not to start a family. Always slightly in awe of my writing, he had agreed that to foist children on me would be little short of philistinism. Once he had asked me if it would stop me working and I had replied that it would not in the initial stages but what then? Sticky fingers on the snowy unused paper, crisps in the works of the typewriter, never mind a brain blown by lack of sleep and worry.

Thinking back on this I felt old and not at all wise.

Outside, in a corridor, could be heard the clanking of buckets. A man bellowed with laughter and was still laughing as he kicked open one of the two swing doors and came into the entrance hall. He dumped down his cleaner's bucket, spilling some of the hot, soapy contents, wrung out his mop and proceeded to wash the tiled floor in the wide sweeping strokes acquired with long experience. I watched, fascinated. Everything, however insignificant, that possesses its own excellence interests me. Ten sweeps and then into the bucket for a swish round, a couple of quick pumps up and down and then wrung out.

I became aware that Patrick watched him, too, and could see in his eyes, even from where I was sitting, the same pitiless glitter they had held while he had described how Peter had been gunned down. I looked more closely at the man washing the floor. He was the fourth crow, the middle-aged pervert of the red greasy hair.

At the same moment that Patrick commenced to stalk him he glanced up and then froze into immobility. But only for a moment. In the next he had thrown bucket and mop and thrust through the swing doors, running like a madman.

Patrick ducked under the mop, unbelievably jumped over the bucket which hurtled towards him at knee level, slipped on the soapy lake, regained his balance and we arrived at the doors together, sending both crashing back against the walls as we ran through. Only a miracle prevented Hudson from going the same way when he stood in front of us, arms wide.

"Cool it!" he shouted and then, when we had managed to stop, "It's fixed . . . he'll be followed every inch of the way. When he goes to ground we drive out and bring him in, and anyone else he's with."

"That one won't run back to mother," Patrick snapped.

"What makes you so sure?" Hudson asked. He took Patrick by the elbow. "All taken care of. Step into my office and I'll arrange some coffee."

Patrick resisted the pressure on his arm. "Sewer rats go to ground in sewers," he said repressively. "He hasn't much brain but he knows that if he leads us to the big time, he'll end up dead."

"Coffee first, discussion later," said Hudson throwing wide his office door.

We allowed ourselves to be ushered within and I was glad to sit in the nearest chair.

"All right?" A reassuring squeeze of my shoulder.

I nodded. Hudson had left the room.

"Lunacy," said Patrick. "Sheer bloody lunacy."

"How much do you reckon Daws has told him?"

Patrick sat down. "At a guess not enough for us to open our mouths over much."

Hudson brought us coffee that had come out of a machine. It was warm and drinkable, just, even though he had loaded mine with sugar.

"Derek Smith," said Hudson. "One of the team of contract cleaners. You were pretty near the mark, Mrs. Cl . . . Mrs. Gillard. He's been snooping around for some time by the look of it. The canteen's been missing cash, too, float money, which was nasty for all concerned. Petty cash has been walking away as well."

"A record for what besides sexual assault?" Patrick enquired blandly, handing over his plastic beaker for a refill.

"Er, quite a few things," Hudson said, going away to fetch it for him.

"Contract cleaners can't be expected to provide a list of personnel just because they're scrubbing out a cop shop," said Patrick when he returned, and with, I thought, unusual generosity.

"It's not the norm," Hudson replied.

"The same truncheon," I said.

"Could be," Hudson said. "As you thought, it had been cleaned. My fingerprints, yours and Stevens'."

Patrick said, "Tell me what Smith was had up for."

"Been in trouble all his life," Hudson said after hesitating slightly. "There were psychiatric reports when he was in his teens after he'd been involved with a gang that had attacked girls. After that and a spell in Borstal he settled down to vandalism, riding in stolen cars, getting drunk and beating up sailors. His most serious offence was ten years ago: someone hired him and another man to beat up their wife's lover. They put him in a wheelchair for life. He got five years for that and only then because his defending counsellor persuaded the jury that it was the other bloke who had broken the victim's spine."

The one who had wanted to rape me, who had watched, sweating, while the others took it in turns to hit Patrick with the truncheon, and had finally beaten him senseless. I didn't want to be near when he was found.

"There are several cases on the files that might be his handiwork," Hudson continued. "We'll find out soon enough."

We sat in Hudson's office for half an hour or thereabouts during which time his phone rang four times. On no occasion did he enlighten us on the information given to him but merely grunted into the receiver and asked to be kept up to date. Then, after the fourth call, he looked at his watch and asked us if we would mind going to the canteen as someone was waiting to see him.

"They've lost him," I said after we'd treated ourselves to much better coffee and a giant Cornish pasty between us.

Patrick made the kind of sound he reserves for female ears while composing obscenities. "If Hudson brings him in, his paymaster'll hit the road for the airport and that's the last thing Daws wants."

"He wants evidence as well," I pointed out.

"Not the same kind of evidence Hudson's after. Daws has to have proof that Trelawney's being paid by the Russians to cause trouble within MI5, not that one of his heavies took apart one of its operatives. Smith won't have that kind of evidence."

"So?" I prompted when he fell silent.

"So nothing . . . we wait and see."

"You hate waiting around like this, don't you?"

He gave me a brief smile. "I don't mind constructive waiting but this is little more than being dragged out of bed to be used in some crack-pot scheme. Smith could have been lined up in an identity parade for us."

This was probably true but I'd heard from Peter that Hudson's methods caused controversy. Also that they usually produced results.

We both lapsed into silence and I sat twisting my wedding ring, not the wide smooth one that had been Peter's gift but a narrower, more ornate and slightly worn ring that had a circle of white skin on each side of it, the one I had given Patrick back the night I had thrown him out.

"Misgivings?" he said suddenly, startling me.

I said, "No, of course not."

He looked up and his gaze focussed somewhere over my left

shoulder. "Hudson's smiling. The rat must have gone back to his sewer."

By the time we had been driven to a wartime concrete gun emplacement on a low cliff overlooking the river Tamar, Hudson's plans had gone seriously wrong. An ambulance was already parked with the cluster of police vehicles, its crew bending over a stretchered still form.

"What's happening?" Hudson shouted, running, while some ten yards away.

Little explanation was needed. Smith had waited until the young constable had crawled into his hiding place within the base of the structure and then pounced, knocking him senseless against a wall. He had dragged him out and used him as a shield to reach the cliff edge then had thrown him to one side and slid down the cliff face to the foreshore below. Everyone had been taken unawares.

"Fractured skull," Patrick said after one glance. He walked to the crumbling edge and leaned over then went for a short distance in the opposite direction to that taken by several of Hudson's squad who were looking for a way down.

"You can't go down there," I called.

"Gillards can go anywhere," was the weird response just before he disappeared.

I ran in time to see him reach the bottom of the thirty foot cliff in a boneless forward roll. It was quite clear how he had done it, the almost vertical slope was little more than a mud slide after the heavy rain and not dissimilar to the initial stage of yesterday's fun and games.

"Gillards can go anywhere," I told myself fatalistically, sat on the edge and pushed off. The world turned with great rapidity for a few seconds and then a hell of a lot of estuary hit me between the shoulder blades, winding me completely.

When I caught up with him he took my arm and drew me down, pointing. "See how the light catches the grass where it's bent over? That's where he trod on it. No, there . . . small shining areas the size of feet."

With some use of the cursed imagination, yes, I could see footprints leading away in the coarse grass just above high water mark. We followed them, Patrick as bloodhound, and they led firstly to a hole in the ground some six feet deep, half filled with plastic bags of rubbish that someone had tried to set alight, and then meandered away westwards. Gulls soared, scolding us as we set off in pursuit. The braver ones stayed on the ground, squabbling over nameless scraps.

Patrick walked fast and by now I was so familiar with his new gait that I only remembered occasionally when otherwise preoccupied that he had an artificial leg. How much the effort was costing him in discomfort was impossible to guess.

The Plymouth to Gunnislake railway line ran along the shore of the estuary and about a mile further on crossed a small river via an iron bridge, a Victorian structure of rust and peeling black paint. The whole area was strewn with rubbish, old mattresses, tin cans, tyres, and when I spotted a dead cat I looked no further than Smith's tracks in the mud.

There was no one hiding under the bridge.

"I'm damned if I'm getting my leg wet in that," Patrick said, grasped the nearest wrought iron supporting strut and swung himself, one hand at a time, across the water.

I paddled, up to my knees, very circumspectly, shutting my eyes to crabs and trailing green slime. Nothing could be done about the smell, however. I just concentrated on not falling in.

"I suppose you were expecting something like this," I said when I had run to catch up, squelching, eyeing apparel even more mud caked than my own.

"When called out at unsocial hours, dress rough," said he with a shrug. "A horse, a horse, my kingdom for a bloody horse."

A hundred yards further on we came to a man digging for bait.

Patrick said, "Seen a chap, medium height with red hair?"

The man, several days' growth of beard, tattered clothes and a Rolex watch, thought about it. "What's he done?"

"I'm not the law," Patrick said patiently.

"Then why d'you want him?"

"To tell him his breakfast's ready."

I said, "He's a child molester."

The man glowered at Patrick, bent to a rusty tin on the mud and came up with a handful of worms. "Red rag," he said belligerently. "Better than lug worm . . . don't fall off the hook."

"So I gather," said Patrick. "You're plundering a rare species. Which way did he go?"

A muddy finger pointed. "Through a tunnel under the railway. Behind those bushes. I know because that's the way I come. You say you're not the law?" He spat on the ground.

"No," Patrick said, beginning to walk away.

"Are you going to take the law into your own hands?"

But Patrick did not reply so it was left to me to thank an eccentric who might or might not have been an ex-con.

The tunnel was for drainage purposes and went diagonally from one side of the railway embankment to the other. I jumped down behind Patrick into the culvert into which it drained and looked through. I could see daylight but the distance seemed far further than the width of a single track railway line.

Patrick threw underarm a large stone the length of the pipe. It rattled hollowly into what sounded like tin cans and then there was silence.

"Can't we cross the line?" I pleaded, shrinking from an environment that promised rats and worse.

"No," was the uncompromising reply over his shoulder as he went in. "Stay there until I say it's safe."

It occurred to me when he was two-thirds of the way through that Smith might be waiting for him on the other side. I crouched down, watching where a circle of daylight had been until a few moments earlier and asking myself how he managed to move so quietly. Then the circle of light reappeared and I heard him kick the cans out of the way.

"Safe and reasonably dry," he promised. "No spiders larger than tennis balls."

I scuttled through on elbows and toes, surrounded by echoes, panic within spitting distance. He yanked me to my feet at the other end.

"I hate small spaces with cobwebs," I said.

"So your complexion would have me believe," he grinned.

Across what seemed to be a boundless open space of playing fields, tiny distant movement distracted the eye; dogs running loose, a couple of joggers.

"He's had a fair start," Patrick said, scanning the perimeters before setting off again.

A small sports pavilion was locked, the windows boarded up

against the attentions of vandals. The toilets, no more than a screened hole in the ground, I gladly left to Patrick's fuller investigation. He entered very quickly and reappeared almost immediately.

Playing fields, allotments, and still Patrick followed a trail. We traversed the patchwork of tiny plots, bright with chrysanthemums and dahlias. All the tool sheds we passed were securely padlocked but he checked every one and also a derelict car body, now a home for snails and yet more spiders.

"He's too unfit to go any faster," Patrick said, indicating a clear footprint in a patch of soft mud. "If he'd been running you wouldn't see the heel like that. There'd be a deep toe print and where the ball of his foot hit the ground."

Then we came to a wider path that led to a road and, waiting for us, leaning on a tree trunk, smoking, Hudson.

"Unless he swam he had to come out here," said the DI. "We've got the dogs on it now. He's gone into the woods over the road."

In all honesty I could detect no smugness, not a hint of derision. But all the same I turned my back on him, ostensibly reading a large notice board that gave details of the redevelopment of several acres of land adjoining the allotments. It appeared to have originally been a sewage works.

Patrick jerked his thumb in the direction I was looking but Hudson shook his head.

"He was seen crossing the road."

"He might have crossed back again," I said.

"If we draw a blank I'll send them in there next," Hudson said, humouring us.

"I think I'll have a quick look now," said Patrick, making for one of several large holes in the sagging wire netting fence.

Hudson said sharply, "I should wait a while if I were you, Major." He stared as if mesmerised when his words were disregarded, the look of a man not used to being disobeyed. Then he swung and bellowed "Rawlings!" causing a constable to come at the run.

"I'm having a shufti round here if I'm wanted," Hudson told him. "Let me have your radio."

I didn't wait any longer but wriggled through another hole in the netting and jogged slowly in the direction Patrick had taken.

Hudson caught up with me after a few yards and grabbed my sweater.

"Mrs. Cl . . . Gillard, you really ought to—" He stopped speaking then, the rest of what he was about to say dying in his throat as Patrick suddenly came through a gap in a brick wall. A request for silence was unnecessary. His eyes said it all.

A wasteland of tall rank grass, ruined single storey brick buildings, their broken windows gaping darkly like empty eye sockets in a skull, doors open or sagging on their hinges, all with their quota of obscene graffiti. Dried up settling tanks were choked with weeds and nettles, the pipes that led to them broken and buried in the soaking wet grass. I tripped over twice, going headlong the second time and muffling a yell as a sharp stone drew blood on my knee.

Smith wasn't in the first building, nor another right next to it, both with most of the slates off their roofs. I went in the first myself when the men had come out and a musty draught brushed my face. The hinges of an unseen door creaked as it gently tap-tap-tapped against the frame, a pile of rags in one corner, and black cobwebs festooned where the ceiling had been.

There was no sound but the swish of our feet through the grass. I kept well back but, to a coward, this had its perils. Every patch of shade, every open doorway, was a hiding place for a monster with long sinewy arms covered in red hair. I already knew what it would be like to have that face close to mine. For the first time in my life I broke into a cold sweat.

Smith wasn't in the third building, a pumphouse with the roof right off. Hudson went in first, shoving past Patrick as he carefully pushed the door back. The latter gave no sign of anger but walked around the outside to a window and dislodged a loose pane of glass. It fell inside and when Hudson emerged he was several shades paler.

Not that he learned. The final building was in far better condition than the others and furthest away from where we had entered. Formerly, perhaps, a staff room or office, whatever it was Hudson walked into it in the manner of one whose turn it was to bat in a village cricket match. When he was level with the open door he was slammed to the floor inside by a savage kick in the small of the back.

Patrick had kicked him. There was a flash as glass caught the light and then the door banged closed. Patrick shoulder charged it open. It connected with someone inside who yelled and tried to use his weight to keep Patrick out. But it was too late, he was already inside. The door swung wide and Smith was ejected violently into the mud. He leapt up and lunged at Patrick with a broken bottle which, had it made contact, would have ripped out his throat.

"Cripple!" spat Smith.

Patrick had blood on one hand but would probably not have heeded had it been severed. He saw when Smith noticed me and began to move in my direction and from that moment Smith had no chance. I could not move, my limbs refused to let me escape, so I was only feet away when Smith was disarmed. At no time did Patrick appear to strike him. It would have been unnecessary, almost wanton, luxury; the man merely had to come within his reach. There, right in front of my eyes, Patrick broke Smith's neck, neatly and quickly, the sound akin to snapping a stick of seaside rock between gloved hands.

He was standing quite still, breathing deeply, when I reached him. Then, he moved stiffly, limping slightly, and went inside to bring out Hudson. The DI was mobile but not over-talkative.

"The bastard kicked me," Hudson said, noticing the way Smith's head lay at a strange angle on his neck.

Patrick gave him the broken bottle.

As Charlie had said, you either loved or hated him, there was no middle course. But at that moment I don't think either Hudson or I could have put a name to what we felt. The one concrete fact was that the footprints leading into the building, imprinted into mud by the doorway and still plain to see after the struggle, were the same as those we had followed all that way.

CHAPTER 17

When it seemed that I could keep my eyes open no longer it was still only four in the afternoon and Daws sat tight in his chair, holding court with Hudson, Patrick and sundry other persons. I had shopped, given them coffee and biscuits, prepared lunch, bread rolls filled with ham and salad; then, as the endless day dragged on, I made tea and was now wondering if I would be expected to fetch drinks. But it was not for me to ask, I reasoned tiredly. We were in Patrick's flat in the Barbican.

As an indication of how weary I was it must be said that it had taken me half an hour to realise that I was within the same four walls where Peter had died. Self-banishment to the kitchen was tolerable because it reminded me of Elspeth, her homeliness shone from every polished tile. No doubt Patrick had called in the family interior designer when he moved in. I could imagine her revelling in fulfilling her ideas free from the constraints on her own purse.

It was all immaculately clean, of course, not even bread crumbs in the cutlery drawer. I found irksome the fact that reaching most of the items I needed involved stretching up to the middle shelf of the wall cupboards, but then again the kitchen belonged to someone well over six feet in height.

If I concentrated deeply on this kitchen there was no time to wonder about blood stains on the living room carpet. Had Peter entered this flat knowing he had only minutes to live?

I switched on the radio and then turned it off again after a baritone had informed me that his love was like a red red rose. A quick search of the cupboards was rewarded by a bottle of sherry, thankfully not cheap. No, a warm, sweet, tawny pick me up for a woman of shrinking nature who had witnessed her first killing not half a day earlier.

Hudson had dealt smoothly and efficiently with the aftermath. He had stared for a moment longer at the weapon that had nearly killed him and then spoken into the radio, one hand massaging his back.

Daws had not arrived until midday, having apparently commandeered some form of military transport that remained unseen. What had been clear from the moment he arrived was that Hudson required him to do a lot more explaining.

I was well into my second glass of sherry when the owner of the flat put his head round the door.

"They're going. Daws wants a word with you."

"There's blood on your tracksuit," I told him. I had noticed it earlier and he could hardly have remained unaware of it all afternoon. A wifely remonstrance, perhaps.

"I'm going to have a shower and change," he confirmed, and went away, limping badly.

Daws was packing a few documents into one of those flat as a pancake leather briefcases that in actual fact hold enough clothes for a weekend ski trip, come from Harrods and cost well into three figures.

"Bad do," he said.

I sat down and made myself relax. If he kept quiet I could go to sleep.

Daws cleared his throat noisily. "Unfortunate end to the affair," he translated.

"Self defence," I said, eyes closed. My cat's whiskers told me that one of his smiles flitted across his mouth and lost itself in the moustache.

"Hardly," said he.

"All right," I said. "Murder."

"Is that what you believe?" he asked quietly.

I said, "Put any name to it you like. A man disarmed a dangerous criminal suspect who had already attacked two people and broke his neck by mistake. Or, he broke his neck on purpose because he's a very strong man with a thing about others who go around sexually assaulting children and crippling people for money. Or, he broke his neck because he'd been one of the gang responsible for him losing a leg. Take your pick."

"It makes no difference to you?"

"He's a soldier," I continued. "Soldiers kill people. They also obey orders. Some time yesterday morning you had a quiet word with Patrick and told him that you didn't want any of Trelawney's hired thugs to be in a position to warn him. When you've written as many words as I have on human nature, you get to be slightly telepathic with those close to you."

Daws gave no indication as to whether I was right or not.

"I'd like you to learn to look at home with a shotgun before the weekend house party," he said. "If you need warm clothes let me know and I'll arrange it."

Mink or thermolactyl long johns? I wondered. I had a feeling it would be the latter and enquired of him where we would have to travel.

"Quite a way," he replied, moving towards the door. "Dumbartonshire. It's all right, I'll let myself out." He paused with a hand on the doorknob. "Ingrid, the invitation is primarily to you on the strength of your writing. If anyone asks, you wrote to the host and told him that you'd just remarried and requested that your husband might accompany you. Sir George was delighted."

"My new husband will have to rattle round the moors in a wheelchair unless his leg heals first," I said, refusing to be impressed. "Perhaps I ought to buy him a motorised invalid carriage and ride shotgun on it with a blunderbuss? That could hardly draw more attention than turning up in the first place."

"It's a bona fida invitation," Daws insisted. "At that distance from home, Trelawney can hardly arrive with a horde of mercenaries. The last person on earth he'll be expecting to see is you until it's pointed out to him that it's Scotland's Book Week. The confrontation's to rattle him. We're hoping to get a lot of information out of him before the weekend's out." He turned to leave and then said over his shoulder, "I've given all the details to your husband . . . get the gun from him."

Daws opened the door, changed his mind about leaving via a cupboard, wrenched open the door next to it and strode out. I heard the front door slam.

Brimming ash trays, a smoke-tainted room, plates with pieces of tomato skin and cucumber on them, a pile of cups and saucers. The party was over and somewhere in the city a mortuary slab had a new burden, perhaps the same slab upon which Peter's body had lain. Good, gentle Peter who had been unable to kill even a sparrow that Pirate had reduced to a bundle of sodden, quivering feathers. Mercifully it had given one last shudder and died.

The killer and the killed, hunter and hunted. According to those who believed as Patrick did, there was a purpose to it all, a divine creation, an artist all powerful who knew when every sparrow fell. If it was all a lie and good people and sparrows together fell into useless black eternity then the lie was the most wicked calumny ever inflicted upon mankind. If it was true . . .

If it was true then humankind would be blessed with a sense of humour. Somewhere, not too far away, that bloody dog still had a thorn in its paw.

I found Patrick in the bathroom, standing in a puddle of pink water in the shower, trying to reach his towel in order to lay it on the floor to sit on.

"I don't mind," I said, having got him safely on to dry land. He had dressings and soft padding ready, and I used my commonsense and bound up the rawness to make it comfortable for him.

"That's really amazing," said Patrick. "Where did you learn first aid?"

"Nowhere," I told him. "I'm just good at parcels. Do me a favour and be Long John Silver for a few days to let it heal." Then I told him about Daws walking into the cupboard and we both collapsed with the giggles; silly, ordinary things that have to happen to people who kill in the name of duty if they are to stay sane.

My request to return to my cottage was met with equanimity and we drove over the moor early the following morning, Patrick quite placid on crutches. I was fairly convinced that Daws had made his wishes known but had no intention to pry.

"D'you mind if I write?" I asked when I had unloaded the car.

"Please never say that," he replied.

"I switch off for days . . . it's anti-social."

"Can we meet for lunch in the pub, dinner where you like, and in bed for whatever?"

I told him that suited me fine.

Surrounded by my own possessions I regained a measure of tranquillity. It was surprisingly easy to take *Moonlake* from the drawer where I had locked it away and I spent the rest of that morning reading it right through. Sure enough, the digression had to be ripped up and went into the wastepaper basket. Not exactly back to square one but many hours of work nevertheless. I left the folder with *A Man Called Celeste* on one corner of my desk after roughing out the whole plot. It would be a very long novel, perhaps the labour of many years.

At a little after one I went downstairs. In the kitchen was evidence of cheese and pickles so I fixed the same for myself and took it back upstairs with a mug of coffee, hoping that he hadn't minded getting too hungry to wait any longer. A sound of loud hammering was coming from the barn.

For the next couple of days I lived in *Moonlake*. I forgot to ask Patrick if he was happy, or myself how a man on crutches hammers anything. It worked out that we went our own way during the day and ate at the local pub in the evenings, I was usually too tired to drive all the way to Plymouth to a restaurant. Even then I was in a dream, immersed in my own creation, so much so that on the second evening he reminded me gently that we were supposed to be on honeymoon and, later took steps to prove it.

His lovemaking still tended to maintain the characteristics of a boarding party storming a pirate galleon, and by the way he sometimes caught his breath, I knew that Horatio did not always return completely unscathed. I didn't ask. He had fitted the problem into the pattern of life and there wasn't the impression of a man coping with pain to give his woman pleasure. Far from it, he was innovative enough the next morning to bring me tea in bed and then demand wages, a quick laughing skirmish that reached a conclusion on the floor.

An hour later all had changed. An Army staff car swept into the yard, its driver bearing a sealed envelope. One small sheet of typewritten paper was responsible for a hurried breakfast for Patrick, coffee and a bolted down slice of toast and honey, while I, despite his initial protests, re-strapped his leg with the protective wadding, far more effectively, I guessed, than he had managed to achieve himself.

Then I was alone. "Go to Maggie," he had said, blowing a kiss. "Take the typewriter." In a nutshell, Trelawney had arrived home early from his holiday and had paid a visit to a naval establishment. Terry, sent to investigate his movements, had requested urgent reinforcements.

Maggie was due to fly out to South Africa for a holiday that day so was more than pleased to be suddenly presented with a resident care-taker.

"Only until I'm given the word to go up north," I warned. I had told her that Patrick and I were going to have a proper honeymoon touring Scotland and that it had been postponed as he had been called away.

Maggie gave me a sideways look.

"OK," I agreed. "I know I'm quite mad."

"Chucking up the writing then?" she wanted to know.

"I've never made a career of marriage," I told her. "Why start now? No, I'm going to try to finish *Moonlake* while I'm here. I might just do it. There are no distractions, no cows mooing under the windows and cats to feed."

At the mention of her bitterest enemies the wolfhound's ears shot up. She was going to another friend which was quite a relief. Being towed around several square miles of London twice a day was not my idea of fun.

"What's so incredible about this guy that you missed before?" said Maggie dubiously. "Fine, he's attractive and can charm the birds from the trees. D'you feel you can handle him a bit better now he's a trifle dented from the war? I know that's a bitchy thing to say," she went on, "but the whole time I've known you you've been thanking your lucky stars you got rid of him."

"The problems we had don't exist anymore, everything's different. Besides," I finished wretchedly, "he needs me."

Maggie made a loud hooting noise.

"You fancied him yourself," I said cruelly.

She laughed again, another synthetic one. "Pax," she offered. "I take it that one of the solved problems is that he no longer wants kids."

"Probably can't," I said. "All part of the South Atlantic

disaster.'' I gave her a few more details, if only to stop her thinking that I had really taken leave of my senses.

Her head went up and down like one of those confounded nodding toy animals you used to see in the back windows of cars. ''But, honey, even if he's still got part of—''

''I'm not even thinking about it,'' I snapped. ''If I get pregnant I get pregnant.'' I could see that she was dying to find out more. ''It's made a difference though,'' I added.

''I'll bet,'' she said, all agog.

''Before he made love to me as though he was writing a thesis on the subject. Now he's just plain randy.'' Why this need to defend myself in such childish fashion? I wondered, as I went into the spare room to unpack. For this reason, a small inner voice insisted. Maggie had always flaunted her own sexuality: with Alan—''No, dear, not your type''; with Peter ''Such lovely big brown eyes, so quiet, so undemanding.'' She had flirted with Patrick, making it blatantly clear that she thought him wasted on me. Plain Jane, an egg-head but didn't know what her body was for.

I was quite prepared to let matters be but it soon became clear that Maggie was either suffering from pre-flight nerves or had recollected, in Panavision, the brush-off Patrick had given her.

''I saw Alan the day before yesterday,'' she said, as if entrusted with vital secrets. ''In the hairdresser's.''

''Is he still going out with that model?'' I enquired, ignoring the mental picture of them sitting side by side under the dryer with their hair in rollers.

''Trollop,'' Maggie corrected starchily. ''No, she sacrificed his company for a weightlifter called Brian who came sixth in the World's Strongest Man competition. Alan's too chicken to try to get her back.'' She paused and I waited for her to come to the point. ''He thinks you're crazy, too.''

I shrugged. ''I can always take his ten percent somewhere else.''

''He seems to be coming to the opinion that you've burned yourself out. I'm sure he's wrong, honey,'' she hastened to add when she saw the effect her words were having. ''I just thought I'd let you know from the horse's mouth kind of thing.''

Maggie had never seen me lose my temper. I informed her exactly what I thought of Alan and his chit-chat with mistresses past or present about the private affairs of clients. Then I borrowed her phone without asking and told him so myself, brushing aside his explanation that it was only concern for my welfare by old friends. After really putting him in the picture I told him that I'd almost finished *Moonlake*, was working on a chart buster, and then fired him, slamming down the phone on him in mid-bleat.

When it became apparent that Maggie was about to giggle I walked out, bored with both their respective stupidity. I spent the rest of the daylight hours behaving like a tourist, seeing tall grey-haired men with a limp at every street corner. I had never been lonely before. I was very lonely now.

Maggie had jetted to the sun when I arrived back, and had left the key with a neighbour. She had also filled the fridge with fillet steak, asparagus, strawberries and clotted cream as a peace offering. When on earth would she learn that she couldn't behave with her real friends as she did with her kinky clients?

It was probably one of the safest flats in London, Maggie's mild paranoia saw to that. There were locks, double locks, burglar proof catches on the windows in case an intruder who fancied himself as Spider Man tried to get to her, a spyhole in the front door. I had just finished putting most of the steak into the freezer when the doorbell rang. Caution made me call to the girl with the flowers to leave them outside on the doormat, lying that I had just got out of the bath and had nothing on.

Yellow roses. From Alan.

The note was in his own flowerly handwriting so he must have ordered them personally from a florist not far away. Regret oozed from every word, he begged my pardon for being such a bastard. Never would he gossip about me again, to anyone.

I had ripped the note to confetti almost before I realised what I was doing. No, from now on Ingrid Langley would manage her own business. The roses I judged to be innocent so I arranged them carefully, Maggie had all the paraphernalia for making an expert job of it in a cupboard under the kitchen sink, Oasis, tape, florist's scissors, the lot. They looked quite something standing on a gold satin cloth on her handcarved teak coffee table.

For six days I worked. I rose at six-thirty every morning, made myself a pot of Maggie's Earl Grey tea and read through what I had written the day before, making corrections. Then I had a bath, dressed and had breakfast. It was only necessary to shop once during this period and then I really went out because I needed some more paper. My conscience told me that I should take exercise but as it rained nearly the whole time I gladly ignored it. I felt good for the first time in weeks, the same glow of well-being that had come upon me in Wales.

On the Thursday, the twenty-sixth of September, I still had not heard from Patrick. The wedding ring from another lifetime kept drawing attention to itself. It felt so different from the one I had worn for only a year, slightly loose now that I had lost weight. I had always removed it to do the housework and, for ten years old, it was quite new looking.

"A second chance, Mrs. Gillard," its tiny glittering facets seemed to say.

That evening the phone rang and I woke with a start, my half-eaten meal cold on my lap.

"Maggie's on holiday," I said sleepily.

The caller was either locked in a small cupboard suspended over a blast furnace or there was something wrong with the line. I gathered, after a lot of shouting on both sides, that it was Sober Simon and he would ring back. Precisely seven minutes later I snatched up the receiver again.

"That was a call box," he explained. "Only half the glass was in it and there's a full gale blowing."

"Where are you, for God's sake?" Unmistakably, the immediate location was a pub.

"Portland, Dorset. Underwater weapons," he said laconically. "Did you get the flowers?"

Gallivanting around indoor assault courses seemed to be doing wonders for my thinking processes. "No," I said.

"Apricot carnations," he said. There was a pause. "It is your birthday tomorrow, isn't it?"

"Yes," I managed to say. "You're very sweet. Thank you."

"There's a chance that this job at AUWE won't take much longer. I can't talk over the phone. If you don't hear from me again in a couple of days, go down to Hinton Littlemoor and ask my father to show you how to use a shotgun."

"Your father!"

"A wow at slaughtering clay pigeons. Get him to drum the

rudiments of it into you but don't stay longer than a couple of days, three at the most. If neither Daws nor I have contacted you by then go home—you can use my flat if you like, Elspeth's got a spare key. Don't stay anywhere for longer than three days. Got that?''

His voice had that whipcrack note it always holds when he's tired and under pressure.

''Of course,'' I said.

''That should take you into the first week of next month. Go to Scotland on the Friday, travel by day, not the sleeper. You'll get the ticket through the post at my flat so you'll have to call in there on the Thursday anyway. I suggest you hire a car in Glasgow. There'll be a map with the ticket, and directions for the journey. Can you remember all that?''

It was etched into my brain with acid. ''Roger,'' I said, and the line went quiet for a few seconds before he chuckled.

''I love you,'' I blurted out, and this time there was a longer silence.

''Not besotted, I trust,'' he said carefully.

''No, I just like your style,'' I countered. ''By the way—what *was* the computer print-out concerning your sperm count?''

He whispered something that I heard quite clearly but was obviously not intended to reach my ears. I could picture him leaning against the wall, thunderstruck.

''You wouldn't be having me on?'' he asked.

''It's probably the trauma of all that's happened lately,'' I said. Ingrid, whose clockwork arrangements had always been something of a joke. You could put the moon right by her, Patrick had once commented when we were first married. To some of his army friends in the saloon bar of the local, of course.

Some more money clattered into the coin box and I knew by the continuing silence that he had been told he wasn't sterile.

''I'd never have an abortion,'' I said. ''Not even—'' I broke off and told him I had heard a ring at the doorbell. Yes, I'd be very careful.

Through the peephole all I could see were red roses. I adopted the same procedure as last time and when the man who had delivered them had gone from sight I brought them in. After glancing at the card I put them on the draining board in the kitchen and shut the door.

"Red roses," I said into the phone. "Two dozen."

That really took his breath away for a moment. If there's one thing Patrick loathes, it's scentless greenhouse roses.

"I didn't ask for roses," he said.

"So you said."

"What does it say on the envelope?"

"To Ingrid."

He swore then, furiously. "I asked them to send them to Mrs. Gillard . . . our little joke."

"I've a funny feeling about them," I said. "They seem heavier than they should be."

"Where are they?" he rapped out.

"In the kitchen."

"Don't touch them! Whatever you do, don't touch them."

I thought deeply. "Shall I drop one of Maggie's long pile rugs over them?"

Another silence.

I said, "I'd feel a ninny if the bomb squad came and—"

"That's what the bomb squad's for," he raged. "God, if I wasn't down in this bloody hole." A lot more words battered into my eardrums but I preferred not to listen.

"I'll put one of Maggie's rugs over them," I announced when I could get a word in edgeways. For the first time in his life the man had flipped.

I picked up one of the oblong crimson and gold Rya rugs and went into the kitchen, holding it in front of me like a shield, careful to hold it high enough to protect my face. From the telephone table the receiver was issuing an urgent summons.

Dewy perfection lay on the draining board adorned with a white satin bow, real ribbon, not the usual stiff papery material. At the last possible moment I folded the rug in half and dropped it, en masse, over the flowers.

There was a loud, stunning crack and my back hit the edge of the open door. I ran to the phone where Patrick was still shouting my name.

"I'm OK," I said, and had to sit quickly on the floor. The rug now had a smoking black hole in it, the kitchen reeking of burnt wool.

"I'm OK," I said again.

"Get hold of Daws," Patrick said.

There was nothing else to say. Neither of us needed to remind·
the other that if he hadn't rung I would in all probability either
be blinded or minus my hands, out there in the smoky kitchen.

CHAPTER 18

I went to Patrick's flat first. Not contrariness on my part but Daws' orders, a precaution while he checked that Maggie's phone hadn't been tapped. I had nearly said to him that it was a little late for checking but this seemed small-minded when he had arrived on the doorstep fifteen minutes after I had rung, and in full dress uniform, straight from a Regimental dinner.

We had raided Maggie's drink cabinet and found some vintage port to make up for what he had missed. After two glasses he had become less twitchy and said that if I went straight to Plymouth he would contact Hudson and ask him to issue me with a bodyguard. The ticket and instructions would be sent to me there. I would know the package by its red string and London postmark. I was to treat all other post with extreme caution.

I travelled south-west by train and caught a taxi from the station. I was weary at the prospect of more travel, cloak and dagger parcels and all the rest of the tomfoolery. Daws had sensed this and tried to make me understand that he was as upset about the affair as I was but it would soon be over. I could remember smiling at him. In truth the man was haggard with worry; not all torture is of the physical variety.

The memory of his drawn face was with me still when I shoved open the door of the Barbican flat, typewriter, manuscripts, cases and all. Without even taking off my coat I went into Patrick's bedroom and to the bedside cabinet, took a key from a hiding place in the base of a lamp standing on it and used it to open a drawer. The cupboard below was a blank and the base of the drawer above it hinged to hang downwards when pressed in a certain manner. I explored the cavity with my fingers and had to push my arm in almost up to the elbow before I found what I was looking for.

Cold, heavy and loaded ready for instant use, Patrick's anti-widower kit—my description, not his.

It lay on the dining table next to my typewriter for my entire stay while I was working, and in my pocket when I went out, immensely comforting. I had received a ten-minute lesson on how to use it, the only lasting impression of which was that it had looked far more at home in his grasp than mine.

I carried on writing, words pouring on to paper effortlessly and tirelessly. On the day after I arrived I worked until two A.M. There was no logical explanation for this other than that it was all in my mind, waiting to be set down and while it was there, rolling around like shifted cargo, it bothered me. In a wild burst of energy I completed *Moonlake* at ten the following night, leaving Becky and the man she nearly lost in each other's arms.

I shed a few tears as I always do when I finish a novel. Now the people with whom I had shared the past few months were no more than figures on paper. We had taken our leave of each other, I to my fate on the hands of H.M. Government, they to a thousand shelves in shops and libraries. The moment of sundering could not be permitted to linger. I checked through the final chapter there and then, tidied the manuscript and placed it in its folder, ready for posting to the publisher. They would get a surprise on this occasion. All but the first two had been delivered personally by Alan. Of course, there was not the slightest reason why I should not take it myself, on the way up to Scotland.

Commonsense prevailed. No, the fascinating and charming lady novelist would not swan into Thorpe and Gittenburg's London office, her manuscript extended in one languid hand. She would grow up and entrust it to the Post Office, recorded delivery. I went to bed.

A Man Called Celeste was more of a problem and I thought about it early the next morning while scuffing my feet along the Hoe. I had roughed it out, or at least I had roughed out a perfectly acceptable plot. The crux of the matter was, did I still want to write it?

Behind me, collar turned up in scant protection against the cold wind, was my protector, of an age and demeanour likely to be shunted into early male menopause if he knew the true identity of the heavy lump in my coat pocket. In the end I took pity on him and went back to the flat. Plymouth was too distractingly beautiful to suit my purpose, the Sound spiked by grey ships that might have come from Portland.

I did half an hour of brisk housework, packed, wrote a little note to my guardian angel to let him know that I was leaving but not saying where my next destination would be—that was relayed only to Hudson, over the phone—and departed by taxi.

There had been no phone calls and only two items of post, a postcard addressed to Patrick from his Great-aunt Jane in Lima and a package tied with red plastic string for me. Inside it had been a single rail ticket to Glasgow Central, two closely typed sheets of instructions and one thousand pounds in used fifty pound notes.

I was in the cottage for perhaps four hours, unpacking, packing and parcelling up *Moonlake* for posting. Patrick had cleaned the car during the two and a bit days I had left him to his own devices, cleaned it and arranged to have it serviced. There was a receipt for nearly a hundred pounds folded up in the glove compartment. So now I owed him rather a lot of money as well as a classical guitar.

In the barn I discovered the rest of his handiwork: a plant trough made from a sheet of marine ply that had been leaning on one wall of the barn for as long as I could remember. Sturdy, built like the *Dreadnought*, it was the most hideous thing I had ever encountered. Curse those woodwork classes while he was in military hospital.

After driving to Hinton Littlemoor in my own car, I was John Gillard's pupil for two days. At first I was reluctant but became more confident after I had been taught to carry the shotgun correctly, negotiate gates, fences and ditches, to load, unload, master safety, etiquette, everything. When he was satisfied with all this I was allowed to fire it a few times and I went home to dinner on the second day with an aching shoulder and a very dead rabbit. The latter had been a complete fluke. The creature had popped up from nowhere and sat looking at me like a lunatic from a ridiculously close range.

I had Terry's company all the way to London, and just before he loaded me into a taxi for Euston he passed over an envelope addressed to me and several dire warnings about speaking to strange men on trains. Then, with a peck on my cheek, he was gone, striding broad shouldered and purposeful through the crowds of travellers.

The letter was from Patrick, handwritten on flimsy Ministry of Defence paper. I began to read, jaw dropping. He had arranged with Alan—here I looked out the window of the taxi until I had come off the boil—that I should sign copies of my latest novel, *One for Sorrow*, the imminent publication date of which had slipped my memory, in Hollingbury and Makepeace, the famous Glasgow bookshop. This was to take place on Saturday morning, the following day. I was to stay at the Central Hotel tonight and he had booked a room for me under my pseudonym. (I'd give him pseudonym! It was my maiden name and well he knew it.)

The black ink went inexorably onward.

Our quarry had paid a visit to AUWE, the Admiralty Underwater Weapons Establishment, where he had asked to see certain documents. His security clearance being extremely high, this request had been granted but the government scientist whose brainchild the folder represented had extracted some of the pages with the most sensitive information before giving it to him. Patrick did not say why.

It had not been the intention to leave Trelawney alone with the folder but he had requested a more comfortable chair so perhaps had had the room to himself for a minute and a half. This much Terry had discovered for himself before glimpsing the three remaining crows going into a pub on Weymouth seafront. Hence his request for reinforcements.

Patrick was staying in Portland in the event of Trelawney's returning either to view or photograph the missing pages. The problem was that Trelawney was perfectly entitled to knowledge of the information concerned as he was involved with monitoring the Russians' progress in a similar field.

I read on.

Trelawney was expected to drive himself to Scotland; he had an Aston Martin and enjoyed giving it its head. There had been prosecutions for speeding. Reliable sources of information prophesied that he intended to arrive at Craigsmuir just after lunch on the Saturday whereupon he would be personally welcomed by Sir George who would conduct him to refreshments and private conversation in the library. The library had already been bugged. I was to make sure that he saw me. Haunt him, my better half said, loiter with malice aforethought to inflict much damage to his cool. He, Patrick, would endeavour to arrive at the house first thing on Sunday morning.

The taxi pulled up at Euston and I had to push all uneasy thoughts to the back of my mind while I paid it off, organised luggage and found my train. I would have to find time to shop for clothes in Glasgow, there would be a couple of hours after the shops opened and before I was expected at Hollingbury and Makepeace. But it would all have to be done by taxi and how the hell I was going to get to Craigsmuir before Trelawney was anyone's guess.

I tracked down my reserved seat, took notepad and pen from my briefcase and started work. Concentration was not difficult where distractions were of a vague, fairly constant nature and I had always found train journeys ideal for writing.

A Man Called Celeste was a problem. Martin Celeste himself was interesting, a pastiche of both Peter and Patrick although exactly whose good and bad points I was using I hadn't examined too closely; that led to less productive trains of thought. The difficulty was that the more I wrote, the more it resembled the events of the past few months and I couldn't plan ahead because I didn't know how it was all going to end. The original rough draft had gone into my mental wastepaper basket days ago.

No, I mustn't let it become a diary.

Why had the government scientist removed some of the pages? Had he taken an instant and violent dislike to Trelawney? If so the man was a master of second sight. Had he been ordered to and if so, by whom?

I shooed away reality and went back to make believe. Celeste's boss, Cartwright, was the villain of the piece and I spent quite a while creating a character study of him—any resemblance to Daws being quite coincidental, I didn't dislike him that much. Cartwright was ambitious and greedy, although the face he presented to the world spoke only of quiet dedication to his job.

We had stopped at Rugby when I became aware of my own hunger and much unwrapping of sandwiches round and about me. I excused myself from the window seat and fought my way to the buffet car, roundly slating myself for not having bought food beforehand.

The inner woman kept on working, noting and recording a female with the most extraordinary hairstyle. She was quite young, no more than thirty, and a real Valkyrie, her hair in chunky blond plaits wound round her head to form earphones. They were greasy, the whole lot didn't look as though it had been undone for weeks. She was probably German, I decided after a second look at her broad posterior while she stood slurping lager from a pint glass. Her companion was disappointing, flabby and with a toothbrush moustache. I firmly suppressed any imaginings as to their activities in bed and bought two ham rolls, soup and some chocolate.

Morecombe Bay came and went, the sky darkening with dusk and rain clouds. Soon it was pouring, blotting out the hills of the Lake District and the only real scenery of the entire journey. I finished my chocolate, walking in my mind's eye with Martin Celeste down a dark alleyway in East London. Halfway down it and nearly into the hands of the men about to abduct him, I realised that I ought to destroy Patrick's letter.

I couldn't find it.

Quite a while later, in my hotel bedroom, I tipped out my bag on to the bed and searched every item of luggage. It simply wasn't there. Had I dropped it whilst paying off the taxi? No, I could distinctly remember putting it into my suit jacket pocket. From there I had placed it in the wallet part of my purse but, aware that I might pull it out with a note, had transferred it . . . where? At that moment someone had asked to see my ticket. Where the hell had I put it?

My handbag was capacious, one of those with zippered compartments on the outside. I turned them all out, finding all manner of amazing things, including a nephew's tooth that he had presented to me on my last visit. James was six and Sally's second to youngest and was going to be an explorer when he grew up. I thought of James and how brave he had been when he had fallen and knocked his front milk tooth out. Here was I half crying because I had lost a piece of paper.

I picked up the phone and dialled Daws' emergency number. For some reason he answered himself this time and I went hot with shame when I told him what had happened.

"Could it have been stolen?" he grated.

I told him that it was quite possible.

"Can you remember all the details?"

I could, but only because most of it had annoyed me so thoroughly.

"We'll assume it was stolen deliberately," Daws said. "It means he's far closer to us than I thought. I'm flying up. Don't do anything until I've seen you."

I said, "But I'm supposed to be signing books tomorrow."

"Oh, carry on with that," he huffed. "Then make your way to Craigsmuir. I'll see you there tomorrow afternoon."

"What about—?" I started to say but he had rung off. What about Patrick? Our cover, such as it was, was well and truly blown.

Patrick had said that he would arrive first thing on Sunday morning. How, for God's sake, when public transport simply didn't happen like that in Scotland? One answer was that he might drive. I doubted it. Another was that he might put his motorbike on the overnight train and ride it from Glasgow. That would mean he'd have to go home first to collect it.

I rang the Hinton Littlemoor number. Elspeth answered. I could not tell her too much but she found nothing odd in my requesting her to inform Patrick, if she saw him, that I had lost the letter he had given me. I explained that I was in Scotland to sign books, adding that it was raining buckets and I was going to blow a lot of money on clothes. She reminded me not to buy her a haggis and we rang off, laughing. So far so good, I had given him fair warning. No doubt he would expect my resignation in triplicate.

It was always possible that Daws would manage to contact Patrick and warn him that his arrival time was now known to the enemy. But surely, I reasoned, once he saw me, Trelawney would put two and two together and expect Patrick to turn up at any time, whether he had arranged to have the letter stolen or not. I began to feel irritated. As a plot to capture a spy it appeared remarkably amateurish. I could have written a better scenario myself, and without resorting to melodrama. And why on earth had so efficient a worker as Patrick committed such sensitive information to paper in the first place? Easy, came the answer, it was known that Trelawney would try to get hold of it.

Which meant, if I was still in full possession of my grey matter, that I had been a sitting duck.

I put my feet up and thought about Trelawney with a curiosity I knew to be dangerous to my peace of mind. Spy, traitor, whatever he was, first and foremost he was unbalanced. Those in the Kremlin paying him must be aware of it and were playing on whatever aspect of his insanity could cause the most damage to MI5. Chaos within, public uproar afterwards, the field was theirs.

We had come a very long way from an Argentinian deserter spinning a tale that had been responsible for a British army officer sleeping with a gun under his pillow. Trelawney had left quite a trail. He had hired men to kill, kidnap and maim, and if I was his contact in this country I would be sweating blood.

Then, the flowers. The only people who had known where I was were Patrick, Daws and Maggie. And Alan. How? Simplicity itself. Maggie had rung him again after I had stormed out and unwittingly spilled the beans. It would not have been too difficult for Trelawney to get in touch with my agent and ask for my whereabouts on some pretext or other.

Over *Fillet de Boeuf*, courgettes and sauté potatoes, I gave the thinking processes a rest and skimmed through a guide book of Scotland I had bought in reception. I hate eating alone in restaurants. One has to read a book to avoid the attentions of raffish commercial travellers. My clothes were still hanging on me like rags over a rail so I filled a few odd corners with fresh fruit salad and cream, following this with a pot of coffee and yet more cream.

Back in my room I wrote for two hours. Celeste was taken to a cellar and I described it in exact detail: newly painted walls in a shade of pale cream, the ceiling white, floor concrete and swept spotless. Not a woodshaving, dropped screw or cobweb in sight. It was part of a house belonging to an obsessively tidy man.

It did me good to write about it, exorcising the remnants of bad memories. There had been no nightmares for a little while and not all the memories were bad ones. Patrick had shown me what real courage and grim resolution looked like and I could paint Celeste in those colours, bright hues that had shone through the horror. And also his own peculiar brand of twisted humour.

I slept well, only missing a companionable warmth next to me. My father had always insisted that I'd end up married. Too cuddly to remain a spinster, he had teased. Although he had died a month before the wedding he had been happy for both of us, approving of Patrick, the only member of my family to penetrate the young man's somewhat lordly manner. He had made us promise that there would be no deep mourning and that the wedding would take place as planned. My mother had been horrified and had wanted us to wait a whole year "out of respect," but she had had other motives.

After a real Scottish breakfast of porridge, kippers, bread rolls and marmalade, I went shopping in Fraser's. Thermolactyl underpinnings against the lashing Arctic rain that still poured down, two lambswool sweaters and woollen slacks to match, a huge hand knitted sweater in Falkland Islands wool, two white silk blouses and an evening skirt in dark green velvet. I relied on mine host to provide waterproofs, and if he couldn't lend me a shotgun I'd go fishing instead. The handgun was still at the bottom of my bag, making my arm ache with the weight.

I enjoyed coffee in the restaurant while they parcelled it all up and then wandered into the book department. Banners proclaimed that it was Scotland's Book Week and the shop had made its own gesture by installing a large comfortable lady writer of cookery books. I bought one of them, seeing pleasure suffuse her face as she signed it for me.

Hollingbury and Makepeace was only a short walk along Argyle Street. On the way I bought a pair of black velvet trousers in a boutique, and some black patent shoes with diamanté buckles. Thus it was that a rather laden lady writer presented herself, several minutes late, within the illustrious portals. The assistant to whom I spoke had clearly expected me to arrive in a gold-plated Rolls with outriders and when I asked her where I could stow my shopping looked as though she was about to burst into tears. I soothed her as best I could, borrowed the staff ladies' room and changed into the black velvet trousers, new shoes and one of the white silk blouses. Then I painted myself to the hilt, sprayed on a generous mist of Patou's Joy, and presented myself for duty.

In the middle of performing another calming operation on the manager, poleaxed at being presented with a romantic novelist and wistfully telling me about his previous singing session with a hirsute mountaineer who had climbed half the Himalayas without oxygen, a vast bouquet of red roses arrived, addressed to me.

Did one clear the shop or merely dive beneath the nearest table?

The manager, confusing frozen terror with bashfulness, summoned chivalry in the guise of his buck-toothed assistant who whipped off the card and gave it to me with a courtly flourish.

It was a very bad moment.

The roses were from Alan. His swan song, he snivelled, every happiness in my new marriage and if I changed my mind about needing his services all I had to do was pick up the phone.

I sat down at the desk provided.

"Are you all right, Miss Langley?" asked the manager.

I conjured up a smile for him. "It's rather hot in here. Do you think I could have a cold drink?"

The shop began to fill with people: genuine fans, the curious and those who had been passing by and saw the crowd. I clutched my glass of tepid Irn Bru and wondered if anyone would buy. The roses lay before me, starting to wilt already. When the first copy of *One for Sorrow* was diffidently held out for me to sign, I did so and gave the customer, a woman, one of the roses.

"From my agent," I explained. "I'm giving them away to the first two dozen buyers."

After that trade became brisk and the roses disappeared quickly.

Just before noon, when the session was supposed to end and warm sherry had replaced my first refreshment, it seemed that we might be giving the books away, so many people were crammed into the shop. The stand with copies of *One for Sorrow* looked distinctly thin in places and the cash register was bleeping away merrily.

The books were placed on my desk and sometimes I only just remembered to look up and note the face behind each sale, and smile before taking up the next copy.

They were all women's hands, mostly hard-working ones. There was an occasional well-manicured be-ringed one and then, lo, hard-working masculine ones, a blushing bricky buying his mother a book for her birthday. When the same thing happened a few moments later I wasn't so surprised.

Except that this time the male hands belonged to the man codenamed Trelawney.

I suppose I stared at him for five seconds or so but have no recollection of any other physical reaction on my part.

"A thousand, thousand apologies," he said, very quietly.

"D'you want to buy this or not?" I snapped, working out an escape route.

"Of course," he murmured, holding out two five pound notes to the girl taking the money.

I signed. Yes, it was my signature that appeared on the fly leaf, not meaningless scribble.

"In one sentence, I can make amends," he said.

He really had the palest blue eyes I had ever come across and they twinkled as he smiled at the assistant when she gave him the wrapped book and his change. Behind him, a woman was getting impatient.

"I'm busy," I said, my own voice sounding hollow inside my head.

He bent towards me. "Daws promised the Russians you had gone over with him," Trelawney said.

CHAPTER 19

He was waiting for me outside Hollingbury and Makepeace, tall, distinguished-looking, a senior member of the Secret Service. He relieved me of most of my parcels and we walked the short distance to where he had parked his car.

"We can't arrive together," I said.

"Most certainly we can," he replied. "Sir George is near the top in MI5. Daws won't arrive until early evening." We were side by side in the front of his silver Aston Martin, he studying me carefully and I returning the scrutiny.

"Every accusation under heaven is in your eyes," he remarked. "Why remain silent?"

"I try never to state the obvious."

"The source of my information was impeccable."

"Perhaps it was the same source that made it clear that you were the traitor."

Trelawney laughed softly. "I hope not."

I said, "You questioned us about Peter who had nothing to do with the department."

"You're right. I know that now. Would you like to ask Sir George about that when we reach Craigsmuir?"

"I'd prefer to hear you attempt to wriggle out of it," I told him.

His fingers tapped the wheel. "Look, Daws has his little unit to hunt out enemies within, moles if you prefer the popular idiom. He gave his word in exchange for a large sum of money that the whole thing, lock, stock and barrel, would be working for Moscow and those that weren't, the ones on the periphery, wouldn't be important enough either to know or matter. Now,

when a member of the group shot and killed two IRA gunmen—
and not just a member of the group but one working directly for
Sir George in a position deliberately designed to attract the attention of the enemy—"

"You've just said that Daws is the enemy," I interrupted.

"Suspected for some time but not confirmed until after that
incident. When Major Gillard shot those two men, a shooting
during which a policeman was also killed, questions were asked
as to what the policeman was doing at the flat and why he had
gone there. Everything had to be investigated."

It was important that I kept my temper. "In the course of
which investigations Major Gillard was beaten so severely that
he subsequently had to have part of his right leg amputated."

"I regret that," Trelawney said, and then cleared his throat.
"I intend to apologise to him when he arrives on Sunday. I must
admit that hiring criminal help was an appalling blunder. I wasn't
party to those arrangements, and it all got a bit out of hand."

"Did you offer to resign?" I asked.

"Yes," he replied. "But none of us is blameless."

"Will I get confirmation from Sir George about what you've
just said?" I enquired.

"Naturally. I can hardly expect you to believe me after what
took place. Would you like to drive?"

So I drove an Aston Martin, first of all to my hotel to pick up
the rest of my luggage and then out on to the motorway past the
airport and towards the black jutting pinnacle of Dumbarton
Rock on the east bank of the Clyde, crossing the river over the
Erskine Bridge. I knew I was handling the car well and not once
did Trelawney offer advice or suggest a route. I had memorised
my map.

After Dumbarton, Helensburgh and then Rhu we were driving
into the Western Highlands along the Gare Loch towards Gare-
lochead.

Patrick had done two hours of duty in Northern Ireland. There
had been plenty of time for him to become a marked man.

I said, "Was it a personal vendetta with the IRA?"

"A compliment," said Trelawney, "you usually have to be
Commanding Officer before you earn that kind of attention."

"Or a member of an undercover unit?" I said.

"Not on this occasion, I understand. A suspect was taken in for questioning. He died. Not unusual in this day and age."

I took one hand at a time from the wheel to wipe the moisture off my palms against my trouser legs. "I take it that Patrick was in charge of the interrogation?"

"He was the interrogating officer."

"Was the suspect a relation of the O'Neills?"

"Their younger brother. He'd been picked up on suspicion of being one of a gang of boys who had thrown petrol bombs at a patrol."

"Boys!"

"He was fifteen. Don't upset yourself. They're vermin."

Craigsmuir Estate was tucked into a glen above Loch Long. The house itself was at the far end of the glen, several miles east, in the hills that lay between Loch Long and Loch Lomond.

Songs of bonnie banks had passed by Craigsmuir House. A granite fortress of a place of an age that spoke of its rôle as a Jacobite stronghold, it faced west down the glen, its back to more granite. As we approached, early afternoon sunshine lit the building through a slit in the clouds and tinted pink stone worn by a thousand Atlantic gales.

The car rumbled over a cattle grid at the massive entrance gates and I kept to a steady fifteen miles an hour, observing magnificent gardens. The drive curved through the grounds and there were heathers and juniper-clad slopes with small waterfalls splashing through them, statuary and acres of smooth lawns. I parked just as carefully, between a Range-Rover and white Rolls-Royce. Perhaps I should not have come.

Trelawney said not a word, unloaded the car of all the baggage and gave it into the care of a major-domo who appeared as if on oiled wheels from the front door. There was no incentive to linger. The wind had already taken my breath away with its purity and keenness, acting on me like immersion in iced water.

I kept my mind on practicalities, admiring the front door. It was solid oak and pitted with what could have been grape shot, the tiny dents slightly to one side of an iron grille. There was no glass behind the grille and one could imagine a draught powerful enough to lift rugs inside. But not so, there was another door within a small vestibule, this fully in the twentieth century, double glazed and with several locks.

"Sir George is in the library," said the major-domo to Trelawney, and then to me, "I'll show you to your room, Mrs. Gillard. I expect you'd like—" He stopped speaking, startled by the swiftness with which Trelawney turned to me.

"We didn't announce it in the *Times*," I said.

At which Trelawney requested that we might be shown to a room where we could talk in private for a while.

"I don't think I have anything to say to you," I said when we had been escorted to a drawing room and the door silently closed.

Trelawney took from the inside pocket of his jacket a piece of paper and held it out to me. My letter from Patrick, slightly crumpled.

"Meadows was fed the information. Major Gillard was ordered to relay it to you in writing."

"Pawns," I said.

"Daws trusts you above all others. I arranged to have it taken from you knowing that you'd immediately inform him of what had happened. So now he will come and can be questioned at length."

"Daws was coming anyway," I said, and then cursed myself for giving away what might be useful information. But he gave no sign.

"He'll be offguard," said Trelawney. He sat down in a green brocade chair and studied me. "I can't understand your marrying Gillard again."

"As you yourself said, no one's blameless."

"Have you never questioned the circumstances of your husband's death?"

"I'd be abnormal if I hadn't," I told him furiously.

"I'd be interested to know how Gillard explained it away."

"It was explained away far more satisfactorily than your need to nearly kill two Special Branch men," I retorted.

Trelawney's eyebrows rose. "I had nothing to do with that. Entirely different people were involved." He got to his feet again. "I want you to know what you've become involved with. Gillard is a trained killer. He was recruited for this job by Sir George for that very reason. He can look after himself, game leg or no. Ask any senior officer in the know: Gillard thinks of little but his personal ambition and keeping in with the right people."

"Thanks for the concern," I said.

"It had a marked effect on him when you divorced him," Trelawney continued. "I sent for his personal file. I wanted to know to whom I was apologising."

"So it's my fault?"

"No. It's not your fault he killed your husband either, but your present behaviour suggests that you're aware of the truth. Hear me out," he said, when I moved towards the door. "Three guns. The IRA gunmen were shot with one: Gillard's. Peter Clyde was shot several times in the back with bullets from the weapons carried by the intruders. You're not telling me Gillard gave them time to shoot Clyde first before he took care of them."

"Peter threw himself over Patrick to protect him," I said.

"Without spoiling his aim by so much as one millimetre?" Trelawney jeered. "Did he love his wife's previous husband that much? I'll tell you what happened. The men burst in, Gillard shot them and then asked Clyde to get their guns. He was only walking with great difficulty, wasn't he?"

I said nothing.

"Gillard was given the guns and then asked Clyde to call the police. He shot him when he went towards the door. Once, with one of the intruder's weapons. Then, when Clyde had fallen, he made his way across the room and put a few more bullets in him where he lay."

"Fingerprints?" I queried after a long pause.

"I told you, he's a trained killer. He'd make sure his prints weren't ever found."

The nauseating aspect of all this was that it was perfectly feasible. It was exactly what I had once pictured. I didn't believe a word of the rest of what he had told me but this had the solid ring of truth.

If this were true, I didn't particularly care about the rest of it.

Trelawney had not given me the letter but had folded it and returned it to his pocket. I said, "You didn't go to Portland. It's a complete fabrication to lull Daws into a false sense of security."

"That's right," said Trelawney.

"Then how did Meadows come to see your filthy henchmen going into a pub on Weymouth seafront?"

"Young and immensely keen." Trelawney shrugged. "Also,

unfortunately, subjected to a severe fright . . . it preyed on his mind.''

''Balls,'' I said, and Trelawney looked extremely startled. ''Balls,'' I said again as I turned to leave the room.

Trelawney said, ''Nothing can alter the fact that it was Daws who ordered the Marines to take the kind of action that would have crippled the only man likely to have found him out.''

Other guests were in the house. Several times while I was washing and changing I heard doors opening and closing. I donned my new blue slacks and sweater and grabbed my bag, hoping that no one would notice how heavy it was. It seemed best to tuck it under my arm in a casual sort of way, casual and passably attractive according to a gilt-framed mirror at the top of the stairs.

I intended to beard the dragon in his lair.

Finding a library in a large country mansion is not difficult when you've travelled widely and have quite a few wealthy acquaintances. Libraries usually have double doors opening inwards and are sited so that they are not a thoroughfare to anywhere else. There was just one set of double doors leading off the large square hall and I crossed the parquet flooring, noticing Persian rugs and an arrangement of bronze chrysanthemums and copper beech foliage in a brass jug. In a room nearby someone was playing the piano.

I entered, prepared to apologise and withdraw immediately if necessary. For a moment I thought the room empty but then saw that one of the leather wing chairs was occupied, cigar smoke wafting above it.

''Surely people with your kind of job shouldn't sit with their backs to the door,'' I said when I could see whom I was addressing. I already knew what he looked like. His youngest daughter had recently married a televison script writer and the wedding had featured on all the society pages.

Sir George rose. He was of medium height, slightly portly, silver-haired and with a face remarkably unlined for his sixty years. Instead of the regulation velvet smoking jacket and grey flannels he wore an Aran sweater and tweed trousers from neither of which anyone had succeeded in removing the morning's harvest of dog hairs.

With not a second to spare, a word from him prevented a canine avalanche from engulfing me. Grabbing collars, he said, "Do help yourself to sherry while I get rid of this lot," and crossed to another door as if floating in a sea of black and gold leaping gun dogs. Two elderly retrievers followed with a couple of tail wags especially for me. The whole pack, I could see now, had been asleep on the floor in front of the log fire.

I helped myself to sherry, a pale, dry luncheon sherry that would do nothing to dispel my tummy rumbles of hunger, and heard him despatch his dogs into the grounds with the weird cries people reserve for their pets when they don't think anyone else can hear.

Sir George returned, rubbing his hands, and warmed them before the blaze. "God, it's cold out there." He reseated himself, waving me to a chair near the fire. "Am I wrong in assuming you prefer to be called Miss Langley?"

"Yes," I said. "The book world refers to me as that. The real me is married to a man recently half killed by someone under this same roof."

He took it well. "Does your writing not take priority?"

I said, "I make rather a lot of money by using my imagination, but sometimes you have to surface and live within reality for a while. Life was all too real when I was married to Patrick before, too real and too raw and I rejected it. That was appallingly selfish . . . you simply can't do that."

"Has he told you that he's working directly for me?"

The room was bugged, I reminded myself, at least according to information that could now be regarded as suspect.

"Trelawney just has. You got yourself a trained killer."

"Together with every other man serving in special operations units," Sir George said. "I'm well aware Trelawney said that to you—I've just finished listening to the tape. No, Major Gillard is working for me because he's none of the things Trelawney suggested."

"No one will ever know what happened in that flat in Plymouth," I said.

"Well, it certainly wasn't the IRA," Sir George said with a smile. "The O'Neill brothers came from a Loyalist family and hadn't been home for years. They'd been doing just about everything illegal for money in London and the South West."

"I expected Trelawney to be in here," I said.

"Everyone's listening to my wife playing the piano for a while, and then lunch will be served." He smiled more broadly. "I think we'll end up by calling it tea."

"This is what baffles the Russians about the British," I said. "A weekend house party to catch a spy, piano recitals and cucumber sandwiches."

Sir George ground out the butt of his cigar in an ash tray and leaned forward. "I admire you. You think he might be a murderer but you're going to see this through. Good! Now let me try to put your mind at rest. I asked Gillard. In fact, I gave him a bit of a carpeting for being careless enough to let it happen. Clyde got in the way. He ran between the Major and those damned thugs and took three shots in the back. I admit I checked the post-mortem findings very thoroughly, just in case. None of the bullets had entered the body at an angle that would suggest that whoever had fired was sitting down. And none had been fired into the body while it was lying down. From that range they would have gone right through and into the floor."

I hadn't known anything about a post-mortem.

"I'm sorry to have to be so specific," he said quietly.

"Spies don't cry," I said, living the lie.

"People of questionable mental balance don't work for me," said Sir George softly. "Forget Trelawney. He tried to impress his new masters and proved himself a damn fool. He only attempted to steal the stuff on Towed Arrays to prove that he was capable of rational behaviour."

"Toada Rays?" I said, blowing my nose.

"Underwater surveillance systems. The equipment's towed behind the ship to detect noises below. It's a passive system."

"A passive system," I repeated solemnly.

"Doesn't ping," he said. "The enemy can't hear it searching for them."

The penny dropped but only because of all those wonderful films starring people like Jack Hawkins and John Gregson.

Cheerfully, Sir George said, "And for that we have to thank Dr. Dougie Irvine. Marvellous chap. You'd never think he was a Civil Servant to look at him—a real wild Scot, looks as if he's come straight from the Battle of Culloden without combing his hair. He didn't like Trelawney's smooth English manners and removed all the important pages. Ought to get a medal in my view."

A knock at the door.

"Are you still game?" said Sir George. "You saw straight through all the lies. He was hoping you'd take the next train home and press for an official investigation into Peter's death."

I was game for the moment. I nodded and then looked at Trelawney as he entered the room, hoping in a mad, wild moment that if I was pregnant it was a boy, another Gillard to hound out the likes of him.

The recital having finished, there was movement in the hall and the room filled with people. Someone let the dogs back in, a posse of lawbreakers, noses into everything, and for several minutes there was domestic chaos.

At last we lunched, a buffet affair in a long comfortable room on the western side of the house. There was tayside salmon with several kinds of salad, gateaux or hot girdle scones with strawberry jam and thick cream. I slipped one ancient golden retriever my last morsel of scone and promptly earned Sir George's wrath for breaking the number one house rule.

"Don't let it worry you, Ingrid," said his wife, Philippa, glamorous and called Pip by all and sundry. "They get half a bullock a day as it is. We can't afford to give them our food as well." She laughed, her voice deep and richly humorous.

Pip had her only son Robert at her side, home from Aberdeen University where he was studying law. He was a son from a previous marriage, she being considerably younger than her present husband. Then there was Danny, Sir George's son from his first marriage and of the same generation as his step-mother and myself, around thirty-five. Danny had a wife, a dowdy little thing who looked downright miserable—mostly, I guessed, because of a child of about four who filled me with horrible qualms as to what might be in store for me.

No way, I decided, several seconds later, no way would I tolerate that kind of behaviour. My fingers itched to spank as the little one stamped on a furry tail when he thought no one was looking. The dog yelped, jumped up and knocked over an antique jardinière, cascading potting compost and a superb carmine Japanese azalea across the carpet. The smooth pattern of hospitality continued without a pause. A bell was rung for a servant to clear up the mess and the child, ignored, kicked at the flocked wallpaper in a corner.

After a while my attention strayed from a discussion on a disastrous pheasant shooting season back to the miscreant who now sat beneath a writing desk sucking his thumb, rocking backwards and forwards with the same kind of boredom one sees in animals pacing their cages in zoos.

"Show me your toy soldiers," I said to him under cover of the conversation. It seemed a safe enough bet. Didn't all the upper classes prepare their sons to be Generals, or was I behind the times?

"Damien doesn't have soldiers," his mother bridled, her pasty face displaying a hint of pink.

Oh ye gods, one of those. "What does he do," I asked, making it my carrying tone, "petit point?"

Pip exploded into a very public snigger so I knew I had at least one ally. The father of the child shot me a look that was impossible to decipher but a hint of gratitude might have lurked within the gloom.

"Damien makes himself useful," said the anti-sexist, anti-racist spokesperson. No Biggles and King Arthur for her child, none of the fierce delights of fortresses on the sand, caves full of goblins to be vaniquished with a magic sword, Darth Vader to be banished to outer space.

"He has a little garden and helps around the house," continued his mother, warming to her theme. "If it wasn't for his asthma he could keep a rabbit but the doctor advised against it." She beckoned to the child. "Damien, come and show the lady how well you know your alphabet already."

I noticed that the father's eyes went ceilingwards, the only ones in the room that didn't fasten unwaveringly on the hapless child. You bloody coward, I thought. No woman would do that to my son.

Amazingly, Damien came, perhaps because of the attention. Even more amazingly, he lisped up to M and then lost interest. His mother shook him lightly to help him concentrate, her reputation on the brink of disaster, and was kicked on the shins. He was borne from the room, tucked under her arm and, judging by the way his yells of anger changed to howls of outrage, she gave him a sneaky wallop when safely out of our sight. I found myself hot with rage, wanting to snatch him from her and give him a ride in a Chieftain tank.

Sir George was telling everyone what a little horror he'd been as a child, stealing from a neighbour's washing line to clothe his Guy Fawkes.

"Would you like to see the garden before it gets dark?" Pip said over several heads to me. "The copper beeches look wonderful at the moment."

I got up, trying not to look relieved, and followed her out.

"Whoopee." she exclaimed gloomily when we had collected coats and were outside on the terrace. "What an utter, utter bag that woman is! How Danny ever came to marry her is the mystery of the century as far as I'm concerned."

"The child's in stage one of becoming a fairy," I remarked heatedly.

She chuckled. "I know what I'll do, spirit him away and let him have a holiday with you and your fabulous husband."

"You've met Patrick?" I said, stopped in my tracks.

"For the first time last night. Didn't George mention it? How remiss of him. He had dinner in London with us before we flew up."

I carried on walking, controlling my every thought and action. "How was he?"

"Dying to renew his acquaintance with his motor bike from what I could gather," she drawled. "He spoke of it at least twice. Said he was going to throw it on the train tonight and ride up from Glasgow." She glanced at me sideways. "I'd never have guessed he has an artificial leg. George told me afterwards. I think I'm rather envious."

She didn't mean it, of course. She knew as well as I did that an estate in Scotland, a penthouse flat overlooking Regent's Park and a house on Mustique didn't come on a Major's pay, special operations or no. Had he mentioned me? I ached to know.

"He was badly injured in the Falklands, wasn't he?" Pip continued.

"Yes," I said. "A grenade." But then again it was probably regarded as outré for men to refer to their wives. I must really bring myself up to date with modern social behaviour.

The copper beeches were indeed wonderful, protected from the worst of the prevailing wind by the curve of the valley. Pip explained it to me, a freak of nature which meant that a few degrees of angle difference in relation to the mountain behind the house would have made the siting of it impossible. Obedient to her pointing finger I scanned the heather-tinted crags jutting hundreds of feet above and then wondered aloud if the tiny speck soaring in a patch of blue sky was an eagle.

"My God, you've good eyes," she said, squinting in vain and then running indoors for binoculars.

It was, circling in lonely splendour, at one with the moving air as a minstrel plays a harp.

"Really beautiful things have their own inherent sense of tragedy, don't they?" said Pip with a nervous smile as if I might laugh at her.

"Like sunsets," I said.

"Like sunsets," she echoed, and changed the subject.

CHAPTER 20

It was just after five when Daws arrived, hurrumphing petulantly at the servant who took his case and almost dropped his shotgun. A front, I knew now, an old duffer figure behind which he concealed the Daws of the steely stare. I found it rather endearing.

"Is that Richard?" called Pip, emerging from her music room through a door behind me.

Caught in the act of peering at him round the grandfather clock near the door of the drawing room, I jumped guiltily but she paid no attention, roving the room restlessly while plumping cushions.

"Yes," I said. "Jet-lagged by the sound of it."

Pip had already changed for dinner which I knew was not until seven-thirty. She wore a long black evening skirt, heavily embroidered with gold and silver roses. As she moved, tiny sparkles caught the light from crystal beads that had been sewn on to represent dew drops on the flowers. A softly draped black chiffon blouse completed the outfit.

She saw me looking at her. "Perceptive Ingrid. No, I can't get used to a life of ease even after five years." She sat on a chaise longue and patted the other end of it in invitation. "Do all authors observe people so closely?"

"Oh dear," I said, seating myself. "I never mean to stare."

"You don't," she assured me quickly. "It's more giving people your full attention in an interested way. You see a lot and say little, filing things away to use in your books. I'd love to be in one of your stories," she laughed, "the youngish wife of an old man who married him for his money."

"But you didn't," I said. "You love him."

"What else do you see in your crystal ball?" she prompted.

"You don't lead a life of ease at all. You're heavily involved with several charities."

"I'm not looking for compliments, Ingrid."

"Your husband doesn't mind all that much when you flirt quite innocently with some of his younger friends."

"That has to be a guess," she protested good-naturedly.

"I listen to what people say," I replied. "You described Patrick as fabulous. The guess involves deciding whether he played along or froze you off, and I'd put a lot of money on the latter."

She went slightly pink.

I said, "Fabulous is an adjective usually used to describe the unattainable."

"What kind of women does he flirt with?" she asked faintly.

"Tarts."

"Tarts!"

"Women who dig him in the ribs, drink too much and tell him dirty stories. He sits them on his knee and then after a while gets bored, dumps them on the floor and goes home."

"How absolutely fascinating," she breathed.

"With ladies he does his virgin knight on the ramparts act. Right?"

She giggled, blushing deeper.

I said, "The real man is utterly different. Sensitive of rebuff, susceptible to a thousand and one conflicting loyalties, and very funny."

"So what brought you together?"

"We were at the same school," I said. "I'm afraid it was probably sexual curiosity."

"One of the best reasons I know of," Pip said emphatically, switching on her hostess smile as Daws entered. "Richard! How lovely to see you."

Daws whisked a tiny parcel from his pocket and dangled it by its ribbon bow in front of her eyes. Inside, and just the right size to be held in the palm of her hand, was a quaint jade, seated beast, a kind of baby dragon with large soulful eyes.

"Richard, this is one of your treasures," Pip whispered.

"I—er—found I had two nearly the same," he said. "It's—er—Ming Dynasty . . . fifteenth century. There's another one quite similar in the Burrell Collection. Don't lock it away. They're meant to be held and enjoyed. Very hard stuff, you know. Won't break easily.''

She kissed his cheek, overwhelmed.

Daws said, ''There may be some . . . unpleasantness before the weekend's out. Perhaps you won't get so annoyed with me now.''

He really ought to find another wife, I decided there and then, someone he could take cocoa to in bed and who would make a better job of ironing his shirts.

Pip thanked him profusely and then excused herself, saying she had to talk to the cook about dinner.

''She knows I want to talk to you,'' said Daws when Pip had gone. ''One interferes with Agnes at one's peril.''

''I might have torn that letter straight up and consigned the pieces to the four winds,'' I said.

''It wouldn't have mattered. Information has been leaked to him that I'm the real suspect. He only fed you all that phony stuff to excuse having it stolen and to try to break up you and the Major.''

''You've only just arrived,'' I said. ''You can't know about that.''

''I flew up last night,'' he said with one of his microscopic smiles. ''There's a modern equivalent of a priest hole just off the library. Both Sir George and I were eavesdropping when he was trying to get you to have second thoughts.''

''Everyone's keeping a low profile,'' I said. ''What are you waiting for?''

''No mystery,'' Daws replied. ''While the letter was being stolen, Trelawney had returned to Portland to get the rest of the information there photographed. We told Irvine to let him get on with it and the Major got several good shots of him snapping away with his nasty, cheap little spy camera. He's bringing the developed film with him tomorrow, then the feathers'll really start to fly.''

''You want to know who his Russian contact is?'' I said. ''The one whose activities are incompatible with his status.''

''Quite,'' said Daws. ''Now, there's a small dressing room next door to the bedroom you're sleeping in. If Meadows sleeps in there, have you any objection to the communicating door being left unlocked—for your own safety?"

"Neither of us sleepwalks so far as I know."

Changing for dinner, I settled for the new evening skirt and one of the white silk blouses, the one with a cowl neckline. Green and gold eyeliner and peach-coloured lipstick made me appear more winsome and lively than I felt. Tucking the gun into a white leather evening bag, I speculated on how much the excellent Philippa knew. She was not the kind of woman to be content with being decorative and making the right noises.

Robert escorted me into dinner and if he discovered a little about *One for Sorrow* and the sequel I planned to write one day, *Two for Joy*, I found out very little about him other than that he loved to travel and was learning German. I could see a generous portion of the family wealth going in his direction. Danny was colourless in comparison and his mother no longer alive to champion his cause.

The meal was quite perfect: tiny vol-au-vents stuffed with shrimps in a delicate cheese sauce to begin, roast haunch of venison with sherry and horseradish sauce, skirlie—pinhead oatmeal fried with onion to form savoury crunchy crumbs, a traditional Scottish accompaniment to roast meats—mashed potatoes and broccoli. To follow were Scottish cheeses, Islay, Dunlop and Cabot, with oatcakes, and an unusual cranberry sorbet.

The conversation flowed around me. I had been placed next to Pip on my right, sitting at one end of the table, and Danny on my left. The meal was served by a maid I had seen earlier and a young man who had the Terry stamp all over him. Sir George's minder, no doubt, learning a few social graces. Everyone called him by his christian name, yet another Peter, and not in the manner of those addressing a servant. It came as no surprise when he joined us for coffee.

All through dinner Trelawney had kept himself to himself, only speaking when spoken to and for some extraordinary reason waiting assiduously upon Linda, passing her the sauce, rowanberry jelly, gravy, then cheese and everything that went with it. Having to watch him, I felt a sudden pang of yearning for

Patrick to be sitting by my side, apeing his insufferable unctu-
ousness.

Now, perhaps lulled by two glasses of claret, I sat back and
allowed myself to loathe him uninhibitedly. It was an intense
black hatred that disturbed me with its virulence. Thus I had
seen Smith killed; this hatred could stand watching Trelawney
being done to death, slowly. Patrick had jerked, trying to stem
the screams of agony, biting his lip until the blood ran . . .

"Are you cold, Ingrid?" said Pip. "You're shivering."

It was a very subtle game of cat and mouse that was being played
at Craigsmuir, the mouse, it seemed, being permitted to wander
among the cats, pulling their tails. I was half expecting, after
dinner, to see Trelawney being discreetly escorted by Terry and
Peter to an interview with Sir George in the library. It didn't
happen. Terry did not even put in an appearance but there was
a green sleeping bag I recognised in the dressing room next to
mine when I slipped upstairs for a short while.

I had a suspicion, no more, that there were more people in
the house than was being made known. My cat's nosiness discovered nothing. The grandfather clock ticked softly, dogs
snored, American voices snarled in a distant soap opera and my
feet made no sound on the thick carpet on the stairs. Perhaps I
had heard the echoes of Jacobite feet.

No visitations, ghostly or otherwise, disturbed my sleep that
night. Whether it was the claret or the knowledge of Terry's
reassuring proximity I was not sure but as soon as my head
touched the pillow it was dreamless oblivion until the maid
knocked with tea at eight the following morning. I got up to let
her in and the communicating door opened a couple of inches.

"I'm decent," I said when I'd found my dressing gown and
shared the tea between the cup provided and a tooth brush mug,
adding when he appeared, "Shouldn't you really be guarding
the Colonel's back?"

"Daws won't be mothered," said Terry. "There's a rumour
that he carries a *kris* that someone gave him in Malaya."

I blew on my tea. "I wish I knew what was going on."

"We can't do anything until the Major gets here with the
proof."

There was a knock at the door.

Terry took his tea, moving silently back into the dressing room. I knew he would stand just by the slightly opened door. But it was he that Peter wanted and there was a whispered consultation in the corridor outside. I heard Terry exclaim, an uncharacteristically strong epithet.

"Regrouping," said Terry, putting his head around the door.

"I have signed the Official Secrets Act," I said.

He considered. "Peter's found a bug in the drawing room that isn't one of ours and wasn't there yesterday morning. No need for headlong panic," he continued, "Trelawney's still in his room."

I said, for some reason not shouting, "He hasn't paid off the crows?"

"No," Terry said. "See you later."

I had planned to wash my hair, take time over my make-up and wear the Falkland Island's wool sweater with cream cord slacks. I did put on these clothes, threw them on, and only remembered to comb my hair as I was going out the door.

There was a council of war in progress in the library. I could hear Sir George's voice addressing persons unknown through the door as I approached. I didn't go in. Daws didn't need me to remind him of our conversation in the drawing room.

"Pheasants are off," said Linda, in the dining room, giving Damien his breakfast. "They're having a confab about it now."

I looked out of the window. The glen was hidden in mist, like milk in a dish, the tops of the hills seeming to float on the surface.

"There's not enough pheasants," she said, more loudly.

"I heard you," I said.

"There's been so much rain the gamekeepers don't think it's worthwhile organising a shoot today, or even in the near future."

Damien was playing trains around his plate with small fingers of bread and honey. Steam trains. It was one small mercy as far as Damien was concerned, his father's passion for steam engines. Danny had enthused at length to me over dinner the previous evening and I, not really giving him my full attention, had nearly put my foot in it when he told me they were going to see the Duchess of Hamilton on the way home by being on the verge of asking him where she lived.

"Does your husband shoot?" asked Linda, appearing desperate to make conversation. Perhaps she had forgiven me.

"Only when he has to," I replied, and then realised the idiocy of what I had said. "No," I amended. "Not really . . . sometimes, for the pot."

At that moment Sir George entered the room, followed by Daws and Trelawney. Good mornings were exchanged, and they set about helping themselves to breakfast from the hot trolley.

"Had something to eat?" said Sir George to me.

"I'm not hungry, thank you," I replied.

"Coffee?"

I gave him a smile, hoping it didn't look as sick as I felt, and poured out a cup. Pip, Danny and Robert arrived almost together so I was able to busy myself giving them some, too.

"Fancy a little rough shooting?" said Sir George, again to me. "We're going to leave the gamebirds alone and let the numbers recover."

"I can usually hit rabbits when they come out with their hands up," I told him and he laughed, tucking into grilled kidneys, bacon and scrambled egg.

"Aren't you going to church then?" demanded Linda.

Pip replied. "We're going this evening to evensong. It's not really on if all of us are out when Major Gillard arrives."

Ouch, I thought, that was Pip becoming just a little frayed at the edges. The hostess surveyed her gathering: the men, including Trelawney, making a hearty breakfast; me moping by the window; Linda, blushing, and trying to persuade Damien to finish up his railway carriages. A look of such acute disenchantment crossed Pip's attractive features that for one heart-stopping moment I thought she was about to ruin everything. But no, she took the green jade dragon from her pocket and smoothed it, frowning.

I finished my coffee and went upstairs to raid one of the bathrooms for aspirin. Crossing the hall ten minutes later, I knew that I wasn't pregnant, as well as being in the first stages of a cold.

Sir George called to me through the opened doors of the library, giving the impression that he had gone in to look for something.

"I *am* going to do something about Trelawney," he said. "Seen my glasses?"

"Does it show that much?" I enquired.

He smiled and resumed his search.

"There are some glasses in your top pocket," I observed.

"What? Oh good grief!" he said, taking them out and glaring at them. "Meadows and Webster are outside now. Just to make sure there are no trespassers."

But Meadows and Webster were in the gun room and by the look of them just back from a Ten Tors Race. Peter heaved himself to his feet with a groan when he saw me and went over to unlock the case that contained the guns.

"Find some waterproofs that fit you in that cupboard over there," said Terry. "The wind'll cut you in half otherwise."

I went on a search for boots, finding a pair of size fives at the bottom of the heap. "I don't really want a shotgun," I said.

"Carry it," snapped Peter, selecting one. "Walk right behind me and Sir George, and if he gives you the chance to shoot something do your best. Otherwise . . ." he shrugged.

"Shut up and do nothing," I said for him. "Sorry you're being cluttered up with a senior officer's trembling ninny." I did all the correct things with the gun and cartridges, right there under his nose, and sauntered outside.

The mist had lifted, blown away by a wind that would batter into nothingness anything delicate, fragile or weak against the bare bones of the mountains. I waved to Pip, well wrapped up in red fox taking Damien for a walk in the garden. Then more movement caught my eye, Robert, Danny, Trelawney and Linda walking up the side of the mountain, the latter sulkily in the rear, disassociating herself from bloodsports.

I took my handbag back up to my room, going round the front of the house and in through the front door, aware that it was always left unlocked during the day. The boots stayed on the doorstep but the shotgun made the journey upstairs, I'm not stupid. It was the work of a moment to transfer Patrick's gun from the bag to the deep pocket of the waterproofs. What Sir George would think of this minor arsenal travelling in his wake I dared not try to imagine.

Finding mine host by the simple ploy of following the soun~ of barking dogs, I caught up with him at the same time as P~

to whom I made a point of flashing a brilliant smile. Sir George called all the dogs to heel and bade them be silent and we set off in the opposite direction to that taken by the others. Deliberately, I understood, to avoid accidents.

We traversed the rough tussocky grass in a small field that ran parallel to the private road and climbed over the stone wall on the other side of it. Now we were on open moorland, Scottish Blackfaces tail-flopping away from us through the bracken.

"Ben Muir," said Sir George, pointing upwards for my benefit. "Over on the other side is Black Mountain and behind it, like a volcano, Ben Lomond. Straight ahead is The Cobbler."

True enough, the wind was cold enough to make my eyes water and I was glad of the long johns that I had put on after breakfast and a woollen hat I had found in one of the pockets of the waterproofs.

"Where's the Colonel, sir?" Peter asked.

"Bird-watching," said his boss. "He and Meadows have taken the Land-Rover down to the loch."

"Crows?" I enquired innocently.

He paused in his stride.

"I invented the terminology," I explained.

After this exchange we walked in silence except for the occasional male exclamation as one of them tripped over a heather root. I watched where I was going. I was carrying a loaded hand gun with no safety catch.

The dogs flowed around us like black and gold silk, never going further forward than their master's heels or more than a few feet away from his side. When we stopped for a short breather in the lee of a large rock they lay down immediately, watching his every movement.

Far below, water glittered in folds of the hills and in the distance was the long blue ribbon of Loch Lomond. Daws and Terry had not gone this far. Sir George had pointed to a small loch, probably too small to be included on most maps, just over the other side of the main road and slightly to the east of Loch Long.

I cleared my throat and both men looked at me.

"Tired?" said Peter.

"Worried," I said. "Patrick said he would be here first thing. To a soldier that means first light. Where is he?"

"No one's expecting him to rush," said Sir George. "Not under the circumstances."

I said, "Is your house haunted?"

"What makes you ask?" he answered carefully.

"Movement," I said. "A general feeling of more feet than people visible."

"Out there somewhere," said Sir George with a sweep of his arm, "are half a dozen members of the Mountain and Arctic Warfare Cadre. They are keeping an eye on Trelawney and sent Meadows and Peter here packing when they fell over two of them in a ditch. But they haven't been near the house."

We walked on, climbing higher but still keeping roughly parallel with the road. Bejabers, hadn't himself been terribly rude to the Marines not all that long ago? And, with all due respect to Sir George, if the Cadre had played strip poker in the middle of the night on the dining-room table, who would have known?

"There's a Land-Rover just turned off the main road." This from Peter, his voice brittle with nerves. He scanned it through his binoculars. "Might be ours . . . too far away to read the number plate."

"It might be Andrew McTavish's, he rents the grazing. Rather battered, short wheel base."

"No," said Peter. "Long wheel base. Possibly ex-army. Good condition."

"Let's take cover," said Sir George, and sent the dogs into a gulley, ordering them to lie down.

We crouched down and watched as the vehicle came about a mile along the road and then pulled into a gateway almost directly below us. No one moved.

"Two of them," Peter reported. "They've got a map out."

Then I heard it, unmistakable, brought on the wind.

Almost without thinking I thrust my shotgun at Sir George and was running down the hillside, jumping boulders, heather clumps and sheep tracks.

I was going to be too late.

All the way down the hill I knew I was going to be too late, floundering over the rough ground, turning my ankles in ruts, the gun banging bruisingly against my side. Simply too late. The bike turned into the private road while I was only a third of the way down. I tried to run and wave but it was impossible. Then I fell, my head crashing against a stone.

The hills spun sickeningly. I got to my knees, saw Peter running towards me, and then the world went mad.

I didn't hear the shots but there must have been several. The bike slewed sideways, straightened, and then the rider was hit and it went into the stone wall. In slow motion, a hideous slowness, the machine climbed upwards and then fell back, pinning the man beneath. It still moved, man and bike sliding along the base of the wall.

I think I screamed for I knew what was about to happen and, as if thought could bring it about, flames flickered briefly and then the road was a wall of fire.

I was still going down the hill, and another part of me jeered at the shambling, screaming woman who stumbled, ran, fell over and kept on getting up until she reached the bottom. There was another fifty yards to go but I could feel the heat. It was no longer a peaceful country lane but despoiled, full of black smoke, the wind now bringing the stomach-churning smell of burning flesh.

Peter crashed into the wall by my side and spread his arms wide to prevent me going any closer. ''Ingrid, don't!'' I ducked under them.

Even through this I registered that he was using my first name. Out of shock? I didn't mind. After this I didn't mind about anything.

With full military honours.

There was only smoke, blackened twisted metal and, beneath, a husk of what had been a man, strangely shrunken. Peter's hands were on my shoulders, trying to pull me away, but I shrugged them off. The horror was stark and somehow pathetic. The plastic visor of the helmet had melted but a small clod of grass survived, steaming a little on what was left of his nose. I looked away. The once mesmeric grey eyes, the irises fleeced with gold, were now only a memory.

With full military honours.

CHAPTER 21

A spectator, I watched the finale, and that other part of me that wasn't Ingrid saw a hunched middle-aged woman wearing a ridiculous woolly hat sobbing under a wall. Dear God, undo this day's filthy work.

The Land-Rover crashed into gear, shot across the road, reversed into the gateway where it had been parked and then sped back toward the main road. Peter drew his gun and took out the windscreen and one of the tyres as it roared past. I flung myself flat as stone chippings and bullets zipped and cracked around my ears.

"You're hurt!" I shouted at him.

"Scratched," he gasped, trying to wipe from his eyes the blood streaming from a cut on his head.

Shots from somewhere up on the hill took out another tyre and then, judging by the way the vehicle accelerated and drove into the wall, the driver. Another Land-Rover howled up the road towards it, braked closed to the wall, and the man in the passenger seat leapt out and over it, using the door as cover.

Terry, moving with deliberate and murderous intent, ran bent double under cover of the wall and, when he was behind the first vehicle, jumped back into the road, blasted open the rear door and lobbed inside an object that wasn't a stone. Seconds later, in a ball of flame, the Land-Rover ceased to exist.

I wanted to be left alone with what was left of Patrick but Peter was pulling me away, pressing his handkerchief folded into a pad on to my temple. Peter was right. There was nothing left now, only his gun dragging down my pocket.

You weren't paid a thousand pounds to sit puling in a ditch.

I looked around wildly but no one had spoken. Daws had driven up and was in the act of leaving the driving seat, eyes on the smoking pyre of the bike, his face ashen. Terry was only yards away from Peter and I, on the same side of the wall.

"Sir George," I said in a voice snatched away by the wind.

"Bloody hell," said Terry, and set off up the mountain.

I went after him, there might be one crow left. The simple arithmetic of murder chimed away inside my head like a hurdy-gurdy. Smith was the first or the fourth, whichever way you looked at it. Two in the Land-Rover—Terry had met no answering fire when he had thrown in the grenade. One more crow might have orders to kill one of the top men in MI5.

He shot Terry when he was two-thirds of the way up Ben Muir towards the gulley where we had left Sir George. Almost at the same moment a shotgun fired, a distinctive roar as both barrels went off. A pandemonium of dogs barking, another shot, and then a shrill stricken yelping.

Terry was hunched by a large boulder, his knuckles white and with blue marks where he had bitten into them. I hauled off my waterproof jacket and threw it over him, putting the woolly hat under his head. The bullet had gone right through his shoulder and he seemed in no immediate danger of dying.

I kicked off the heavy over-trousers as well and the welling-tons went with them. Old, over-worked clichés came into their own. I had nothing to lose, come hell or high water.

The dogs were still barking, a high frenzied clamour that rang in staccato echoes around the surrounding peaks. The shotgun fired again and then again and again.

Patrick's Smith and Wesson and I went up the hill and I shrank into every clump of heather and behind every bracken stalk. Then, a ricochet chopped away a small piece of lichen from a rock near my head and I wedged myself into a space between two massive tombstone-shaped chunks of granite. Not for long. Another shot showered me with stone splinters.

I looked up and saw a movement. When he showed himself again I fired at him, lying flat on my stomach. Too far away and wide but it made him run, scurrying along the line of the hill. I took another shot at him and then desisted. I had no idea of the present whereabouts of Sir George. Another quick sprint upwards and I found him, crouched in a hollow just below the gulley, one of his dogs dead by his side.

There was no time to make conversation, we were pinned down. Swearing under his breath, Sir George let off both barrels in the direction of the fire but a shotgun was useless against a rifle. I waited until he fired again and then bolted upwards for the gulley.

There he was, well out of range of the shotgun, silhouetted against the sky on the rim of the gulley. We both fired at the same time and his bullet thumped into the turf at my feet. I flung myself down and rolled away. His next shot came even closer, whistling past my cheek.

He stood up on the rim of the gulley, mocking me, and then raised the rifle to his shoulder.

Two-handed, I fired.

He didn't. He jerked, spreadeagled into the morning, and pitched forward, rolling and crashing down through rocks and grass to thump at my feet like a sack full of wet leather. I thought I saw his chest heave a couple of times and thereafter there was no movement at all. The last crow, the one who looked like an East-Ender, bouncer type, with yellow eyes.

"Ingrid . . ." said Sir George, out of breath.

"I didn't kill him," I said quickly. "The Cadre did. He was shot from behind." I glaced back towards the hollow. "I'm so sorry about your dog."

Sir George put his coat around my shoulders and I wore it down the hillside, reassuming also the identity of the middle-aged woman who had to be practically manhandled into the Range-Rover when it came, driven by an appalled Pip. She had had no time to find someone to look after Damien who bounced up and down, chortling gleefully, and wanted to go and look at the bonfires.

Peter and Sir George brought down Terry who could walk, after a fashion, while Daws went back to make contact with the Cadre. Peter pointed out a couple of them to me, pieces of hillside that got up and walked towards the road. Robert, Danny and Trelawney had already reached it, Linda still bringing up the rear.

"They can walk," said Pip.

I turned in my seat as we drove away, aware that Peter was giving Terry morphine and remembering myself standing by the side of the road, gazing down, forever gazing down.

My love is dead.

"That is bloody marvellous," said Terry slowly, hitting cloud nine.

"Ingrid!" Pip was shaking me gently, offering me a hip flask.

We were at the house, the car empty but for the two of us. I shook my head.

"Please try."

I took it from her, sitting there in my muddy clothes and soaking wet feet in the passenger seat. "He's dead," I said, giving it back to her.

Pip took a solid swig of whisky. There was nothing she could say to help me so she put an arm round my shoulders and we stayed there, parked in the gravelled forecourt in front of the house. I became aware of Damien playing in the back with some decoy ducks he had found on the floor.

Slowly, they began to trickle back. Daws arrived first in the Land-Rover, bringing with him the body of the crow and the commander of the Mountain and Arctic Warfare Cadre group. They went straight indoors after Daws had thrown a blanket given to him at the front door over the body.

My brain ticked away, recording, noticing, filing and processing. I couldn't switch it off. It recorded that Robert was walking behind Trelawney, Danny hand in hand with Linda, almost dragging her along. Even from a distance she looked as though she was crying.

"I can't cry," I said.

Pip swallowed another large mouthful of whisky. "I wish I could," she said.

An ambulance came speeding up the road, followed by a police car, both with sirens wailing. They overtook the rest of the group from the Cadre, all busy removing bracken and foliage from their battledress.

"The quietness ends," said Pip as they stopped. "Are you still strong?"

No, I wasn't strong.

"That's my Hamish!" Pip exclaimed, snatching up the bin-oculars.

"Hamish?" It seemed churlish not to make some kind of response.

"The garron," she cried. "He's used to carry down the deer. God help anyone if that pony breaks its knees on the road." She opened the door and jumped out.

There was no doubt about it, Hamish was coming home. Permitted to hurry rather than urged, it seemed, he found an-other gear and broke into a rolling canter, his large hooves fling-ing granite chippings in all directions. When he got closer I could see his small pointed ears pricked and his nostrils flaring as he snorted, joyfully playing the warhorse.

The bastard, how could he?

How could he bring back a quite forgotten memory of Patrick on holiday when he had borrowed a friend's daughter's pony, far too small for him, and careened around the paddock on it, no saddle, no bridle, just loose-limbed oneness with the animal. There was no saddle on Hamish either, and control was being achieved with a short length of rope looped round his nose.

There were cowboy whoops from the Cadre as their comrade in arms clattered past but they got out of the way quickly enough. Five walking. I counted them again and then joined Pip on the gravel. She handed me the binoculars but my hands were shak-ing so much I couldn't hold them.

Hamish made straight for us, no doubt thinking of sugar lumps. He slowed, sides heaving, the rope quite tight above his nostrils. It was quickly released when he came to a standstill.

Death is a horseman, I thought, looking at the man in combat gear with his face blackened, holding his sniper's rifle one-handed. Death had come for me, just the two of us in the whole universe, death with his grey eyes flecked with gold.

"I knew you'd never die with your boots on," said Patrick.

He dismounted, breaking the spell, and for a little while nei-ther of us were strong, clutching tightly, party to one another's grief for Charlie. Then he scrubbed at his face with both sleeves, removing most of the camouflage paint, and went over to where Terry was being placed aboard the ambulance.

Pip let Damien out of the car as his parents approached and

he bounded towards them. Trelawney intercepted him and scooped him up.

"Put down that shotgun or the boy dies," said Trelawney to Robert. He had a gun, the muzzle pressing into the side of Damien's head.

Robert laid it down on the gravel.

"And you," Trelawney called across to Patrick. "Put the rifle on the ground."

Patrick turned, possibly unaware of what was happening. The shock of recognition hit both men with a force that was tangible.

"I'll count to three," said Trelawney.

Slowly, a frame at a time, Patrick stooped and placed the weapon on the gravel. He walked a little closer. No one else moved or spoke, not even Linda, her hands belled, fists at her mouth.

"Now any other gadgets you might have."

The tableau continued, even more slowly. With the deft insouciance of a master conjuror Patrick emptied his pockets. A grenade, ammunition, a knife, more ammunition of another kind, a small flare canister and then, with a shrug and a broad grin for Damien, holding both man and child as a weasel hypnotises a rabbit, with a flourish his handkerchief, a large round pebble rolling from it on to the ground to lie with all the rest.

Damien squealed with the fun of it all.

Patrick dropped his handkerchief and moved as if to retrieve it.

"Leave it!" Trelawney barked.

In straightening, Patrick contrived to take another step in Trelawney's direction.

"Make sure those soldiers know what's going on," Trelawney said. "I want them out of the way and a clear road ahead. I'll leave the boy when I know I'm not being followed."

Patrick made sure they heard, emphasising the child's life was at stake, and the Marines laid down their weapons and stood in a line by the entrance gates.

"The cream," sneered Trelawney. "And you can't do a damn thing."

They were the last words he spoke. No sooner had he placed Damien in the passenger seat of the Range-Rover and walked around the front of it to get in the other side when the commander of the Cadre group shot him from an upstairs window.

Patrick got to Damien before his mother, swung him up on to his shoulders and took him away for a ride on Hamish, who dozed where Pip had left him, tied to a tree. He brought him back a short while later, the child filthy and waving a homemade bow and arrow, his hair adorned with feathers, yelling that he wanted a pony of his own. Quite, quite corrupted.

Within that time the police had departed, following the ambulance with Terry, and another ambulance had come to remove the bodies. Daws insisted that Charlie was not to be carted, pell-mell, with a quartet of murderers and ended up taking the remains in their plastic body bag to the mortuary himself. He drove out of the forecourt slowly and grimly, taking Peter with him on Sir George's orders to have his head wound cleaned and dressed at the hospital.

The Cadre went, too, their commander shaking my hand and regretting that he was unable to wait and shake Patrick's. Cool, he said, really cool. The man on the stretcher had alerted the police by the door and a chain of silent information, sign language, had sent him up to one of the front bedrooms. There had been plenty of time, and while a voice like a diamond cutter had told him everything he wanted to know he had opened the window. Cool, he repeated. Bearing in mind the rivalry, it was as good as being mentioned in despatches.

CHAPTER 22

I kept very close to Patrick as we entered the library. Actually to hold his hand or tuck my arm through his, weak and ludicrous actions in the present company and circumstances, was the real need, and, finely tuned as always, he turned to me just inside the door, put an arm around me quickly and gave me a kiss redolent of moorland ditches and Hamish. I was surprised but not offended when he bestowed the same upon Pip, just to his left.

Overstrung, shocked and tired, the five of us sat down and carried on being exquisitely polite to each other. Patrick caught the mood, taking himself and his muddy camouflage clothes to an upright wooden chair away from upholstered ease. Then, when Sir George was still only halfway through his task of providing everyone with a consoling glass of brandy, Patrick broke all the conventions of polite social behaviour and started talking.

"This morning," he said, "a friend of mine rode my motorbike to enable me to be elsewhere. Yesterday I assured him—gave him my word—that he would come to no harm even though he might be in some danger. There would be plenty of back-up. There was no bloody back-up! Just after he was killed I took a quick shot at a man who stood up on a ridge, thinking that I was providing a little supporting fire, and killed him. I've since discovered that this one shot stood between life and death for my wife. No fucking back-up. Gentlemen, you have my resignation."

The atmosphere in the room became like treacle, lightly chilled.

Patrick's gaze came to rest at a point on the wall just above

230

Sir George's head. "My criticisms do not extend to the Cadre. They were ordered to watch the glen itself for intruders on foot and keep a close eye on Trelawney. It was not part of their brief to man a road block or keep a physical presence on the slopes of Ben Muir. This latter I decided to do."

"They were classified orders," Sir George commented, handing a glass of brandy to Patrick after the briefest hesitation.

Daws cleared his throat. "I thought it best that all exterior surveillance should be in possession of code words. No point in having a shooting match between the wrong people."

Patrick gave Sir George a shark's smile. "At the time they had night sights and I was mounted on a pale grey pony. A section of stone wall armed with a rifle asked me my business and then took me to his leader, a worried individual who expressed a fervent hope that the gaps in security were being plugged by other arrangements about which he knew nothing."

For a moment no one spoke.

Pip said, "Your responsibility surely, George?"

In all likelihood, I reasoned, but he didn't have to explain to his wife in front of two subordinates.

Sir George glanced quickly at Daws as if for moral support and said, "I must confess, my dear, that in not anticipating the danger to myself I placed other people's lives at risk. But you must remember that the Major had said that he would be riding the motor bike . . . I assumed that he would take adequate steps to protect himself." He looked across the room to Patrick. "Your offer of resignation is not accepted."

I said, "Does that explain why Peter ran down the hill after me instead of sticking with you? You didn't realise that your own life was in danger?"

"It wasn't uppermost in my mind," he agreed. "I ordered him to follow you."

How very strange, I thought, but kept quiet for the moment. Patrick couldn't resign for both of us.

"The important thing is the proof," Sir George said to Patrick. "Do you have it?"

Patrick took an envelope from his pocket and gave it to him, watching, quite inscrutably, while it was torn open and the prints it contained were thumbed quickly through.

Daws said, "What about the shots he took of the Towed Arrays documentation . . . the stuff he went back to Portland for?"

Patrick dug in another pocket and held up a roll of film between thumb and forefinger.

"Where did you get that?" Sir George said sharply.

"I removed it from Trelawney's room last night while you were all having dinner."

A peremptory hand was held out. "I'll look after it."

Both items went into a wall safe behind an early Dufy but no one relaxed when the picture was back in place.

I said, "I'd like to know why Trelawney brought the film to Scotland in the first place. I also want to know why Peter and Terry didn't find that gunman on the hill beforehand. I'm assuming that Patrick didn't find him due to the size of the area which he would have had to cover on foot."

"Answers are not required," Patrick said quietly. "What you are listening to is Mark Langley's daughter *demanding explanations*. She already knows the answers: she has his brain. He was a Chief Superintendent of Police."

I took a large sip of brandy and came to within an ace of choking. My father had been a stockbroker by the name of Gerald, and Patrick well knew it.

"Well then," said Daws, looking at me, "what is your opinion?"

I was frantically wondering if Patrick's warning had been to discourage me from having any opinions at all when he took another roll of film from his pocket and commenced to toss it up and down one-handed, idly.

"What is that?" asked Sir George.

"The film from Trelawney's first trip to Portland," answered Daws.

Sir George looked appalled and for a moment lost for words. "You mean that it wasn't destroyed as I ordered?"

Patrick continued to play catch. "No, it had been given to a Russian working as a cabin steward for Aeroflot."

"The bastard," Sir George muttered.

Daws said, "The meeting was filmed. It wasn't Trelawney who made the handover." He turned back to me. "Now, please carry on with what you were about to say."

Seven words had given me carte blanche. I said, "Trelawney

brought the film to Scotland because he was to meet his contact here. It simply wasn't worth the risk otherwise. And I can only think that Terry and Peter didn't discover the man on Ben Muir for the simple reason that they'd been ordered to ignore it. They fell foul of the Cadre on the other side of the glen . . . they weren't out long enough to have covered the entire area.''

Daws said, ''The explanation given to Meadows and Webster for the curtailed search being, of course, that the Cadre were already in position on Ben Muir. Webster was glad. He had the discovery of the listening device in the drawing room to worry about. Quite unnecessarily as it happened: the Major planted it as a pre-arranged signal to myself and Meadows to let me know that he was on station.''

Before anyone else could speak Pip stood up slowly, staring at her husband. ''It was you, *you* had Trelawney killed, but before that you betrayed him. You gave him his head so that his activities would draw attention away from your own. All those things that you said Trelawney had done and told me to keep to myself—murdered Ingrid's husband because he'd alerted the Cornwall police after he'd seen a couple of local thugs getting into a car belonging to Trelawney; nearly killed Ingrid and Patrick—it was all done with your connivance and blessing. He did all the dirty work and in the end you used him to try to prove to the world that the Russians were gunning for you, thus ensuring your integrity for all time.'' She looked around the room, seeming to realise for the first time that she was standing. ''What a tragedy that it was Flash who had to be shot instead of you.''

I was expecting her to leave the room but she reseated herself and gave her attention to Daws' gift, the jade dragon, clutching it tightly.

''A magnificently concise exposition of the charges against you,'' Daws said to Sir George, but he was fully occupied in fielding another shark's grin from Patrick. Not a knight of the realm, I told myself, a traitor.

Patrick said to him, ''Part of my job was to keep you sweet and unsuspecting. You really thought you had MI5 in the palm of your hand when you personally paid for me to go to the States for the best artificial leg in the world. After I'd identified Trelawney all attention was deliberately given to him but the defector hadn't mentioned any other names, only yours!''

I thought about Peter, and how perhaps casual enquiries by the police in Cornwall as to the identity of some of the estate workers being employed by a certain respected country gentleman had signed his death warrant. And I thought about Charlie, who had suggested that he ride the bike from Glasgow. For Charlie, permission to stay in Britain had not been so important as repaying his debt to Patrick.

Patrick had told me about it as we had come indoors: how Charlie had tried to escape after his interrogation in the Falklands, snatching a grenade with the intention of warning his own side and seen it bounce off a rock and roll right back through the door of the hut.

Patrick was as good as his word and resigned. But, two weeks later, the all powerful one to whom the defector had given his information persuaded him otherwise and he was immediately reinstated on a part-time basis. So I perform my small services for Queen and country and take him with me to provide support. The rest of the time he is my agent and is currently arranging a television dramatisation of *Barefoot Upon Thorns*. Earning his ten percent.